Meant

to be

Kept

Meant to Be Series
Book One

By AMELIA FOSTER

Meant to be Kept

Limitless Publishing, LLC
Kailua, HI 96734
www.limitlesspublishing.com

Formatting: Limitless Publishing

ISBN-13: 978-1-64034-510-2
ISBN-10: 1-64034-510-8

Chapter One

Izzy

Folding the last t-shirt and laying it on top of the pile, Izzy glanced at the clock above the couch. A slow smile crept across her face. Three more hours and Tanner would be home. Two days had felt like an eternity while he'd been gone.

But tonight, she hefted the laundry basket onto one hip and headed to the stairs. Tonight the kids were at his parents' house and it would be just the two of them. The first time in far longer than she cared to admit.

The roaring sound of a loud truck engine made her jump just as she reached the top step. Her brows drew together. That sounded like...but it couldn't be.

Izzy flew down the stairs and ripped open the front door. She beamed when she saw the bright June sun reflecting off Tanner's obnoxious yellow truck as it sped up the long driveway, dust clouds rolling behind the tires. Her feet were fixed until he

1

parked in front of the house. As the driver's door opened, she bolted down the porch steps and ran the few feet to the truck, launching herself into his arms before he could even shut the door. She wrapped her arms around his neck and her legs around his waist.

But even her overwhelming excitement couldn't disguise the change in him. Instead of enfolding his body around hers as he had for so many years, his back stayed straight. His strong arms held her loosely, not pulling her close.

Izzy leaned her head back, hands braced on his shoulders. The expression on his face had the same effect on her as a dip in the lake on a January day. "Tanner?"

He gently pried her off him and made sure both her feet were on the ground before he spoke. "Belle, we need to talk."

Her throat closed at his tone. She took a step back and then another. "No, Tanner. No, we don't need to talk. You need to hold me and tell me you missed me and we need to go in the house and make up for the past two days, but we definitely don't need to talk."

Tanner closed the truck door and shoved his hands in the pockets of his khaki shorts with a heavy sigh. He dropped his gaze to the ground. "Come on, Belle. Let's go inside."

Izzy's stomach churned, and she held her arms around her midsection. Her mind flew in a million directions. They had been married for nearly eight years, and in all that time she hadn't had a single doubt or concern about their relationship—until now.

He's sick.

The company took a massive hit.

Wyatt had an accident.

An avalanche of worst case scenarios flooded her mind. The one person she needed was standing just a few feet in front of her but seemed miles away. She wanted nothing more than to reach out to him, but everything about him from his voice to his posture screamed "closed." Something he'd never been before.

"Belle," his voice softened a fraction, and he put a gentle hand on her back, "let's go inside and sit down. I really don't want to talk to you out here."

She allowed him to steer her toward the house and up the porch steps, unable to slow her racing mind. A nervous laugh bubbled up as they crossed the threshold. "Tanner, you're really scaring me."

He stood near the far corner of the gray overstuffed couch and gestured for her to sit down. She couldn't remember ever feeling this overwhelming sense of trepidation in Tanner's presence. He had been her safe place since the first time his lips touched hers a month into her freshman year of college.

After a moment's hesitation, she finally sat down. When he sat next to her, he gently wrapped his hand around hers and pulled it lightly until it rested on his knee. For a brief second, her heart lifted at his touch. But then the complete absence of warmth registered and she felt her heart breaking all over again. "Please, Tanner." Her voice cracked. "Just tell me."

His mouth opened, but he seemed to think better of what he was going to say. "Where are the kids?"

Izzy's eyes dropped to her free hand, nervously playing with the hem of her shorts, and tears prickled the back of her eyes. "At your parents' for the night. I asked them to watch the kids so we could have some alone time and…"

Tanner nodded, his eyes fixed on their joined hands. "Belle, I did something." The words came out in a rush, and when he finally looked up, his blue eyes were tortured. His grip on her hand tightened infinitesimally. "Before I say anything else, you need to know I didn't sleep with her…"

From her head to her toes, Izzy was numb. His mouth was moving and she knew there were words coming out, but all she could hear was the distant sound of ringing in her ears. She didn't move. Couldn't move. She could barely remember to breathe in and out.

Izzy blinked and focused on him, narrowing her gaze. She pulled her hand free from his and slid to the opposite side of the couch. "What do you mean you didn't sleep with her?" she bit out between clenched teeth. "With who? And if you didn't sleep with her, what *did* you do with her?"

He swallowed, his brow knitting together. "I don't know her name. I-I-I don't know what happened. Not exactly. Wyatt won the whole thing. He got the big belt buckle and decided we needed to go out to celebrate. And he was probably self-medicating some bruises after eight seconds on particularly nasty bulls three nights in a row. I don't even remember how much we drank—"

"I don't even care. What did you do with her?" She wanted to shout the words, but she could do little more than whisper.

"Wyatt had this group of...fans, I guess, following him around, and he pulled me on the dance floor with all of them. I had a few more beers while we were dancing, and I-I don't really remember what happened next or how it happened, but the next thing I knew, Wyatt was pulling me away from some blonde girl that was holding onto my arm and he said I was..." He swallowed again. "Kissing her. Touching her."

Izzy wanted to run away. She wanted to throw up. She wanted to throw *something*. Preferably at his lying, cheating head. She wrapped her arms around her stomach again, trying desperately to shield herself from some of the pain ripping through her body.

She focused on a small speck on the area rug beneath her feet. Leave. He had to leave. He had to get out of their house and just leave. A familiar memory tugged at the corner of her mind, but instead of seeing herself watching her father drive away, it was Ava and Noah with tears streaming down their faces watching as Tanner left.

No, he would stay. For now.

"Belle." His voice cut into her thoughts. "I'm sorry. I can't possibly apologize enough. I guarantee I hate me more right now than you do." He ran his hands through his light brown hair. "I'll spend the rest of my life making it up to you, Belle. I'll do anything..."

She jumped up. "Bring your bag in." She

5

focused her attention on the large window at the front of the house. "I'm doing laundry."

When she turned to leave, he stood and grabbed her arm from behind. She spun around and wrenched it away, looking him in the face for the first time since he made his proclamation. "Don't touch me." She ground out the words. "You don't get to touch me after you touched *her*."

As the tears streaked down his face and his knees hit the floor in front of her, she felt a pang in her stupid heart. Today marked the fifth time in the twelve years they had known each other that Izzy had seen Tanner cry. "Belle, please." His head fell forward. "Tell me what to do to fix this. I'll do anything, Belle, anything. Just tell me what you want, what you need. I promise I will fix this."

Her fingers itched to run through the hair on the bent head in front of her. As much as she wanted to hate him right now, this was Tanner. And she only had that one simple fact to blame for the softening of her voice. "I don't know what I want, and I don't know what I need, but right now you just can't touch me."

Izzy ran up the stairs into their bedroom and pressed her back against the closed door. She managed to find the lock on the knob behind her and click it into place before sliding down the door. The sobs she was barely able to contain in front of Tanner rolled through her body.

She drew her legs up and laid her forehead against her knees. She would have to face him, and face this, soon enough. She would have to figure out what she wanted, what she needed, and what, if anything, Tanner could do. But right now all she was certain of was that she needed silence and to never, ever hear him call her Belle again.

***

Twelve years ago

Izzy slid her aviator sunglasses into place over her chestnut eyes and stole another look across the quad. There he was again. Nearly every day he was sitting at the same place with his back pressed against the trunk of a tree, long legs stretched out in front of him, reading a different book. He never seemed to be in a hurry and was never bothered by any of the commotion around him, while she scurried to get from one class to another.

She glanced down at her black watch and bit her lip. She had nearly thirty minutes until her next class started, and it was only five minutes away…

Nope. She shook her head and continued down the path. She could never approach him. Even if she could see the cover of one of her favorite books in his hand. Even if the wind ruffling hair that was just a little past due for a cut was possibly the cutest thing she'd ever seen. Even if she liked the way he smiled at the book while he was reading.

She had been at Wake Forest for only two weeks and, although most of that time her head was buried in textbooks, she knew who was important, and Tanner Carlisle was important with a capital "I." He was a key player on not only the football team, but the baseball team. He was the shining hope for the fledgling athletic department. Easily the most well-known guy on campus.

Izzy forced her eyes to the ground as she walked by and tucked a stray wave of dark brown hair behind her ear. She was the antithesis of everything he represented. She had yet to attend a single game or frat party.

Her father's decade of guilt had manifested in his willingness to pay for a private dorm. It was her sanctuary. Her days consisted of running from one class to another while cursing the double course load she'd requested, studying in the library, or eating alone in her room as often as possible.

She'd have time for a social life once she was done with college and was teaching at some school in North Carolina, hundreds of miles from her parents and their bitter arguments. Isabelle Ricci would make friends and fall in love in four years. But right then she needed to get to Early American History class early before someone took…

"Hey."

Lost in thought, she hadn't noticed someone keeping pace beside her until he spoke. She turned her head to politely rebuff whoever was talking, but as her eyes traveled up the black shirt and collided with bright blue ones, her words and feet halted at the same time.

Scratch that. It wasn't someone. It was him. "Hi." The single word finally came out.

Perfect white teeth flashed at her, and he stuck out his hand. "Tanner Carlisle." His slow drawl dragged out his last name slightly, and it was the most charming sound Izzy had ever heard.

After a couple of beats, her brain finally kicked in and she slid her hand into his. "Isabelle Ricci." She grinned back, feeling foolish, but completely unable to stop herself. "But everyone calls me Izzy."

"Pleasure to meet you, Isabelle Ricci." He pulled his hand back and hiked his backpack higher on his shoulder, inclining his head to the building a distance behind her. "Are you going to Trib?"

She could only nod in response, once again feeling at a loss for words. This was ridiculous. He's just a boy. Just another dumb jock who relied on his good looks and gift for…whatever he did in sports. She straightened herself to her full five-foot four-inch height, which still failed to bring her to his shoulders, and summoned her confidence. "Yes." She congratulated herself on her strong voice. "Early American History with Mr. Calhoon."

"Great, I'll walk with you." He held a hand out in front, encouraging her feet to finally start moving again.

Just like that, he fell in step beside her and asked about her major, her dorm, where she was from, and almost everything besides sports or himself. Izzy was confused and, if she were being completely honest, mildly in awe. Every time someone tried to pull him away he would smile and wave them off, never once stepping from her side.

Izzy turned to face him when they reached the door of Tribble Hall. "You never said what class you're taking here." She waved her arm toward the large brick building.

"That's because I'm not taking a class here." He

ducked his head and offered a crooked grin. "My next class is Global Marketing Strategy over in Farrell Hall."

Izzy had spent the entire summer memorizing the campus map in an effort to bolster her confidence. She pulled it out of her memory bank, and her eyebrows drew together. "But that's in the opposite direction," she argued. "And that's quite an impressive class."

He raised his eyebrows and offered an amused look, pointing at himself as he took a step back. "Not just a dumb jock."

Heat started to creep up her neck. "I never…"

Tanner threw her a wink. "Thanks for letting me walk you to class, Isabelle. But I think you need a new nickname."

Izzy captured her bottom lip between her teeth for a minute. This ought to be good. "Yeah? What's that?"

His smile widened. "Isn't it obvious? Belle."

She popped a hand on her hip and opened her mouth to make a sarcastic response. It had to be some sort of derogatory joke.

Tanner took a few more steps backward, not breaking eye contact. "It means beautiful, doesn't it?" He lifted his hand with a small wave as he turned. "See ya around, Belle."

Chapter Two

Tanner

He could hear the muffled cry from the bottom step. She couldn't possibly forgive him for this. Hell, he couldn't forgive himself.

No, losing Belle was not an option. He'd fix this. He'd prove that even though he screwed up, he still loved her more than life itself, and he would fix this. That was his job. He was the oldest, the heir to the company his father built, and the one who could take care of everyone. Especially Belle. He moved up the stairs slowly, quietly.

At six-foot two, he couldn't sneak in anywhere, but if he could find a positive aspect to her gut-wrenching sobs, it was that they were loud enough to drown out his steps as he approached the bedroom door.

The last thing Belle wanted was him anywhere near her. It didn't take a genius to figure that out. But for more than a decade, when she needed something, he was there. When she was sad, he made her feel better. When she was crying, he held her. He was there. Every damn time he was there.

He softly dropped to his knees on the opposite side of the door. This wasn't like every other time. Another hiccuping sob sounded through the closed door, and in a move he thought impossible, his heart shredded more. This time the cause of her heartache lay squarely on his shoulders.

Tanner put his hand against the door, resting his forehead beside it as gently as possible. He wanted to find someone willing to punch him. He wanted to beat his head off the doorframe. More than anything he wanted to turn back time and never leave for that ridiculous bull riding tournament. Or go back to his hotel instead of following his brother to the bar. Or…

No amount of wanting could fix what he'd done. He turned around and leaned his back against the doorframe, closing his eyes. No, she wouldn't want him here, but he wasn't leaving her.

Why? The question had repeated over and over in his brain the entire trip back from Nashville. He left hours earlier than he'd initially planned, driven by the need to see her. She wasn't just his wife; Belle was his best friend. When she smiled, he still felt that flip-flop in his stomach. When she cut that sensuous sideways look his way, every part of him jumped to attention. Twelve years and two kids had done nothing to lessen his desire for her. She was still the sexiest damn thing on two legs and so much more than he deserved.

None of which answered the question of why. Belle was perfect for him. He had known that from the first day he met her. In spite of the churning in his gut, a small smile played about his lips. She still had no idea he had spent nearly two weeks planting himself in the quad in between classes to make sure he was in her line of sight as much as possible. She never knew that on the fourth day back at Wake Forest he saw her for the first time and was almost positive that was when he fell in love. She certainly didn't know that he personally threatened half the football team when a kicker started running his mouth about the hot freshman brunette with olive skin.

He screwed everything up because he wanted to go shot for shot with his brother. He wasn't embellishing in the slightest when he told Belle he hated himself far more than she ever could. At least he hoped it was true. He hoped somewhere in her heart she could still love him and find some way to forgive him.

Lost in thought, he hadn't realized the sobs from the other side of the door had silenced. Gingerly, he pressed his ear against the wood to see if he could hear any movement. Seconds ticked past, and he swore if he didn't hear at least a rustle from the room he'd break the damn door down to make sure his Belle was okay.

The click of the lock registered just in time for Tanner to jump to his feet and take one big step back from the door before he fell through. If he thought he was gutted before, that was nothing compared to how he felt looking at Belle's gorgeous brown eyes turned red and swollen. Every fiber of his being was screaming to hold her and he barely

13

controlled the instinct.

"I, uh, I…" He shoved his fingers through his hair. "Listen, I know you don't want to see me or touch me or talk to me, but dammit, Belle, I can't sit downstairs knowing you're up here crying. I just needed to be near you."

He wanted her to scream at him. Throw something. Hit him. Do all three. Hell, he didn't care. He deserved it. But she just stood in the doorway staring blankly at him, not a trace of the sparkle that always lit her eyes. "Did you bring your bag in?"

His brow drew down, and he shook his head. "My what?"

She folded her arms in front of her, and the shielded posture made him wince. This was not his Belle. She never closed herself off to him. Just ten minutes ago, she jumped in his arms when he got home. And his cowardly ass couldn't bring himself to hold onto her the way she deserved. What had he done?

"Your bag? Your suitcase? Did you bring it in?" With each question, her eyebrows lifted, but her expression remained impassive. "I need to finish doing the laundry and I'll throw your clothes in with the last load."

Clothes? He had done something unthinkable, unimaginable, possibly unforgiveable, and she wanted to wash his clothes. They needed to talk, she needed to call him every name in the book, they needed to work this out because there was no way he was going to let Belle go. And she wanted to do laundry.

Belle waved a hand over to the stairs. "Is it in the back of the truck? I'll just grab it."

"No." He nearly shouted the word and stepped in front of her, blocking the stairs. "No, Belle. I'll get it, I will, but we need to talk. We need to fix this. *I* need to fix this. Tell me what to do, Belle." She lifted her desolate gaze to meet his. Broken. His sweet, fiery, beautiful Belle was broken, and it was all his fault. He really did need someone to kick his ass.

"Don't call me Belle again." She pushed past him and walked down the stairs, taking the air out of his lungs with her as she went.

***

"Aren't you tired of this yet?"

He shoved his book in the side pocket of his backpack and grinned at Belle. "Nope. I'm getting caught up on all my reading so I can keep up with you."

The truth was he had been late to football practice the past three days, but she didn't need to know that. They could start without him anyway. He was only the quarterback. The team captain. Really not necessary.

She shifted on her feet and bit her lower lip. "I'm not going to go out with you, Tanner."

Her words stung, but he affected an unconcerned smile. "That doesn't mean I have to stop asking, Belle. Besides, I won't be able to sleep tonight unless I walk you to the library and know exactly what book you pick this time." That was a lie. He'd sleep like a baby and dream about the girl currently shooting him down again.

A tint of pink tinged her cheeks. Damn, that was cute. She grabbed his arm and pulled him around the side of the building, gaining a little more privacy than the front steps could afford.

"Why?" She crossed her arms and lifted her eyebrows meaningfully.

He shrugged with as much nonchalance as he could muster. The truth was pretty simple. He had no clue. Was it the fact he caught her reading the same books he loved in the cafeteria on the extremely rare occasion she was there? Was it because the first time they talked she claimed almost all of his favorite movies as her own? Maybe it was because he never knew what sarcastic comment she'd lay on him next? Or simply because she was the hottest damn thing he'd ever seen?

Whatever the reason, for the past three weeks, he couldn't think of anything other than the petite brunette with light brown eyes. His usual patience flew out the window with her, and his initial idea to entice her to come to him was quickly abandoned in favor of walking her to and from her classes as much as possible between his own.

She narrowed her gaze and pursed her lips. "Why, Tanner? Why do you spend every free minute waiting out here just to walk me from one building to another?" She rolled her eyes and huffed. "And why in the world do you call me Belle?"

With every word she spoke, his eyes followed the movement of her lips. Her perfect Cupid's bow mouth covered in a light pink gloss caught the rays of the late September sun and seemed to sparkle. He dropped his backpack to the ground and took a step closer.

"Why? Because every night when I go to sleep, I think about what your hair would feel like between my fingers. Because I can't stop wondering what it would feel like to hold you in my arms. Because I have an insatiable need to know what your lips taste like. Because, sweetheart, you drive me absolutely crazy."

He took another step forward, and her backpack joined his on the ground with a thud. He cupped her cheek with one hand and the other rested on her hip as he backed her against the brick wall of the building. At that moment, he could care less if anyone saw him. His heart soared at finally being exactly where he dreamed, with Belle in his arms.

Tanner lowered his head until his lips were a breath away from hers. The eyes that had haunted him for weeks were wide with excitement, her pupils dilated with desire. Yeah, she felt the same way he did. "And I have to call you Belle. You're the most gorgeous woman I've ever seen."

Before she could answer, his lips touched hers. Lightly at first, barely meeting, until he felt the little gasp from Belle and her hands went around his neck. He groaned against her mouth and deepened the kiss, pushing her harder into the wall. His hand moved from her cheek to the long brown waves that were every bit as silky as he'd imagined. He tangled his hand in her hair as he cupped the back of her head.

17

His tongue ran across her bottom lip, and the corners of his mouth quirked up when her fingers crawled up the back of his neck into his hair. She slowly opened her mouth beneath his, inviting him in shyly. Tanner dug his hands into her jean-clad hip, and he nearly fell to his knees at the first taste of her. His most vivid fantasy couldn't compare to the sweetness that was the reality of Belle.

He had no idea how long they stayed connected before he had to pull back and suck oxygen into his lungs. He leaned his forehead against hers. After a few more deep breaths, he was confident enough to speak. "That's why, Belle."

Her swollen lips turned up in a small smile. "Those marketing strategy classes are working. I'm definitely sold."

Tanner chuckled and pulled his head back slightly. "So I can keep calling you Belle?"

A spark lit up her eyes, and she tugged his head back down. "As long as you keep kissing me like that, you can call me Belle forever," she murmured before their lips met again.

Chapter Three

Izzy

"Do you want me to leave?"

Izzy dropped the washing machine lid down with a loud bang and spun around to face him. "No." The word erupted from her mouth without any help from her brain. "No, I don't want you to go. I-I don't want the kids to come home without you here."

Tanner leaned his shoulder against the doorjamb. "What about you Be-Isabelle?" His blue eyes dropped to the floor for a moment before pinning her with a beseeching stare. "Do you want me to leave?"

Did she? Her first thought was exactly what she had said. Her broken heart was screaming "no." Her mind wasn't quite as convinced. She opened and closed her mouth several times trying to formulate an answer.

"I don't want to." His words were barely above a whisper, but the note of agony made her wince. "The last thing I want right now is to leave. I want

19

you to hit me, scream at me, or throw something, but I damn sure don't want to leave." His hand reached out to touch hers, but he pulled it back at the last minute, folding his arms across his broad chest instead. "But what I want doesn't matter. What do you want? I'll do whatever you want."

Her lips curved, but there was no warmth in the haunted smile. "I've thought about throwing something at you." Izzy sighed and rubbed her temple where the throbbing grew. "It's really inconvenient to have you as my best friend. It's really, really pathetic that you've been my entire world for so long that I don't know if I want you to hold me or if I want to lock you out of the house."

She snorted and shook her head. "You were, ya know? You and the kids were my entire world. Nothing made me happier than taking care of you and the kids because I thought," she made a strangled sound in the back of her throat, "I *thought* you were all in just like I was. I had no clue that less than forty-eight hours away from me, from us, would be enough to make you willing to throw it all away. Tanner, you didn't just screw up our marriage. You ruined my entire life."

Izzy watched as Tanner's face paled with every word she spoke. The part of her that was urging her to forgive him, let him hold her and kiss away every tear, ached at the sight. She was growing to hate that part of herself.

"You were my everything and I was…what? Easy enough to replace in two days? Pretty forgettable when some girl in a tight skirt—"

He crossed the few feet separating them and

grabbed her face, cradling it between his hands. The back of her legs hit against the washing machine at the movement. His eyes were wide and tinged with panic. "No, Belle, no. Dammit, this had nothing to do with you. *I* did this. *I* screwed up. You are smart and sexy and damn near perfect. I'm a selfish, thoughtless asshole that will do anything in the world to make this right."

Because his words left her speechless, because she didn't have the strength to fight with him at that moment, and just because it was Tanner, when he lowered his head to touch his lips against hers, she did nothing more than melt into his kiss and his arms. *This is Tanner*, her heart reminded her as his mouth caressed hers. Her hands found his chest and crept up and around his shoulders.

She felt wetness against her cheek, and the ache in her soul deepened with the realization the tears were from Tanner. Her dry eyes started to fill again, and she couldn't stop herself from pulling him closer.

This is Tanner.

And less than twenty-four hours ago he was holding someone else. Kissing someone else. Pressing every inch of the body she knew so well against someone new, someone who wasn't her. *Did he touch* her *the way he is touching me now?*

She pushed against his shoulders and broke their kiss. She clamped her lips between her teeth and bit back the urge to say every thought that had been racing through her head. As much as she wanted to know, knowing might kill her.

"I don't want you to leave." She tightened her

hand against his chest, gathering a fistful of his blue shirt. "But I can't do that again either."

Against her mind screaming at her to stop, she ran her free hand over the light brown, closely trimmed facial hair covering his square jaw. Her forehead dropped against his chest and her tears started to fall, soaking the front of his shirt. In that moment she needed nothing more than a best friend. Someone to tell her to walk away from him. Someone to tell her to forgive him because it was one mistake in twelve years. Someone to tell her what to do so she didn't have to make this decision herself.

But because Tanner had been so busy and someone needed to take the kids to their practices, rehearsals, and recitals, her friends had fallen away.

Izzy slipped past him and stood in the laundry room doorway for a few beats. "I don't want you to leave," she repeated and swiped the tears off her cheeks. "But I don't want you in bed with me tonight. I can't be that close to you right now."

"Right now, or forever?" He shook his head and rested a hand on the churning machine in front of him. "I know, I know I don't have a right to ask that."

Her eyes drifted to the small window where the sun was starting to fade. "I don't even know if I'm going to sleep tonight, much less what's going to happen tomorrow." She dared to peek at Tanner. He had both hands braced on the washing machine and his head was hanging down. "Tomorrow we'll figure out what we're going to do."

"I know what I'm going to do. I'm going to

regret this for the rest of my life and love you long after I take my last breath." He turned to her with a helpless expression on his face. "That's what I'm going to do, Be-Isabelle. I'll, um, I'll finish this." He waved behind him. "You can go to bed. And please try to sleep."

She nodded and turned, climbing the stairs quickly. How could she remind him that she never slept well without him beside her? She slid between the pale yellow sheets, not bothering to take off her t-shirt and shorts. Izzy pulled his pillow flush against her chest and inhaled the cedarwood and musk scent that clung to it…and the tears started to fall again. She couldn't possibly live without this smell and this man in her life.

***

Tanner kissed her deeply. "You are required to be at every game from now until forever." He punctuated each word with another kiss, and Izzy couldn't help but laugh. "That was the best I've ever played. You're my good luck charm. I'm dead serious, sweetheart. My family? Jinxes. Every last one of 'em. They're only allowed to come to my last game of the season."

Her fingers dove into his hair, still damp from a quick shower in the locker room after the game. "You were great tonight. And there is a little bit of an ego rush to know the handsome quarterback is my boyfriend."

His blue eyes sparkled and he tugged at her waist, pulling her tighter against him and pointedly ignoring the other players slapping his back as they passed. "Handsome? Why sugar, you're gonna give me a big head talkin' like that." He embellished his drawl and made her laugh more.

Izzy stepped back and linked her hand with his, turning to the parking lot and dragging him with her. "Come on, MVP, dinner's on me. You've got to be starving. I'll even drive so you can rest."

"Damn straight I'm hungry. I'm nearly emaciated." Tanner lifted his shirt and ran their joined hands over his muscular midsection. Izzy let out a small gasp at the contact, and Tanner grinned at her. "Did ya say something, Belle?"

Relief flooded through her when they reached her car. She shook her head and pulled her hand away, pretending to dig in her purse for her keys. "Nope. Where do you want to go for dinner?"

He plucked the keys out of her grasp and unlocked the driver's door, opening it for her. Before she got in, he grabbed her hand, slid the keys into her palm, and turned her to face him with only the door separating them. "What are you hungry for, Belle?" His voice deepened with passion, and he lowered his head to brush his lips across hers before trailing down her neck.

All logical thought and sense of where they were standing fled. He affected her in a way no one before him ever had. It was thrilling. It was terrifying. If she didn't watch out, she'd wind up falling in love with him.

Finally able to calm her breathing enough to speak, she swallowed deeply and hoped her voice wouldn't give away any of her thoughts. "Tacos."

His lips immediately stilled at the single word. After a few beats he started laughing and stepped back. He waved her into the car and shut her door before crossing around the front and falling into the passenger's seat. "You're pretty damn cute, ya know that, Belle?"

A blush crept up her neck as she guided the car carefully away from the stadium. "And you are a terrible passenger for distracting me."

But throughout the short drive to the all-night taco place, and while he easily devoured six tacos by himself in record time, the idea of falling in love with Tanner kept echoing through her mind. Was that what it was called when you found it adorable that he could sit there for several minutes, oblivious to the spot of taco sauce on his cheek? Was love what made her stomach fill with butterflies every time she heard him call her Belle? Or the warm feeling that spread through her when he kept looking up in the stands during the game to make sure she was still there?

They had only been dating for a month. She shook her head and pulled into her parking spot. It wasn't possible that she loved him.

"You really should let me take you back to your dorm." She chewed on her bottom lip. His head was leaning against the headrest and his eyes were closed. He looked exhausted.

Tanner shook his head, not moving it from the seat or opening his eyes. "Nope, I can walk back. And there's no way I'm letting my girl walk to her dorm in the dark alone."

Izzy snorted and rolled her eyes. "All I have to

do is manage a treacherous fifty feet from my car to the door. In a nearly straight line. You, on the other hand, will have to go clear to the other side of the campus. Besides, your girl is from New York. She can take care of herself."

He rotated his head slightly, popped one eye open, and offered her a lazy grin. "I know and that makes you hotter." He lifted their joined hands to his mouth and kissed the back of her hand. "But you don't have to anymore."

Just like always, he held open her door and made sure her car was locked before handing her back the keys. He held her hand tightly in his until they reached her dorm. "Thanks for dinner, Belle." He turned her to face him and locked his arms around her waist.

"D-do you want to come in? I-I don't m-mean like that. I'm not ready for that. I-I just…" She slid her arms up to his shoulders and fought the urge to bury her hot face in his chest. "I don't want to say goodbye yet."

Tanner brushed his lips across hers, took the keys from her hand, and unlocked the door. He lifted one eyebrow and grinned. "One condition."

She rolled her eyes and pulled out of his grasp long enough to walk into her room and close the door behind them. "So that business major of yours rears its ugly head again. Go on, let's hear the counter offer."

He collapsed on her bed and stretched his long body out, cuddling her memory foam pillow. "Geez, Belle, even your pillow is amazing. Okay, counter offer." He propped himself up on one elbow and patted the small space beside him. "I stay for a while as long as I get to hold you."

Izzy laid down next to him, running a hand down his cheek. "Just lay here? All night?"

"Just lay here," he confirmed. "For as long as you want."

She captured her bottom lip between her teeth. She wanted him next to her tonight, all night, and preferably every night to come. But there was no way she'd say that out loud. "All night."

He heaved a dramatic sigh and pulled her even closer, tucking her head under his chin. "Fine, but you're gonna owe me for this, Belle."

"Oh really?" she questioned with a soft kiss against the cotton material of his shirt. "For giving you the gift of my single room and amazing pillow for the night?"

"For getting me used to having you in my arms all night. It's going to ruin me for sleep for the rest of my life."

His last words ended on a mumble, and Izzy was incredibly grateful when he began snoring just a few moments later. She didn't want to have to admit the impact his words had on her. And she certainly couldn't admit to feeling exactly the same way.

Chapter Four

Tanner

Three o'clock in the morning.

He turned his back on the clock and resumed his pacing. Sleep was a waste of time. He needed to focus on figuring out how to fix this. He ran his hands through his hair and linked his fingers behind his neck. He could sleep when Belle—no, Isabelle—was beside him in bed again. Geez, it hurt to think of her as anything other than Belle.

He paused in front of the couch, hands resting on his pajama-covered hips. He rolled his shoulders, dropped his head forward, and sighed. "I've got to fix this."

Tanner gave up walking and sat down heavily, his head resting against the back of the couch, staring sightlessly at the ceiling. He screwed up. Hell, why did he even go in the first place again?

Oh yeah, he thought it would be fun. He thought for one night he could stop being the responsible, reliable Tanner Carlisle and be as stupid and

28

reckless as his brother. Yeah, that worked out so well for both of them.

He rotated his head to the right and checked the time again. Four o'clock.

If this were any other day, Belle would be getting up at five o'clock. A smile curved his lips. She would wake up, give him a soft kiss, and remind him that he needed to get up in another hour. By the time he finally ventured downstairs, Belle would have already run five miles on the treadmill, would have breakfast ready, and would be packing his lunch.

How could he possibly screw up this badly and still have the audacity to ask for her forgiveness? What an arrogant prick. He didn't know what he wanted more in that moment: to win her back or let her find someone who would treat her a hell of a lot better than him. Someone who would actually love and respect her enough to keep his damn hands to himself.

Quickly he answered his own question. Win her back. That was the only acceptable option.

Tanner turned and stretched out on the couch, his self-appointed bed for the night, his feet dangling off the end. He could have just as easily slept in the guest room upstairs, but that would have been too close to Belle. He didn't think he could last the night separated from her if there was only one wall between them.

Especially not if he heard her crying again. If she cried.

Shit. Of course she would cry. He threw an arm across his eyes. He betrayed her. He took her love

29

and trust and destroyed it in one night. With one dumbass decision.

He jumped to his feet and began pacing again. He couldn't sleep. He couldn't relax. He damn sure couldn't sit still.

"I have to fix this," he murmured to himself again, taking large strides around the living room. "I have to win her back. She fell in love with me once, I know…"

His words and his feet stopped simultaneously. Memories of the beginning of their relationship filtered through his mind. The promises he made to himself not to repeat the mistakes Wyatt had made with Georgia in high school. The mistakes Wyatt still regretted to this day. Tanner made sure he listened and paid attention and never let Belle feel insecure in their relationship.

For the first time since his brother pulled him away from the overly affectionate blonde and told him what he'd done, he felt a stirring of hope in his heart. It may have been more than a decade ago, but he had won her heart and her trust once.

Yeah, and he could do it again.

A genuine, damn near giddy, smile spread across his face. He ran back to the couch and grabbed his phone from the table. Time to work on the plan.

***

Monday night Tanner lay on his back in Belle's bed with his left arm wrapped around her, holding her close to his side. The same way he spent nearly every night.

His hand tightened on her shoulder slightly, and she turned her head, resting her chin on his chest and smiling. Damn, he loved that smile. Hell, he loved every single thing about her from her chestnut brown eyes and wavy chocolate hair to the soft snoring sounds she made when she slept. He just hadn't told her.

Yet.

"What are you thinking about, baby?"

Every time she called him "baby," his entire body reacted to the term of endearment she'd recently bestowed upon him. He cleared his throat and tried to focus his mind. "Well, Thanksgiving is this week, and I was just wondering what you were doing. You, uh, you didn't mention going home."

Her lids lowered, covering her eyes and frustrating Tanner. He could practically see through to her soul when he looked in her eyes, and he knew she was keeping something from him. "I-I just planned to stay here. Have a delicious cafeteria-created meal of what I *think* will be turkey."

He hooked a finger under her chin, forcing her to lift her gaze to meet his. "What aren't you telling me, Belle?"

She sat up, tucking her legs under her and holding his hand tightly in hers. "Holidays aren't great for me. My family is very different from yours, Tanner."

He stuck his free arm behind his head to give himself a better view of Belle and stroked the back of her hand with his thumb. "My family's not perfect."

Her teeth captured her lower lip again, and she

kept her eyes fixed on their joined hands. "But they're together. They're still married. They don't..." She sighed heavily but didn't continue.

Their families had only been a passing discussion until now. He wasn't comfortable with the thought of Belle at the practically deserted school over the holiday weekend. And he really couldn't stand not seeing her for nearly five consecutive days. "Sweetheart, you can tell me anything."

"I know." Her voice was a soft whisper. When she finally lifted her eyes to his, he thought his heart was going to break with the moisture threatening to spill from her eyes. "But this is bad."

Tanner sat upright on the bed to face her, crossing his legs and holding both of her hands firmly, offering silent support. He hadn't seen Belle this upset before, and it made him feel sick.

It wasn't like he hadn't been around crying girls before. He shifted on the bed at the all too recent memory of his brother's girlfriend standing on their doorstep in tears when he left her without saying goodbye six months ago. The same day Tanner promised himself he'd never treat the girl he loved that way.

But this was his Belle. This was different than Georgia. Worse. She was his girl and she was hurting and he needed to fix it. Simple as that.

She was the first girl he loved and he had every intention of making her the last as well. There was no way he would repeat the mistakes he'd seen his younger brother make in high school. He'd never leave Belle alone and crying. He'd never let her feel abandoned and unloved.

"It's stupid to be this upset about it still," she started slowly, still looking in his eyes. "I-I was only eight so…I don't know, I guess it just didn't seem like anything was wrong. It seemed like it all happened so suddenly, but now I'm older and I wonder if it was actually a slower breakdown." Her voice trailed off on a huff.

He shook his head. "Sweetheart, I'm not following."

"I was playing on the front porch; it was a really hot summer day. I remember it all so clearly. And everything seemed *fine,*" her face took on a distant expression, "until I heard a loud crash."

Tanner moved his back against the headboard, stretching his legs out and pulling her with him into his arms. He needed to hold her while she spoke, maybe even more than she needed him.

After a few moments of silence, she spoke again. "My dad, he walked out. My mom followed him. She stood at the top step of the porch, screaming at him that he ruined everything because he couldn't keep it in his pants. That she would never let him see me. That she would take everything. That she hoped his little slut would keep him happy."

He searched his mind for words to make it better. He felt every bit of her pain as she spoke, and he wanted nothing more than to take it away from her. Before he could think of something appropriate, something comforting to say, she lifted her head and looked at him with the saddest eyes he had ever seen.

"They still fight and try to pull me into it.

Constantly. Anytime they are in the same room. My graduation was a disaster." A small hiccup accompanied fresh tears in her eyes. "He never looked back, Tanner. He left and never looked back. He sent money and showed up for the special occasions, but that's it. I mean, just because he and my mom got divorced, why did he leave me?"

If he thought his heart was aching before, it completely shattered at her words. He slid them both down the bed a little as he turned so he was hovering over her with a hand cupping her cheek. "I wish I could answer that for you, Belle, and you have no freaking clue how much I wish I could take your pain away." Tanner took a deep breath and hoped he wasn't completely screwing this up by saying it now. "But sweetheart, what I can tell you is that I love you with my whole heart. I'm never leaving you, and I damn sure am never going to hurt you."

Her eyes grew wide, and she cradled his face in her hands. "You love me?"

A small smile curled the corners of his lips. "I haven't had any experience, so I must be pretty bad at showing it. Hell, yeah, Belle. I love you."

She pulled him down and pressed her lips to his, but Tanner couldn't let himself drown in Belle like every other time. He felt something wet on his cheek. Shit. She was crying again and she hadn't told him she loved him back. He screwed up. *Don't act like Wyatt*, he coached himself. *Just be patient.*

Finally she broke the kiss, and before Tanner could launch into a speech assuring her that it was perfectly fine if she didn't feel the same way, Belle

34

beamed up at him with the brightest smile he'd ever seen. "I love you too, ya know."

Words failing him, Tanner leaned down and kissed her again. He felt her hands slide down the front of his t-shirt and make contact with his bare skin beneath. The breath left his body in a *whoosh*, and he pulled back from her. "Belle…"

Her cheeks flushed and her smile turned shy. "I-I want to, Tanner. I think I'm ready."

Every single cell of his body reacted to her words, and it took all his self-control to pull her hand from under his shirt. He couldn't give in to his desire. She was too emotional, and when they finally got their first time, there was no way in hell he was going to let there be any room for regret from her.

The crestfallen expression on her face made him groan and lean his forehead against hers. "I want you with every fiber of my being, sweetheart. More than you know. But not right now, Belle. Not tonight. Not when you are feeling sad and happy and confused. Tonight I just want to hold you."

Her eyes still held a tinge of uncertainty and…shit. Rejection. He rolled his eyes and pressed her hand against the front of his painfully tight jeans to offer physical proof of his need for her. "I want you more than I've ever wanted another woman in my life and more than I'll ever want another woman again. But Belle, our first time is going to be special. I've screwed up a lot of stuff, and that's one thing I want to do perfectly."

Tanner could practically see the switch flip in her brain as his words registered. Her smile reappeared, and Tanner flopped onto his back, pulling her tight against his side. They lay together in silence for a long time before the reason he even started the conversation popped back in his mind. He smirked up at the ceiling and ran a hand up and down her arm. "I deserve a reward for the immense amount of self-control I just exhibited, don't you think?"

She lifted her head from his chest and raised an eyebrow at him. "And you've already decided what that reward should be, I assume?"

"Business one-oh-one, sugar," he drawled. "Never ask a question or make a suggestion without knowing the answer and the exact outcome."

He could see the smile tugging at her lips, even though she was trying valiantly to remain stoic. He loved to use his negotiating skills almost as much as Belle liked teasing him about it. It was one of his favorite parts of their relationship. "Go ahead."

"Come home with me for Thanksgiving." It wasn't a question. No way in hell was Belle staying on campus. "You can experience the unique crazy that is the Carlisle family. If we're lucky, Aunt Sharon will have a few too many. That's loads of fun."

The amusement disappeared from her face, and for a moment he thought she was going to refuse. "You really want me to go home with you? And be with…your family?"

He smiled and tucked her head against his chest. He wanted to tell her that this was the first of many holidays he expected her to be with him. He wanted to tell her he couldn't see his daily life without her in it, much less every special occasion. He wanted to tell her he wanted her with him forever. But he settled for simple. "Yep."

"Okay, baby." She sighed contentedly against his chest and promptly drifted to sleep.

Chapter Five

Izzy

Her heart leapt into her throat and her traitorous body hummed as soon as she rounded the corner into the living room. Tanner, still every inch as gorgeous as he'd been in college, was sitting on the couch clad only in pajama pants, sound asleep with his head leaning on the back of the couch. His hand rested on the smartphone on his bare chest that, if it were possible, had only grown broader and stronger over the past dozen years.

His light brown hair was tousled, and her fingers itched to bury themselves in the thick mass. The lashes that were ridiculously long for any man rested against his tanned cheeks, and she groaned.

Izzy held onto the wall for support. She wanted to run her fingertips down his thick bicep. She wanted to plant soft kisses along his shoulders. She wanted to walk over and straddle his lap and…

Had she *done that?* The thought pummeled her heart and her mind at the same time. *Had* she *run*

*her hands across Tanner's well-defined abdomen?
Had* she *trailed her hands up his strong back?* Izzy felt sick again.

Her gaze traveled down her own body. She had less than zero desire to run today, but nevertheless she pulled on spandex shorts and a knit tank top and ran five miles on the treadmill. She had managed to lose most of the weight after she had the kids, but her abdomen still wasn't as tight as it had been. Her hips were still a little wider. She still wore clothes two sizes bigger than she had in college.

Was that why? Was that why Tanner had wanted someone else? She felt nauseated again.

She crossed the room and sat on the coffee table in front of him, biting her lower lip. She wanted to hate him so much right now, but it was still Tanner sitting in front of her. Reaching out, she tapped his knee lightly. She didn't trust herself to touch his bare skin.

He slowly lifted his head, eyes growing wide when he saw her. He scrubbed a hand across his face and down his bearded cheek, offering her a sheepish smile. "Mornin', Belle. Did you sleep, sweetheart?"

Belle. Sweetheart. Two names she'd always cherished now sliced through her heart, but she couldn't bring herself to chastise him. It felt as good to hear as it hurt. "A little." She looked down at her lap and nervously ran her hand up and down her mostly bare thighs. "The, um, the kids are going to be back in a little while, and I think we need to, um, I think we need to figure out..." She gestured between the two of them.

"You're right." He leaned forward, resting his forearms on his knees and bringing his head close to hers. "Can I...can I hold your hand?"

Her heart constricted. *Was this ever going to stop hurting?* "I-I think I need space. I don't think I can figure this out with you so close."

Tanner nodded and moved to the other side of the couch. His face registered a brief flicker of hurt before he offered a weak smile. "Whatever you need, Belle."

Izzy stood and walked over to the window, shaking her head. "That's not what I meant, Tanner. I need..." Her throat closed around the next words, and she tried to find something, anything, outside she could focus on. "I-I need you to leave. A-and I need you to stay."

She spun around, tears falling down her cheeks, and every ounce of the pain and anger she'd so carefully avoided last night began to bubble. "I can't look at you! I can't touch you, I can't hear your voice, and I really can't hear you call me Belle one more time. The guy who called me Belle? He promised he'd never hurt me. He walked around every underdressed, oversexed girl that threw themselves at him after each game to get to me. For weeks and weeks he was happy to lie next to me without anything more than a few kisses. That," she spit out the word, "is the only person allowed to call me Belle."

He stood from his seat on the couch, looking totally shell-shocked. Even though a small voice in her head told her to stop, once she began to voice her heartache, she couldn't stop. "I don't know what

I did or what I didn't do to make that guy leave." She hiccuped and wound her arms tight around herself. "And I don't know who you are."

Before the last words had even left her mouth, he strode across the room until he stood in front of her and grasped the tops of her arms. "Don't. Don't say that. Don't you dare believe any of that. You have been the best thing to happen to me since the first time I saw you. Don't think for one minute that this, that *any* of this, is you. I'm the only one responsible for being here right now."

He pressed his forehead hard against hers, his breathing as labored as if he had just finished a marathon. She had to close her eyes at the agony reflected in his. "This is your call. Whether I stay or whether I go. I'll do whatever you want. I'll even sign d-divorce papers if you can't forgive me." A tear streaked down his cheek as he stumbled over the words.

Izzy's eyes flew open and her hands immediately went to his face and she held him close. "No, Tanner." Words died on her lips, and she circled her arms around his neck as she dissolved into hysterical sobs against his chest. She couldn't help it. She needed him as much as she hated him right now.

"Shit, sweetheart, I can't imagine my world without you beside me." He choked out the words, tightening his arms around her waist. "But I can't hurt you anymore. If you want me gone, I'll go."

She pulled back a little from him. "I just need space to think. That's all. I d-don't w-want a d-d-d..." She fell against him again, unable to even say the word.

The sound of a car traveling up their driveway registered to both of them at the same time, and their arms fell as they jumped apart. He jerked his chin toward the small half-bathroom just outside the living room. "I'll let them in if you want to wash your face off or something."

Izzy nodded and caught him grabbing his t-shirt off the back of the couch and sliding it on. *Why couldn't he have slept in the stupid shirt?* she wondered bitterly, as irritated with her body for craving his as she was at the man himself.

She regarded herself carefully in the mirror above the pedestal sink in the small half-bath. Dousing her face with three handfuls of cold water had almost erased the red rims and bags. She practiced the carefree smile a few times before greeting her kids.

After several hugs and simultaneous chatter about all the things they had done with their grandparents, Izzy noticed a strange look pass between her in-laws.

"Ava, Noah, come show Grandma that new slide Uncle Connor added to your playground." Tanner's mother grabbed each child by the hand and let them lead her.

Before Izzy could say anything, they disappeared out the back door. She turned around and swallowed when she saw the furious expression on her father-in-law's face as his gaze moved from one to the other before landing on Tanner.

"What the hell did you do, son?"

***

The third time Tanner laughed at her, Izzy dropped his hand and smacked his arm. "It's not funny!"

"Aww Belle, it's damn near hysterical." He continued to chuckle as they took the exit off Interstate 40 for Asheville. "Just when I thought you couldn't get any more adorable, you get all worked up over meeting my parents."

She laced her fingers through his again and turned to look out the window in an effort to hide her flushed cheeks. She wondered absently when she'd get used to his charm and stop blushing with each compliment. "It's important, baby. I just...I just want them to like me."

"Not a chance in hell they're gonna like you, Belle."

Her eyes widened, and she whipped her head around to face him. "You've spent the past three days telling me not to worry and assuring me everything would be okay, and now, *now* you feel the need to tell me there is no way they are going to like me?"

Tanner lifted her hand to his lips and brushed a kiss across her knuckles. "They aren't going to *like* you, sweetheart. They are going to *love* you." He flashed her a cocky grin. "Not as much as I love you, of course, but they are going to love you nonetheless."

Izzy settled back in the leather seat of Tanner's Jeep with a small smile tugging at her lips. "You're a jerk, you know that?" Only to herself could she admit that his encouraging words did, indeed, boost her confidence.

And that confidence disappeared as soon as they pulled into the driveway of his parents' house. Her dad had always been very successful and, even after the divorce, she'd lived in comfort, but nothing had prepared her for Tanner's home.

"Tanner…" She couldn't even utter more than his name, suddenly sick to her stomach.

"What's wrong, Belle?" He guided the Jeep around the curve in the long, cement driveway. His tone was completely nonchalant and completely irritating.

She blinked a few times as they crested the top of the drive and the house came into view. Her mouth was dry and her voice hoarse when she finally spoke. "You live in a mansion."

He threw the car into park in front of the wide stone steps leading to the front door. Tanner's brows drew together. He leaned over the center console and regarded the two-story red brick house sprawled out in front of the passenger's window. "Nah, it's not a mansion."

Izzy turned in her seat and pinned him with a look full of disbelief. "We drove through a wrought iron gate, up a two-mile long driveway, and I'm fairly certain somebody named Jeeves is going to be opening the front door any second to welcome the young master home from university."

After several beats of silence, Tanner erupted with laughter. He grabbed both sides of Izzy's face and pulled her in for a warm, sweet kiss. "Not a mansion. No staff. No pretentious family. Just a bunch of people who have spent the past two months hearing about my amazing girlfriend and can't wait to meet her. Even more tomorrow, when the rest of them show up for Thanksgiving."

She smiled against his mouth and linked her hands behind his neck. "You've been talkin' bout me?"

He hummed in the affirmative as she deepened the kiss before pulling back slightly. "You may want to stop there, sweetheart. Even though there aren't any servants waiting in the wings, I can almost guarantee there are half a dozen people gathered around those windows."

Her cheeks burned, and she buried her face against his chest. "You could have said something sooner," she mumbled against his blue-checkered button-down shirt.

Tanner did nothing more than laugh and plant a final kiss on her temple before tugging her into the house behind him. Despite the nerves leading up to meeting the Carlisle family, Mike and Tracy quickly made Izzy feel like more than a welcome guest—they made her feel like she was exactly where she belonged.

As Tanner assured her, there were no servants waiting in the wings. Other than Tanner himself, who made a point to make sure Izzy did nothing. When he carried her bag to her room, she was grateful. When she wanted a drink of water and he practically knocked over the chair he was sitting in to get it, she thought it was sweet. But when he tried to fill her plate for her at dinner, she flashed a sweet smile to the rest of his family and begged to be excused before pulling him from the table.

She dragged him down one of the long halls before ducking into an alcove beneath the stairs, confident they were out of earshot. "Tanner. What was that?"

A look of utter confusion descended on his face. "Dinner? With you and my family?" He shook his head but took the opportunity of their secluded space to pull her close and bury his face in her neck. "I mean if you want to do something else…"

Izzy smacked his shoulder and pushed him away, unable to stop the laughter that accompanied it. "No! And I mean with the waiting on me hand and foot thing. I appreciate that you like doing stuff for me, but baby, your family is going to think I'm some sort of spoiled princess."

"Too much?" He winced before flashing her the sad puppy dog eyes that wormed their way straight into her heart.

She held her thumb and forefinger a half an inch apart. "Just a little." Not wanting to hurt his feelings, she wrapped her arms around his waist and stood on her tip toes to offer a kiss. "How about after dinner we go into one of the other million rooms in this place not occupied by various members of your family and watch a movie?"

The look of chagrin disappeared at the suggestion, replaced quickly with a mischievous smile. "Have you been reading my business textbooks, sweetheart? Because you are getting pretty damn good at this negotiating thing. Maybe you'll have to join Dad's company with me after graduation."

Izzy clamped down on her bottom lip. Was he really planning on still being with her in four years? Sure, he said he loved her, and she loved him more than she thought it was possible to love another human, but...

Her thoughts contorted her face into a mixture of concern and disbelief. She could tell the exact moment Tanner read her expression. "Belle, what's wrong?"

"You still want to be with me?" The words tumbled out before she could cover with an excuse. She found it nearly impossible to keep anything from Tanner. "I mean, when we graduate. And after. You still want to be with me?"

Every feature on his face from his strong brow line to his square jaw softened. A small smile she had never seen before lit his lips and his eyes. "Sweetheart, I don't know how to tell you this without scaring you." He shook his head slightly. "Belle, I love you and I just don't see a life for me without you in it. Forever. I know this seems too soon—"

Before he could finish his thought, she leapt into his arms, wrapping her own around his neck and her legs around his waist. She wanted to tell him how much that meant. How she had been uncertain in every area of her life and in every relationship other than theirs. How every dream she had always held for her future suddenly included him in it. But she couldn't. "Me too," she whispered in his ear.

He sighed softly in reply and just held her until a loud growl made them both pull back. Pink appeared on Izzy's cheeks once more, and she glanced down at her abdomen. "Sorry?" She wrinkled her nose.

Never letting go, Tanner held her close and walked them both back to the dining room with a chuckle, only releasing her just outside of the entryway. "All right, all right, go fix your own plate, Princess Belle."

She winked before turning into the dining room. "Princess? That would make you Prince Charming, eh?"

After a cheerful family dinner the likes of which Izzy had never experienced before, she shooed him out of the kitchen, assuring him she could help his mother put everything away and load the dishwasher by herself while he chose a movie. She couldn't help that her eyes tracked him as he left the room. Or that the entire evening had left a grin on her face she couldn't lose.

"You're good for him," a voice behind her commented softly.

Izzy straightened from her position stacking the plates in the dishwasher. "I'm sorry?" She certainly couldn't have heard Mrs. Carlisle right. Tanner was the perfect boyfriend. He didn't need any improvement.

A warm smile graced her lips, and she tucked a stray curl of light brown hair identical to Tanner's behind her ear. "You're good for Tanner. He's never been this excited to come home. He's never brought anyone here, even when he was in high school, and he has never looked so peaceful and relaxed. I swear that child was born to carry all the responsibility on his shoulders." She tilted her head and looked at Izzy thoughtfully. "Yeah, you're good for him."

As her words sank in, warmth spread through her chest. He really did love her. He really did think she was special. They were special.

"We're good for each other."

Chapter Six

Tanner

Belle looked like a deer in the headlights. Tanner cursed himself ten different ways in his head. He debated the right way to answer his father before heaving a sigh and looking directly at Belle as he spoke. "Something I'm going to regret for the rest of my life."

Despite being over thirty years old and built almost as big as his hulking father, Tanner still felt like a child when Mike Carlisle fixed his disapproving glare directly on him. He opened the front door and practically shoved his son outside. "I'll deal with you in a minute," he growled as the storm door slammed closed.

He closed his eyes and inhaled deeply. The voices from the other side of the door reached him easily. He hadn't intended to eavesdrop but...

"That no good, lousy son of a—"

A small sniffle was followed by a forced laugh. "He's your son, so that's more insulting to you and

Mom than to him."

He could hear his father huff. "Izzy, honey, tell me how you're really doing."

Silence. It stretched for so long Tanner began to think they had walked away, but then a hiccuping sob ripped through the air and his heart. He really was a no good, lousy son of a bitch. Maybe his father could be talked into kicking his ass. The idea made Tanner snort. That would take exactly zero convincing.

"He didn't sleep with her and I am so grateful for that." Belle's tortured voice was so soft it barely reached his ears. "But he just fell into the arms of someone else. After twelve years together, eight years of marriage, and two kids. He just so easily walked away from all of that to someone whose name he doesn't even know."

"You can come stay with us. For tonight, for the week, hell, for the rest of your life if you want."

Tanner paused with his hand on the doorknob. Hell. No. Belle was entertaining the idea of letting him stay. It wasn't out of the question. No way was he going to let his dad take her away from him before he could even start to win her back.

"No." Her voice sounded slightly more controlled, and his movements stilled. "No, he's...I mean we..." She sighed, and Tanner found himself holding his breath for her next words. "Dad, he's Tanner. We've been together for nearly half my life. And there is no way I'm going to let the kids go through what I went through until I've had time to think about it all."

He softly let out the breath he didn't even realize

he was holding. She wasn't going to leave. So wrapped up in his relief he missed the next words Izzy said. Shit. Was she still going to make him go? He knew he had no damn right, but he found himself getting irritated that she kept changing her mind.

The sound of his father's steps getting closer made Tanner jump as silently as possible over to the other side of the porch and grip the railing.

"You're too damn old to be listening in on someone else's conversation." His father stood beside him and shoved his hands in his pockets. Neither looked at each other, pretending to memorize the same view of the mountains they'd been looking at for the past six years since construction finished on the house.

Tanner swallowed hard and leaned on the dark wooden railing. "I didn't hear everything. Is she…" He closed his eyes and sighed. "Is she kicking me out?"

Mike shrugged his shoulders. "That's between the two of you. But, son, dammit. Why the hell did you go and screw around?"

Why. The same question Belle wanted answered. Hell, the same question he wanted answered. "I don't know," he enunciated each word. "Wyatt wanted to celebrate his win and one drink turned into more than I can count, and he had this group of fans following him and I just…" He released the rail and ran his hands over his face. "I just screwed up."

"You need to fix this before you lose the best thing in your life."

Tanner rolled his eyes at his father. "Don't you think I know that?" He had repeated nearly the exact same words to himself nearly all night. "I've got a plan. Belle just has to let me try."

Finally his father turned and pinned him with a disgusted look. "That girl doesn't have to do a damn thing." He poked Tanner in the chest with his index finger. "You have to fix this. I don't care if you have to crawl up the Looking Glass Rock Trail on your knees to get her to forgive you, just do it."

He raised his eyebrows and propped his hip against the railing. "Hike up a six-mile trail with a fifteen hundred foot or so elevation gain on my knees? Yeah, this isn't going to be that easy."

His father offered a snort and headed back toward the house. He pulled the glass door open, then regarded his son silently for a few moments. Tanner tried to ignore the desire to squirm under his father's scrutiny. "You don't deserve easy, son."

With a groan, Tanner turned and rested his forehead on the post. "I know I don't deserve easy. But I can't lose her. I have to make this plan work." He tapped his head against the post a few times before straightening up and squaring his shoulders. "And the plan starts tomorrow."

***

"Do you trust me?"

Tanner just stared at Belle in complete disbelief. Did he trust her? Was she kidding? He rested against the front of her car, cold from the December air. "Of course I trust you."

53

A note of mischief lit her eyes. "So I can blindfold you and drive you to an undisclosed location and you'll be totally okay with it?"

"Uhhh," he glanced down at the strip of material in her hand before looking at her smiling face again, "yeah. I guess so?"

He questioned the decision the entire drive to wherever Belle was going. They had just finished their last day of class before winter break, and he was looking forward to spending every moment he wasn't at football practice with Belle. Being kidnapped, however, did not figure into his plans.

The tail of the blindfold was tickling the back of his neck, his sense of direction was out of whack, and it felt like they had been driving for hours. *Nah, this isn't going to work.* He opened and closed his mouth, trying to think of a nice way to shut this down.

"We're almost there." She squeezed his hand excitedly.

That was all it took to silence his complaint and make him smile. She had been acting secretive and downright giddy for days. At the time he had chalked it up to the upcoming holidays, but now he realized it was because she was planning something for him. Damn, he loved this girl. And he wasn't going to ruin anything she worked on by whining.

"Okay, stay right there," she instructed sternly, throwing the car in park. Before he could respond, she had climbed out, rounded the car, and was tugging on his arm to lead him to what he could only hope was their final destination.

Wordlessly she led him a few feet and through

what sounded like sliding doors. A quick turn to the left and they suddenly stood still. "Are we there? Can I take this off now?" He failed to keep the hopeful lilt from his voice.

A ding sounded just then and she pulled him forward again. Familiar sounds of tightening cables greeted his ears followed by a *whoosh* and movement that made him feel slightly unsteady.

"Are we in an elevator?" His mind began cataloguing the places Belle could possibly want to bring him that included an elevator.

She hummed in the affirmative against his cheek, offering a gentle kiss, and then dissolved into giggles. Belle giggled. She never giggled. She'd laugh, mostly at him when he wasn't trying to be funny, she'd chuckle and shake her head at his bad jokes, but Belle never, ever giggled. What the hell?

They came to a stop, and when the doors opened, their little game of follow the leader resumed. He swallowed back more complaints that wanted to bubble to the surface.

Less than two minutes later, after she had helped him out of his coat and took off her own, Belle untied the blindfold, and Tanner was oh so glad he had bit back every damn word. His eyes swung around the hotel room, drinking in every detail from the candles on the dresser and end tables to her memory foam pillow he loved so much on the bed. No wonder she had disappeared for so long this morning.

Finally his gaze settled on the petite brunette standing by his side, fidgeting with the cloth that had been used to cover his eyes. She bit down on her lower lip and lifted her shoulder slightly. "I-I don't know if you want to, I-I mean m-maybe I should have asked, but I thought—"

His mouth covered hers in a hungry kiss, cutting off her words. He wrapped his arms around her waist and lifted her off her feet, eliciting a squeak against his mouth. Driven by the hunger that had grown over their months together, he set her on the small desk to their left and let his hands travel under her shirt and across her silky skin. He nudged against her knees, encouraging her to open them. She groaned when he pressed against her.

Slow down. Somewhere in the recesses of his mind, logic kicked in. This wasn't a random hook-up. This wasn't a one-night stand. This was *his* Belle, and this was her first time. He needed to make this good for her.

The very reminder that he would be the only one to know what Belle looked like after he stripped her clothes off, the sounds she made as he kissed every inch of her body, and what she felt like when he finally slid inside her fed his already healthy ego. A cocky smile spread across his face as he pulled back slightly to look at her.

Her cheeks were tinged with pink and her eyes were wide with desire. "So that's a yes, then?" she asked in a breathless voice.

Tanner cupped her face in his hands and ran his thumb over her bottom lip. "Oh sweetheart, 'yes' is only the beginning."

She covered his hands with hers and looked deep into his eyes. "I love you and I want to be with you so badly, but I-I've never…and you've…and…"

She huffed her frustration. "I don't want to do anything wrong."

He dropped his hands to her waist and pulled her tightly against him, lifting her off the desk. He carried her to the bed and gently laid her on the maroon cover, bracing himself over her on his elbows. "Belle, you can't and won't do a damn thing wrong. Sweetheart, everything you do already feels so good."

Tanner sat up, resting on his calves, and grabbed the hem of his shirt. Before he could tug it up, Belle scrambled to her knees and put her trembling hands over his. "No!"

The single word had the effect of ice water. Shit. She wasn't ready. His hands fell to his side, and he forced what he hoped was a comforting smile. "It's okay, Belle. If you aren't ready, we can just—"

"Oh no." She shook her head and bit down on her bottom lip. "No, baby, I'm ready. I just wanted, well, what I mean is I was hoping…" She sighed. "Can I do that?"

Dammit all to hell, this girl was going to test every ounce of self-control he possessed. "Yeah." His voice was strained. "But only if I get to take yours off next."

Belle grinned and shook her head. "Oh, that business degree of yours."

She slid the shirt up and over his head, her hands brushing against him as she did, and her eyes grew at the sight of him without a shirt on. When her tongue darted out to lick her lips, Tanner couldn't help but groan in response.

She obediently raised her arms. "Okay, baby,

your turn."

Shit. They had only gotten two pieces of clothing out of the way and he was already feeling the pain from his suddenly too-tight jeans. As soon as her shirt was lying on the floor next to his, she pointed to the offending pants. "Next."

Tanner tried to think of something, anything that would make his body slow down as she pulled off his pants. Seeing his grandmother in a bikini. Seeing anyone other than Belle in a bikini. Dammit, that didn't work. Now he was picturing her in a bikini.

Belle laid back on the bed, and he peeled back her jeans to reveal the black and gold underwear that matched her bra. His brain finally kicked in, and he grinned. "Wearing the team colors, sweetheart?"

She raised her eyebrows and smiled, rolling onto her stomach once the pants had been tossed to the side, showing off the number 76 emblazoned on the back. *Dammit all to hell.* This was going to be a short night if she kept this up. "Turn over, Belle," he instructed in a hoarse voice. He covered her body with his and began kissing her forehead, nose, lips, and trailed his way down her jaw line. "How the hell did you get my number across your ass?"

Belle offered a throaty laugh that caught slightly as he slid her bra straps down her arms and followed his hands with his lips. As soon as he released the hook, she buried her fingers in his hair. "Some secrets are meant to be kept."

"That's true," he agreed, lavishing attention to her chest with his lips and tongue before moving lower. "Like the secret of how you taste? The secret of how you sound when you scream my name? The secret of how you feel when you're drenched in sweat and wrapped around my body? Yeah, sweetheart, those are all my secrets to keep."

He slid the ego boosting but oh-so-unnecessary underwear down her firm legs, planting gentle kisses on every inch of skin he exposed. Her soft gasps brought a smirk to his lips.

Make it good for her. Hell yeah, he was going to make it good for her.

His fingers and his lips worshiped her smooth, silky core languidly for long moments, until her quiet moans reached a fevered pitch and she cried out his name.

Tanner slid his body back up hers and planted gentle kisses along her shoulder and neck as the shudders started to subside from her body. She dug her fingers in the hair she loved to play with and pulled him up to her mouth. After a long deep kiss, she pulled his head back. "I need you, baby."

He was fairly certain he'd never removed his boxers faster or less gracefully as he kicked them away, but her words acted like gasoline to the fire of his desire for her. He couldn't move fast enough and...

Shit. Shit, shit, shit, shit. He stilled as he hovered over her.

"What's the matter baby?" She slid her still shaking hands over his shoulders and down his arms.

"Protection." He practically spat the single word. He'd never been without a condom before, but for nearly four months, it had only been Belle and he'd never needed anything and never intended to do anything with her without careful planning and preparation and…shit.

A slow smile spread across her face, and she put a hand on his cheek. She lifted up enough to plant a moist kiss to his lips. "I started birth control last month."

He dropped his head between his shoulders and rested his forehead against hers. He really didn't need anything else to test his ability to go slow with her. Feeling her skin against his without anything in between? Damn. Maybe he could recite banking laws in Switzerland.

Calling on every iota of self-control he had in his body, he slid slowly and gently inside her, wincing when he saw her brows pull together and her lips turn down. He stilled, giving her time to adjust. "Are you okay, Belle?"

When she lifted her eyes to him, the love he saw reflected back took every molecule of air from his lungs. "I know you won't hurt me, baby. Keep going."

His chest swelled with pride at her uninhibited trust, and his body began to move in and out with very little input from his brain. Each stroke brought the same thought to his mind: *Damn, I love her*.

Although he thought it completely impossible, icy warmth spread through his body at the exact time Belle's eyes widened. The sound of his name erupting from her lips was mixed with his own guttural cry.

Completely drained of all his energy, Tanner fell

to the bed beside her on his back and drew her close to his side. Belle threw one leg over his thigh and rested her head on his bare chest. They lay there for a long time, the silence punctuated only by their heavy breathing, trying desperately to return to normal.

"Tanner?"

Her soft voice carried up to him, and he struggled to open his eyes. "Yeah, sweetheart?"

She propped her chin on his chest and looked up at him. The uncertainty and downright fear in her eyes felt like a knife to his heart. "Was that...I mean I loved that, but was that good? F-for you? W-was I okay? Was I good enough for you?"

Good enough? He rolled her beneath him and held her chin firmly with one hand. "I've never, and I mean *never*, known anything in this world that could compare to you, Belle. I meant what I said, sweetheart. I want you with me every day for the rest of my life. Hell no, you're not good enough; you're too damn good for me. But since I'm one lucky guy, I get to keep you anyway. Forever."

Her smile made him feel like he was ten feet tall, and he fell into the deepest sleep of his life holding her by his side. Exactly where she was going to stay.

Chapter Seven

Izzy

When her alarm rang at five o'clock in the morning, what felt like twenty minutes after she'd finally fallen asleep, Izzy reached one hand out to slap it off. She rolled over and buried her face in Tanner's pillow, drifting back to sleep surrounded by his scent.

When Tanner's normal wake-up call sounded an hour later, she pushed the off button and pulled the covers over her head with a groan. Just a little longer. She'd stay in bed just a little longer, then she'd be rested enough to get up and smile in front of the kids.

But when the smell of bacon wafted in the room some time later, Izzy sat straight up in bed with a frown. Her feet hit the floor, and she padded over to the bedroom door, cracking it slightly. Was that maple syrup?

She crossed her arms over the tank top she had slept in and glanced down at her shorts. They had coffee cups with little wings and clouds printed all over them. Two days ago she would have thought nothing of it.

But today? She suddenly and irrationally wondered what *she* had worn. Did she wear skin-tight jeans and a low-cut top held up by thin spaghetti straps? Or a white strapless western dress with brown cowboy boots?

The thought made her stomach churn and, despite the fact she hadn't eaten yet, she felt certain she'd be sick. Instead, she squared her shoulders and marched down the stairs resolutely. If Tanner thought one stupid little breakfast was going to make her forget that he had his lips on someone else and his hands on someone else, he was definitely…

Her eyes fell on the virtual buffet laid out on the kitchen island. A single plate surrounded by dishes of pancakes, French toast, bacon, sausage, and nearly every piece of fruit she could dream of was laid out before her. A steaming cup of coffee and a small glass of orange juice sat beside the empty plate.

"What?" Her voice sounded tight even to her own ears. "What is this?"

Tanner spun away from the stove, carrying a dish piled high with scrambled eggs. "Good mornin' swee—I mean Isabelle." He offered a small smile. "Did you sleep well?"

Izzy shook her head, both as a response to his question and in disbelief of the scene before her. "Tanner, what is all of this?" She repeated the question, unable to think of anything else to say. Just then the realization they were alone struck her.

"Where are the kids?"

"Breakfast," he answered with a smile, "for you. And they are with Uncle Connor."

She quickly swallowed the mouthful of coffee before she spit it out and plopped on one of the high stools at the island. Tanner was the oldest of the four boys and, while Wyatt was easily the least concerned with safety, none of his brothers could be labeled responsible. "Uncle Connor?"

Tanner held up a hand. "Don't worry. They are going to breakfast and then going swimming at my parents' house. There will be actual adults there to keep him in line and the kids safe."

"W-why aren't you at work?"

He shrugged and propped his hip on the opposite side of the island. "I'm taking some time off. There have to be some perks to being the boss."

Izzy's eyes grew wide for a moment before she shook her head and looked down. Honestly, the more time she spent in his presence the more confused she became. It would be better if he just went to the office. "Tanner, I—"

He leaned forward, resting his forearms on the counter. "Just give me five minutes before you say anything." He nodded his head toward the plethora of food laid out before her. "And eat while I talk. You didn't eat anything yesterday."

Her mouth opened to argue until she thought back over the day before. He was right. As if the realization kicked her body into action, her stomach growled and she slowly started putting food on her plate. She held it up once it was full to show Tanner. "Happy?"

64

He regarded her solemnly for a few seconds. "I have a proposition for you."

She nearly choked on the eggs in her mouth. *Is that the pick-up line he used on* her? She closed her eyes against the thought, wondering if she could ever have a normal conversation with Tanner again without these thoughts assailing her. "Okay…"

"Keep eating." He nodded toward her still full plate. "Our anniversary is coming up."

Izzy rolled her eyes and chewed on a strawberry. Of course she knew their anniversary was soon. "Yeah, I know. Next month."

"It's in forty-three days," he recited immediately. Tanner had never forgotten their anniversary, but she had to admit the fact he knew the exact number of days was impressive. And, if she let herself be honest, it tugged at her aching heart. "So I'm asking you for forty-three days."

Her fork, laden with a syrupy square bite of pancake, stalled halfway to her mouth and she stared at him. "You're asking for forty-three days for what?" She stuffed the bite of food in her mouth and set her fork down. Any appetite she'd had disappeared.

"To show you that, in spite of my," he shook his head and dropped his gaze, "behavior, you and the kids mean the world to me. To show you that I love you with every part of me. To show you that you can trust me again."

Tanner rounded the island and stood beside her. "Belle, if I woke up tomorrow and found out I lost the company, the house, and that yellow truck you love so much, but I got to keep you and Ava and

Noah? I wouldn't miss a thing. I know what I did undermines that, and maybe even before that I wasn't showing you the way I should have, but you and the kids are my top priority."

Cautiously he reached his hand out and laid it on top of hers. "So I'm asking you not to make any decisions one way or another for forty-three days. I'm asking you to take a chance on me and let me do the rest. At the end of that time if you want me to leave, I'll go."

Izzy closed her eyes against the conflicting emotions rolling through her. Why did Tanner have to be—Tanner? She swallowed a few times and tried to summon as much strength as she could to open her eyes and meet the sapphire ones staring back at her. There really was only one answer she could give. "Okay," she answered softly.

A mixture of relief and trepidation washed over his face. "Okay?"

She nodded, feeling slightly more confident in her decision.

Another wide grin settled on Tanner's face. "Today is day one. Go get dressed."

***

"What the hell was that?"

Tanner practically slammed the door to her dorm shut and dropped his duffel bag on the floor. Izzy had her back to him, stuffing papers she needed for class tomorrow in her backpack. A grin tugged at the corners of her mouth, but she schooled her features into a nonchalant expression before turning to face him. "What was what, baby? Did you have a bad practice?"

He took three large strides over to her, locking an arm around her waist and lifting her against him. He spun them both around so she was caught between the wall and his hard body. She let out a little squeak and tightened her thighs around his waist.

His blue eyes were stormy with desire. He lowered his head and practically devoured her mouth. Izzy knew it would be the worst possible time to laugh, but she was slightly giddy her plan had worked so well. When his tongue took possession of her mouth, however, any idea of laughing was quickly replaced with her overwhelming need for Tanner.

"Did I have a bad practice?" He repeated her words back to her in between kisses. His hands quickly pulled her short, thin nightgown over her head and his eyes drank in every inch of her olive skin. "You put a picture like that in my bag and you expect me to concentrate on baseball? Shit, I'm gonna get cut from the team after my performance today."

She slid her hands under his shirt and lifted it over his head. Her stomach clenched. Suddenly the idea that had seemed so playful and fun felt like a huge mistake. "I-I'm sorry baby, I never realized—"

He cut off her words with another hungry kiss. "If I do get cut, it'd be the best damn reason." His lips made a trail down her neck and shoulders. "Holy hell, Belle, that was the sexiest picture I've ever seen and you weren't even in it. I'm not sure if I'm disappointed by that or friggin' grateful."

When she had found the white matching bra and panty set with red stitching to resemble a baseball, she knew she had to buy them and get his jersey number embroidered on the back. The idea to take a picture of them laid out on her bed and throw it in his duffel bag for the first day of baseball practice had been much less thought out. She chuckled at his comment. Obviously it was going to pay off for her big time.

His hands moved down from her waist and under her thighs, sliding backward, finding nothing but bare skin.

Tanner lifted his head from the shoulder where he was leaving a trail of bites and looked in her eyes, a mixture of confusion and need reflecting back at her. "You were seriously sitting in this room waiting for me to come back, wearing only a nightgown, and not a single piece of clothing on underneath?" His hands gripped each cheek tightly as he spoke.

Izzy couldn't even remember how they managed to slide his sweatpants and boxers low enough, but it didn't really matter once he drove deep inside her. She gasped at the passion-fueled force. Tanner always treated her like a porcelain doll. He would spend long moments exploring and tasting every part of her body bringing her to frantic climax several times. Not today. Not this time. And she was so relieved.

Her grip tightened in the hair at the nape of his neck and she pulled him hard against her. She needed this, she needed him, more than she needed her next breath. The force of each thrust felt like she was going to go through the wall holding them up.

He dug his fingers deeper into each of her hips, and she was convinced she'd wind up with bruises. She smiled against his lips. She had been waiting for this side of Tanner to show up. If she had known all it would take was one little picture, she would have done that weeks ago.

She pulled her head back as far as the wall would allow and looked into his eyes. Every other time he whispered words of love and adoration. His eyes reflected the truths to her. But today all she saw was his desperate need.

Feeling slightly drunk on her passion, Izzy tightened her inner muscles around him as he moved inside her. His eyes widened and he dropped his head against hers. "Shit, sweetheart, I'm not gonna last much longer if you keep that up." He bit her shoulder a little harder than normal. "Been thinking about your tight little body wrapped around mine all friggin' day," he mumbled against her skin.

His words were the switch to her release, stronger than it had ever been. She pulled his mouth up to hers to silence unintelligible screams and felt a surge in her ego as she felt his deep groan.

Tanner's kisses turned soft and less demanding. After several long moments, he seemed to gather his strength enough to pull them both off the wall and gently lay her in bed before climbing in beside her. His gaze washed over her, lingering on the red bite mark on her shoulder and the finger

69

impressions left on her thighs, before he pulled the covers over her body. "Shit. I'm an asshole." He whispered the words more to himself than her.

Izzy pulled his face close to hers and brushed her lips across his. "Why would you think that, baby? That was incredible."

"That was reckless. Rough." He shook his head. "I'm sorry, sweetheart."

She tugged on his arms until they were wrapped tightly around her. "Baby, that was exactly what I wanted. I'm not an antique vase that will break if you blow on it wrong."

His blue eyes, still tinged with concern, grew wide. "Y-you wanted—"

"I wanted you to know you have me. Any time. Any where. Any way." She grinned when his mouth fell open. "Although you may need to give me a tiny bit of time to rest if you're gonna do that again. Which you are, you know. Doing that. Again."

Tanner chuckled and held her close against his chest. After a long silence, he finally spoke again. "Belle, there was something I've been thinking about."

Her eyelids heavy, she snuggled in closer to him. "I told you, baby, just a little rest."

When he laughed again, she felt the rumble all the way to her toes and smiled to herself. "Yeah, we'll get to that, but I was thinking about the summer."

Izzy's eyes flew open. That was something she had intentionally not been thinking of. It was an impossible situation. She had no desire to go back to New York, but there was no way she could afford to stay in North Carolina unless she lived in her car. More than anything she definitely didn't want to spend three months away from Tanner. Her heart ached at the very idea.

"I want to get an apartment." He made the declaration with very little preamble. "And then we can just stay there once school starts again. I mean, we've been pretty lucky we haven't gotten in trouble yet for all the time I spend here, and there really is no way in hell I am going to let you spend every night alone so—"

"No," she cut him off. She lifted her head and stared at him. What was he thinking? She worked part-time in a coffee shop. There was no way she could afford to share an apartment with him. And he might hate living with her. He might find her cooking disgusting and her overzealous cleaning habits annoying.

His eyebrows flew up. "No?"

She shook her head. "No. Unless I start making way more than minimum wage, I can't get an apartment."

"Sweetheart, I'm working at my dad's company over the summer. He's training me to take over once I graduate. Hell, he's gonna lease office space here so I don't have to commute or move back home. Trust me, I'll make more than enough to take care of us. You can work if you want to, but you won't have to."

Izzy jumped out of the bed and grabbed her discarded nightgown off the floor, not willing to do battle sans clothes. She paced the small room a few times before turning to face Tanner, his head

71

propped on one arm, watching her silently. "But what if this doesn't work?"

She finally spoke her biggest fear out loud and hated the vulnerable feeling it left. She wrapped her arms around herself and looked at the floor. In less than the space of a heartbeat, her arms were pulled apart and placed around his waist as he drew her close.

"Belle, you and I are a forever thing. I know you're scared, but I'm just asking you to take a chance on us and let me do the rest."

Izzy laid her head against his chest with a sigh. There really was only one answer she could give. "Okay."

Tanner hooked a finger under her chin and gave her a cocky grin. "Now, about that rest time…"

Chapter Eight

Tanner

She's nervous just sitting in a car with me.

Tanner called himself every colorful name he could think of and then created a few new ones simply because he deserved it. Belle had been fidgeting with the hem of her white lace tank top the entire ride. As much as he wanted to be hurt or irritated, there was not one part of him that could blame her.

But as soon as he took the downtown Winston-Salem exit, Belle sat up a little more in her seat and her hands suddenly stilled. Her eyes widened and she turned to face him. "Tanner, are we…"

He couldn't tell if she was excited at the idea of going back to WFU or disappointed. Shit. He really didn't need to screw up their first date. Well, their first date after his epic failure. "Yeah, we're going back to school." He managed a small smile. "Happy?"

A huge smile spread across Belle's face, and she

fixed her eyes on the road in front of them. Before she turned her head away, he caught the sparkle in her eyes and breathed a sigh of relief. The first date wasn't going to fall apart before it started.

"Happy? This is great! Tanner, we haven't been back in three years." As soon as the words left her mouth, her expression fell. "You've been too busy to go to games anymore."

He opened his mouth to argue. There was no way it had been three years.

When they were dating, Belle had transformed into a bigger football fan than him, and not just because he was on the team. Ever since they graduated, they had gone to as many of the home football games as possible, and five years ago they started buying season tickets. She even wore face paint and ridiculous faux hair hats. Yeah, he was busy last year, but they went the year before. Didn't they?

Dammit all to hell. She was right.

"I'm sorry, sweet—" He caught himself and covered the endearment with an awkward cough. "I'm sorry."

Belle lifted her shoulder in a half-shrug and looked out the passenger's window. When he took a right and the entrance came in view, she let out a small sigh. "I've missed this place." She said the words so softly, he wasn't sure if she was talking to him or herself.

He lifted a hand in greeting to the security guard as they drove through the gate. He kept a light smile on his face, but his mind raced. The words kept repeating over and over in his head. *You've been too busy*. Shit, shit, shit. Maybe he had more to make up for than he'd ever thought.

Tanner shook his head and threw his truck in park. He needed to stay focused. Focused on their date and completely focused on Belle. He hopped out of the truck and rounded the front as fast as he could to reach her door before she could exit on her own.

A small smile tugged at her mouth as he offered his hand to help her climb down. She bit down on her lower lip and slid her hand into his. "Thanks, Tanner."

Instead of releasing her hand when her feet hit the ground, Tanner intertwined their fingers and felt gratified to have even the small contact with Belle. When was the last time they simply held hands? Heat that had nothing to do with the June sun began to creep up his neck. He couldn't remember. That was pretty damn embarrassing.

Belle turned her head and her smile grew as she realized where they were going. "The quad by Trib Hall?" When he only nodded in response, she let out a happy sigh. "My favorite place on campus."

Damn, he loved that smile. "It is? I never knew that." He was ashamed to admit it out loud. Twelve years together, four of them spent right on this campus, and he never knew it was her favorite spot.

And then she laughed. Tanner felt like his heart was going to beat out of his chest. It had only been a few days, but it felt like years since he heard her laugh. "Of course it is. It's where we met."

"Well," he began, pointedly ignoring her sharp intake of breath as they rounded the same tree trunk where he had spent several days of his junior year positioning himself to gain her attention, "there may be a few details about that you don't know."

He had called in a favor with an old professor to get on campus over summer break, then given his youngest brother, Dean, detailed instructions on exactly how to set everything up. When he saw the red checkered cloth spread on the ground and the food laid out to precision, he breathed a sigh of relief. Even Belle's favorite purple gerbera daisies were laid in the middle of the cloth.

She released his hand and dropped to her knees, bringing the bouquet close to her nose and inhaling deeply. She looked at the small sandwiches, fruit, and cheese with a mixture of hunger and awe. "I have no idea how you managed this, but I love it."

Tanner took a seat beside her before his knees buckled under him at the sight of her light brown eyes glowing. When was the last time he had done something special for her? "Some secrets are meant to be kept."

The words left his mouth without a second thought, but when the look in her eyes changed, he realized what he said. And the memory of the first time they made love came rushing back. His body automatically responded by tightening as every kiss and touch flooded his mind. Belle bit her bottom lip and lifted a shaking hand to his cheek.

Tanner turned his head slightly and planted a warm kiss on her palm. As much as he wanted to do more, he pulled her hand from his cheek instead and held it clasped in his. Just like he did when they first started dating, he had no intention of rushing Belle into anything.

He cleared his throat. "But you get to hear one of those secrets right now."

Storm clouds began to form behind her eyes, and he cursed himself again. Shit. She probably thought it was something bad.

"I sat here on purpose," he spoke quickly, hoping to dispel the fear evident on her face. "The day we met? That wasn't the first day I saw you."

Belle squinted at him. "What do you mean?"

Tanner chuckled lightly and dared to take hold of her other hand. When she didn't pull away, he slowly released the breath he had been holding. *Hell, this is more nerve wracking than our real first date.* "I saw you on the fourth day of school. I started sitting here as much as possible to try to get you to come over to me."

Her eyebrows shot up, and after a brief pause she started laughing. "What? You did that on purpose? Why? And why didn't you ever tell me?"

"I was used to girls coming up to me and I thought you would, eventually." He dropped his gaze, a light flush staining his cheeks, and rubbed his thumbs across the backs of her hands. "But I didn't want to wait any longer. I didn't tell you because..." he shrugged, "...because once you were mine, that was all that mattered."

They sat there for a long time in silence, just staring at each other and not finding a single reason to speak. Finally a small smile spread across her face. "So far, you're pretty good at this, um, whole trial period thing."

Tanner picked up a strawberry and held it up to

her with a grin. "And you're pretty damn perfect at this whole loving me thing."

***

He gripped the square white box a little tighter in his hand and took a fortifying breath before turning the knob to go into Belle's dorm. Well, their dorm really. He rarely slept anywhere else.

The wide grin he had on his face evaporated when he saw Belle sitting on her bed, forehead on her knees, sobbing. What the hell? He'd only been gone a few hours.

He threw the box on the desk and shot over to the bed, collecting her in his arms. "Belle, sweetheart, what's wrong?"

She curled into his embrace and buried her face in his neck. She didn't answer. As a hiccup broke free, Tanner wondered if she could even speak.

Rage started to build with his confusion. Whoever did this, whoever made his Belle cry, was in for some serious issues. With him. The most heartbreaking thing he'd ever seen was Belle falling apart in his arms. Someone was in for an ass kicking.

After what felt like hours of listening to her sob while he held her against his chest, she finally started to calm down. He stroked her hair softly and kissed her forehead. "Okay, sweetheart, now can you tell me what's wrong?"

She sniffled and lifted her head from his red shirt, now sopping wet from her tears. His heart fractured at her swollen, red-rimmed eyes. "I-I talked to my dad. I told him. I-I told him about our apartment a-and that he wouldn't h-h-have to pay for the single room next year because we were just going to keep it when school started again and…"

Her voice broke as another wave of tears began. Tanner tucked her head under his chin and pulled her closer. He ran his hand down her back and made soothing sounds, as much for himself as for her. He loved Belle with all his heart, and he was pretty sure driving to New York and punching her dad in the nose was not the most endearing thing he could do. He needed to get his anger under control.

"What'd he say, Belle?" he asked between clenched teeth, bracing himself for an answer he knew he wouldn't like.

She shook her head against him. "I can't tell you."

Well, that was irritating. He shifted uncomfortably and adjusted her on his lap. She couldn't tell him? What the hell was that supposed to mean? He wanted her to tell him everything. Bring him every problem. Let him take care of her. Didn't she trust him?

Belle lifted a hand to his cheek and offered a watery smile. "Don't think that."

His brows knit together, and his mouth turned down. "Don't think what?"

"Don't think I don't trust you." She spoke his exact thought back to him. "I do, baby. But if I tell you, you're going to try to fix it. Even if that means doing something crazy." She planted a soft kiss on his lips. "And I love you for taking such good care of me, but this is something I have to fix on my

79

own."

Tanner cupped her cheek. "I promise I won't do anything crazy, sweetheart. Just tell me." He silently cursed her father ten ways from Sunday, not only for hurting her but for ruining the surprise he had. Asshole.

Belle took a deep breath. "My dad said if I don't live on campus, if I move in with you, he isn't going to pay for any of my college anymore. I-I have to try to get loans or financial aid or something. I never had to do that before and I don't know where to start and I have to get something quick because I don't want…" A single tear streaked down her cheek. "I don't want to leave WFU, and I can't leave you."

He leaned his head down and slowly, gently, his lips moved against hers in a reverent kiss. "You're not going anywhere, Belle. We'll go to the financial aid office tomorrow and figure this out. I'm not letting you leave."

He didn't bother mentioning that he would work three jobs to pay her tuition, if that's what it took. Hell, he'd borrow the entire damn thing from his dad and work for him for free for the next ten years if he had to. No way in hell he was letting his Belle leave or worry about it for another minute. He was Tanner Carlisle; he took care of the people he loved. And he loved her beyond all sense and reason.

"Speaking of not leaving," he reached over the end of the bed and grabbed the small white box from the desk, not letting her move off his lap, "there's something you need."

Her eyes clouded with confusion and trepidation

as she examined the small square. "What's this?"

He grinned and kissed her. He would never get tired of the taste of her lips or the soft sounds she made when their mouths met. "The best way to find out is to open it, sweetheart."

Belle frowned at the key and keychain inside the box. She pulled it out carefully and examined it. Her sharp intake of breath made his smile wider. "My heart has found its home." She read the silver engraved bangle before lifting her eyes to his again.

"This is the key to our apartment, sweetheart." He put a hand behind her head and tilted it to give her a deep kiss. He hoped she was as excited as he was, and he hoped to hell her father hadn't ruined what they were building together.

She smiled softly, and his heart stopped beating at the sight. "You're pretty good at this whole taking care of me thing."

Tanner swallowed down the emotion clogging his throat. "And you're damn near perfect at this whole loving me thing."

Chapter Nine

Izzy

Izzy rearranged the flowers in the vase again. Tilting her head a little, she smiled, finally happy with the outcome.

Their date, their first date, had been four days ago, but just thinking of the picnic lunch made her smile grow. He'd thought out every detail more than she thought possible. From her favorite sandwiches to the bouquet of purple daisies— everything was perfect.

He had been attentive and thoughtful the entire day. Even after they came back home, he made her a cup of chocolate mint tea and offered to put her favorite guilty pleasure reality show on instead of the baseball game she knew he'd rather watch.

She captured her bottom lip between her teeth. He was like the old Tanner. She hadn't even realized how long it had been until he started doing all those little things again.

Shaking her head, she pulled open the freezer

drawer on the refrigerator and began searching for something to make for dinner. Before she could decide, she heard the thunderous sounds of Ava and Noah running down the stairs and couldn't help but roll her eyes.

"Hey, guys, what do you want for dinner?" she called out, her eyes never leaving the freezer as they bounded into the kitchen.

"Daddy said not to let you make dinner," Ava offered.

Noah nodded his head furiously. "Yeah, Daddy said we're—"

Before he could finish, his sister clapped a hand across his mouth. Izzy turned to face the kids with a frown. "Daddy said we're what?"

Chagrin washed over their faces and they glanced at each other, communicating in the silent way only twins could. In full ownership of her older sister status, even if it was only by mere minutes, Ava took the lead. "Daddy said not to let you make dinner and the rest was supposed to be a surprise."

Izzy fixed her hands on her hips and regarded them solemnly, fighting the urge to grin. She'd had the fleeting thought that Tanner had been so proud of his first attempt at winning her over he hadn't planned anything else. After the one day off, he'd returned to the office and, she assumed, life would just be the way it was before anything happened. Obviously she was wrong.

Her heart soared a little as she shut the freezer and heard the kids scamper away. On autopilot, she turned on her electric kettle to heat water for tea. Her mind was consumed with the same conflicting thoughts that had been plaguing her all week.

Tanner kissed someone else.

Tanner touched someone else.

But, then again, Tanner had spent the past three years distancing himself from his family, working more and more. Was it really that big of a surprise?

She poured the hot liquid over the teabag in her cup and began slowly sipping on the steaming brew. Maybe if she would have said something sooner, argued just a little harder about all the time he spent away, maybe he never would have…

The slamming of the screen door pulled her from the dark thoughts and nearly made her spill her hot drink. Her eyes grew wide, and she glanced at the clock on the stove. "Tanner?"

He tugged his tie off and threw it over one of the barstools surrounding the island. "Afternoon, sweetheart." He embellished his drawl with a grin. "Where are the kids?"

It took several minutes for Izzy to register his question. He was home. In the middle of the day. There was no emergency, no event planned, he was just…home. "Um, u-upstairs. They're upstairs in the play room. You're home?" Her thoughts tumbled out of her mouth without any input from her brain.

He sauntered around the island until he was standing in front of her. Gently he lifted the mug from her hands and set it on the counter behind her. "I'm home." He nodded along with the confirmation. He gripped each of her now-free hands in his and took another step closer to her, now only a breath away. "Tell me to stop, Belle, if you don't want this."

Do I? Do I want him to stop? His head slowly started to lower toward hers. She released his hands and put hers on his shoulders, immediately halting his movement. Then she smiled and slid her hands behind his neck and pulled his mouth the rest of the way to hers.

Oh, she'd missed this. She couldn't stop the moan from escaping her lips when he wrapped his arms around her waist and pulled her against his body. She ran her tongue across his bottom lip and smiled when she felt him shudder. She'd missed this.

But instead of his hands dropping lower or trailing kisses down her jaw and neck like her body was screaming for him to, he softened the kiss before pulling away. "It's good to be home."

Izzy felt confused and rejected when he kissed her once more softly and stepped away. Didn't he want her as much as she wanted him?

"So did the kids spill all the details?" he asked as he grabbed an apple from the basket on the counter. He leaned back against the island and took a big bite, grinning around the mouth full of fruit and juice.

She wrapped her arms around her unsettled abdomen. "Nope," she answered with as much brightness as she could muster. "They just said not to make dinner."

Tanner set the apple on the counter beside him and stepped in front of her again, hooking a finger under her chin to make her look at him. His playful expression had disappeared, and she read the concern etched on his face. "Hey, don't think that."

"Don't think what?"

He leaned his head down to brush his lips across hers, bracing himself on the counter on either side of her. "Don't think I don't want you more than any woman in the world and any woman I'll ever meet. Holy hell, sweetheart, you drive me crazy." He took another step closer until she felt the proof of his desire pressed against her stomach and gasped a little. "I toss and turn every night thinking about you lying in bed without me, wondering what you're wearing, wishing I could touch your skin. But not until you're ready."

They spent several long minutes staring at each other before his cocky smirk slipped back in place. "Now, I'm going to take the kids out to rent a movie and pick up a pizza. We're making Thursdays family movie night from now on."

In spite of their passionate exchange, an impish grin spread across her face. "So we're having family movie nights now?"

Tanner laughed, and it vibrated through her, doing nothing to lessen the desire churning inside. "Yeah, we are." He winked before he stepped back. "I'll rent some crappy adventure movie for us to watch after the kids go to sleep and we can practice making out on the couch."

Izzy's eyebrows shot up as he retreated up the stairs to collect the kids. Despite the warring emotions still swirling through her, she couldn't help but laugh. Making out with Tanner had never been just making out since the first time they made love, but she knew tonight would be different.

She just couldn't decide if she was grateful he was taking everything slow with her or highly annoyed at the knowledge she was going to go to bed alone again.

***

Izzy rearranged the dishes on the table for the fourth time. In spite of her fears, living with Tanner had been so easy. She smiled and bit her bottom lip as she looked at the table one more time before turning her attention back to the stove. She peeked at the chicken baking in the oven and hoped he would get home before it dried out.

Today was their first day back at school and Tanner's course load this semester was unreal. She couldn't help but worry that between his classes and football, he was overdoing it.

Just as she poured the pasta into the strainer in the sink, she heard the front door of their apartment click closed followed by a heavy sigh. "Belle?"

She poked her head around the corner and smiled at him. "I'm in the kitchen. Dinner's ready, baby."

He crossed the floor quickly and locked his arms around her before stealing her words, her thoughts, and her very breath with a passionate kiss. She pushed her fingers into his hair, pulling him closer against her, and smiled against his lips when she heard the deep groan.

"Holy hell, sweetheart, I don't know if I can handle this," he finally gasped when they broke apart. "You make me dinner every night." He dropped a quick peck on her lips. "You pack food for me every day to take to practice." Kiss. "And you take care of every other…appetite. You're damn close to perfect."

Izzy laughed and pulled him into the kitchen. "And since this is the first day of your senior year with the most ridiculous class schedule I've ever seen, you get your favorite."

Tanner closed his eyes and lifted his nose, inhaling a deep breath of the tomato, basil, and oregano scented air. "Chicken parmigiana?" His smile fell a little as he looked at her seriously. "This was your first day back too, Belle. You didn't need to do all of this."

She just shook her head, kissed his cheek, and pushed him into one of the chairs at the small table. Their apartment was cozy, at best, but she loved every inch. Even when she had to dance precariously around the table to set a plate in front of Tanner or when she had to have him move his chair to the side to open the refrigerator.

"Is it good?" she asked with a small laugh after he inhaled half of his plate before she could even sit down.

"Damn, woman, just when I think you can't possibly get better." The words were mumbled in between mouthfuls of food, and Izzy laughed harder.

When he'd polished off a second helping, he sat back and patted his hard six-pack abdomen with a heavy sigh. "I'm gonna wind up getting cut if I gain much more weight."

She abandoned her own seat and half-full plate to sit in his lap and loop her arms around his neck.

"I'm glad you liked it, baby." She dropped a soft kiss on his lips. When his arms tightened, she deepened the kiss and speared her fingers through his hair again. She ran her tongue across his bottom lip, relishing the shiver she felt from him, slightly drunk with the knowledge she could drive him as crazy as he did her.

Tanner groaned into her mouth and pulled away. "Sweetheart, this is my last night free from practice for a while."

Izzy frowned, sitting back slightly, and she battled against the feelings of rejection that always seemed to simmer just beneath the surface. "I know, baby." What was he saying?

A soft smile spread across his face. "Oh, that's definitely happening tonight, sweetheart. At least once before Coach starts kicking my ass so bad I can't move when I get home."

She flashed him a mischievous grin and quirked an eyebrow. "You don't have to be the one doing the work, baby." She leaned down and nipped at his earlobe, eliciting another groan from Tanner.

He barked a short laugh. "Damn, my sweet Belle has turned into a greedy little vixen. What the hell did I ever do in my life that was good enough to deserve you?" He cupped her cheek. "But what I meant was I want to just sit with you for a while tonight. Watch a movie or read a book or something. I want to spend a little time with you before all hell breaks loose."

Her heart constricted painfully. Tanner had a way of saying all the things she never knew she needed to hear. "That sounds perfect, baby." She dropped a kiss on his cheek and tried to hide the effect his words had on her. She'd never had anyone in her life that just wanted to be with her without wanting something. In that moment, she felt certain there was nothing in this world strong enough to make her stop loving him.

He slid her off his lap and stood, planting a kiss on the top of her head. "Go pick a movie and I'll clean up." He turned to clear the table but then turned back to her with a smirk. "Make sure you pick some crappy adventure so we can practice making out."

Chapter Ten

Tanner

Connor threw the queen-sized inflatable mattress in the back of Tanner's truck with a muttered curse. "I like how you screw up your marriage and we're the ones doing all the work."

"What the..." Tanner rammed his brother's shoulder with more force than necessary. "I'm not asking you to do a damn thing. I just wanted to borrow this mattress for one night. I'm working my ass off to prove to Belle that I deserve a second chance and that she and the kids are more important than anything to me. So back the hell off and get the friggin' air pump."

His brother shoved him just as he finished talking, and Tanner stumbled back a couple of steps. "You're the biggest dumbass I've ever seen. Izzy practically worships the ground you walk on. She doesn't complain about a damn thing, even when you're gone constantly, and the first chance you get," Connor pushed him again, "the first chance you get, you shove your tongue down some buckle bunny's throat. What the hell?"

Connor's words held a stronger punch than his fists ever could. Tanner's breathing was shallow. "How long?"

He pushed his fingers through his hair and regarded Tanner with a sneer. "How long what?"

"How long have I been a total prick to her?" He sat on the rear bumper of his truck and braced his hands on his knees. Belle wasn't the only one who saw a change in him. Well, shit. "I've been looking for someone to kick my ass. Wanna start the line?"

Connor sat down beside his brother. "You know, you owe Wyatt big time for grabbing you before you did anything you couldn't fix. You can fix this."

The fear that plagued him every moment of every day for the past week bubbled to the surface again. "And if I can't? Shit. I haven't even taken her to a game in years, and she never said anything. She never complained, never yelled, never got mad. What kind of lousy asshole treats a woman that damn perfect that way?"

He chuckled at Tanner's discomfort. "You. But now that you know, you can do better."

Tanner shook his head and looked over at Connor. "When did you get so damn smart?"

Connor clapped him on the back and stood up. "I've always been the smartest. You were just too arrogant to notice. Now get the hell out of here and make Izzy fall in love with you again, because if I don't get her scalloped potatoes at Christmas dinner like always, I'll take you up on that ass kicking."

A fresh cloud of shame rolled through Tanner as he ran the last few errands he needed to before tonight. For several years he'd been too occupied with work to take Belle to any football games or go to Noah's soccer games and, shit, he only showed up for one of Ava's piano recitals. When the hell had he become *that* guy?

He threw the bags filled with twenty various pillows in the back of his truck ruthlessly. Son of a bitch. He tossed five packages of queen-sized comforters on top of the pillows and climbed in the truck, slamming the heel of his hand against the steering wheel for good measure.

How many times had he promised Belle he would take care of her? That he'd never walk away? That he'd never treat her the way her father...

Oh. Hell.

He was behaving just like her father. Ignoring everything important and letting his hands go every place they didn't belong. The one thing he swore that he'd never do, not just to her but to himself, he had done.

The realization made Tanner more determined than ever, not just to prove himself to her, but to prove how much better she deserved. And how much better he could do. He'd spent the first several years they were together trying to find any and every way he could to make her feel special. She deserved it, and he loved doing it for her. When did he get lazy and stop trying?

Tanner drove past their house and down into the field behind it, far enough to be out of sight of anyone inside. He checked his watch quickly. Shit, it was already four o'clock and dinner was at six. He needed to be back.

He shoved the mountain of pillows and comforters inside his truck and laid the air mattress out, then flicked the switch on the small air compressor to start it inflating. He hopped down from the bed and pulled the long box out of the back seat of his truck with a grin. Belle was going to love this part. Carefully sliding all the components out, he was grateful there were only a few pieces and quickly assembled the telescope.

When the thought first occurred to him of using the time between his confession and their anniversary as a way to win her back, he had a lot of thoughts on the best way to use that time. Ideas of taking her for an extended stay at a resort in the Bahamas, renting out the movie theater and spending an entire day watching movies significant in their lives, or touring castles in Europe for weeks on end all floated through his mind.

But that wasn't Belle. She wasn't impressed by the amount of money he spent on something. What she loved most was when he took the time to create something just for her. And that thought alone had been the catalyst for every date he planned. As he spread the stacks of covers on top of the air mattress, he grinned to himself, feeling just a touch of pride. Tonight might be her favorite.

He glanced at his watch again, a little after five. Tanner ripped open the plastic bags covering the last few pillows and threw them on the pile. Okay, maybe twenty pillows was a tiny bit of overkill, but he wanted to do whatever he could to make this comfortable for Belle.

And if all went well, he'd be holding her in his arms by the end of the night.

Tanner trekked back to the house and couldn't help but smile that he walked through the door two minutes before six. He was still on time for dinner.

The smile stayed fixed on his lips through dinner and as the kids wrangled both he and Belle into a game of Twister in the middle of the living room floor. It grew bigger when Belle led the kids upstairs to bed a long time later and a soft knock came at the door.

His youngest brother stood on the threshold with a backpack hitched over his shoulder. "Reporting for duty," Dean quipped as he pushed past Tanner, bumping his shoulder intentionally.

Tanner rolled his eyes and sighed. Obviously all his brothers were firmly in Belle's camp.

Just then, Belle descended the stairs and visibly brightened when she saw Dean. As ridiculous as it was, Tanner felt a stirring of jealousy at the sight.

"Dean," she wrapped his brother in a warm hug, "what are you doing here?"

The younger man squeezed her back tightly and for much longer than Tanner was happy about. "Ask Casanova over there," he answered with a lift of his chin in his brother's direction. "I'm going to head up to the guest room and read for a bit."

Belle's face clouded with confusion as she watched him climb the stairs, and she turned her gaze to Tanner, her face asking an unspoken question.

"We've got a date, sweetheart." He grinned at

the excitement lighting her eyes. "Dean is going to stay with the kids."

"Where in the world are we going at this hour?" She didn't sound upset and easily slid her hand inside his as they walked out the door. Definitely making progress.

He flicked on the flashlight in his hand and held her close to his side, squeezing her hand lightly as his only response.

Yeah, Belle was going to love tonight's date.

***

"Last week you all agreed to twenty each."

"New week, new price. You've been shadowing Dad long enough to know renegotiations happen all the time."

Tanner shoved his fingers through his hair and locked his hands behind his neck, facing off against all three of his brothers. Shit. He did not have time for this. "Fine, I'll pay thirty. Hell, I'll pay you fifty bucks each if you get to work and stop your bitchin'."

Wyatt, the self-appointed spokesman for the group, quirked an eyebrow for a moment. Then he offered a grin and stuck his hand out. "You got a deal, big brother."

He smacked away the hand and grabbed the drop cloths off the couch, throwing them at Connor and Dean. "You two cover everything in the bedroom. And I mean everything, got it? No half-assing this project."

Tanner turned to Wyatt and pulled him out the

front door of the apartment. "And you, Mr. Ringleader, are gonna help me carry all this shit out of my truck. We've got six hours until she gets home, and I'd like all of you assholes to be long gone by then."

With barely an hour to spare, Tanner managed to get all three of his brothers to finish the job at hand and clean up every single speck of dirt. After a speedy shower, he stood in front of the bathroom mirror buttoning the long-sleeved sapphire-colored shirt, leaving the top few buttons undone. Belle always liked that. He was just adjusting his cuffs when he heard Belle's keys in the door and grinned. Showtime.

He sauntered into the living room, his smile fading momentarily when he saw how exhausted she looked. "Happy birthday, sweetheart."

Belle smiled lightly, but his heart constricted when he realized it didn't come close to touching her eyes. "Thank you, baby, but I told you last year, I'm not really that into birthdays. Well, not my birthday. I can't wait to get out of this uniform and take a long hot shower and—"

"Get ready to go out to dinner," he cut her off. When her mouth fell open and Tanner was certain she would argue, he stepped in front of her and wrapped his arms around her. "Listen, sweetheart, it's your birthday and I want to take you out to dinner. That's all. Just dinner, okay? Nothing big, nothing extravagant, just dinner."

Pouting playfully, Belle wound her arms around him. "You don't play fair." She stood on her tiptoes and gave him a quick kiss before releasing him and walking toward the bedroom. "Fine, let me just go find something—"

"No! No, no, no, no, no." He leapt over the back of the couch to stop her in her tracks. "W-what I mean is, I got something. For you. To wear." Tanner closed his eyes and willed his mind to concentrate and, hopefully, form a cohesive sentence. "I bought you a dress. And shoes. As a birthday present. They're in the bathroom."

Finally a genuine smile spread across her face, and he almost sighed in relief when he noticed the twinkle in her eyes. "You bought me a dress, huh?"

Tanner steered her toward the bathroom door and gave her ass a soft swat. "Yes, sweetheart. And everything you need is in the bathroom. That's the only place you need to go. Just to the bathroom. Now, scoot, we have reservations."

As soon as it was safely closed and he heard the shower turn on, Tanner leaned against the bathroom door and released the breath he had been holding. He could do this. He just had to get her out of the apartment without her wandering into the bedroom. No big deal. He could do this.

But every thought of keeping Belle out of the bedroom fled twenty minutes later when she emerged in the sleeveless, sparkling, and far shorter than he'd imagined, black dress he had picked out. His mouth went dry when she rounded the couch and the long expanse of her olive-complected legs came into view, topped off by the strappy silver heels he was relieved to see fit.

"Damn. Sweetheart, you look so good I'm pretty sure it's my birthday instead of yours."

She laughed and tilted her head back, her long, wavy locks falling over her shoulder. She put a hand on his shoulder and kissed his cheek. "I love it, baby. Thank you." Belle tucked her hand in the crook of his elbow. "Now, let's go. I'm suddenly famished."

As much as Tanner wanted to sit back in the upscale restaurant and enjoy the view of Belle across the table, he felt restless and uneasy. What if she hated his surprise? What if she was disappointed? Belle didn't even want to celebrate her birthday, but what if his gift screwed it up more?

Lost in thought, he almost jumped when her soft hand covered his. "Baby, what's wrong?"

"Nothing, sweetheart. Not a damn thing." He nodded over to her mostly empty plate. "How was your dinner? Do you want dessert? Do you need another drink?"

Her finger traced over the back of his hand in a random pattern, and she flashed a mischievous smile. "Dinner was great, I don't need anything else to drink, and I think dessert at home would be better, don't you?"

Well, hell. The greedy little vixen showed up again, and he couldn't help but grin. "Yeah, sweetheart, let's go home."

Home. Bedroom. Surprise.

And just like that, his nerves shot through the roof again. As he drove them home, he began mentally reciting all the very calm, very understanding, and most definitely very gracious responses he could offer if she hated his surprise.

He paused outside their bedroom door and turned to face her. "Okay, I know I *said* I just wanted to take you to dinner for your birthday, but I may have a little surprise for you."

Belle scrunched her nose and looked so damn adorable, he nearly forgot everything he was going to say. "Baby, you are sweet and smart and the hottest guy at this school, but you are pretty bad at keeping a secret. I figured there was something lurking in there." She looped her arms around his neck and grinned. "So what is it? Chocolate-covered strawberries? Rose petals covering the bed? Some sexy, lacy lingerie?"

He planted a deep, passionate kiss, bending her backwards slightly over his arm. "None of the above, sweetheart, but I hope you like it."

Tanner flipped the switch to kill the lights in the living room and swung the bedroom door open. He followed her inside and hoped the sharp intake of breath was from pleasure and not utter disappointment.

In the room only lit by the faint glow from above, Belle swung her eyes from left to right along the ceiling, taking in every detail. "Tanner." She finally breathed his name, reaching for his hand blindly, not willing to lower her gaze. "You gave me the entire sky."

He chuckled and wrapped his arms around her waist from behind. "Nah, not the entire sky." He rested his chin on top of her head. "I was thinking about how much you love to lay out under the stars at night, so I decided to bring the stars inside for you to look at whenever you want."

And he had done just that, hanging glow-in-the-dark wallpaper across the entire ceiling of their small bedroom. Screw the security deposit. The smile on Belle's face as she kissed him and pulled him toward the bed was worth losing every penny.

Chapter Eleven

Izzy

All the air left her body in a whoosh and Izzy blinked a few times, certain she was seeing things. When the telescope and the mountain of blankets and pillows filling the bed of Tanner's obnoxious yellow truck didn't disappear, she spun around to face him.

"Tanner." She breathed his name and lifted her hand to his cheek. So many thoughts ran through her mind, but none formed into coherent words. Instead she wrapped her arms around his neck, feeling closer to him than she had all week. Closer than she had in years.

His deep chuckle vibrated against her, and she closed her eyes, reveling in the sensation. "I'm glad you like it, but we haven't even gotten to the surprise yet, sweetheart."

She pulled back but held onto his shoulders. "What do you mean? We're going to lie under the stars together on a huge pile of pillows and you even got a telescope which is something we never had before. Tanner, what more could there possibly be?"

"Well, I'm glad you asked, sweetheart." He stepped away from her with a grin and pulled something off the driver's seat of his truck. When he turned back around, her eyes widened at the present wrapped in dark blue paper. "A little something for you."

Izzy shook her head, not accepting the proffered gift. "It's not my birthday." Her brow furrowed. "And it is still, what, thirty-six days until our anniversary? So why am I getting a present?"

A brief flash of disappointment flitted across his face and served to only deepen Izzy's confusion. But just as quickly as it had come, it disappeared. "No, it's not your birthday or our anniversary or Christmas, even. You're getting this because you deserve to get something you love simply because you love it, not just because I'm sorry for what I did. Which I am. Extremely."

She couldn't help the small smile that tugged at her lips when she finally took the nearly flat rectangle from his grasp. She took a few steps closer to the truck, needing the help of the interior light. Izzy's breath caught when she pulled the paper away. She looked from the gift she held in her hands to Tanner's expectant face and back several times before jumping in his arms, still clinging to the picture frame. "Tanner." She choked out his name past the tears clogging her throat.

His grip on her tightened under her thighs, holding her close.

Izzy put her hands on his shoulders and pushed back enough to look in his face, tears streaking down her cheeks. "You bought me a star." A bubble of laughter escaped past the happy tears. "First you bring the sky inside and now you buy me a star."

He grinned and carried her around the bed of the truck, setting her down on the tailgate before climbing up beside her. "Come on, sweetheart, let's lay down for a bit. Unless you want to look for your star. I got the telescope to see if we could find it. Or we could look for what—"

She put a finger against his lips, silencing the stream of words. A tiny part of her enjoyed seeing always confident and capable Tanner just a little nervous. She slid back on the inflatable mattress and laid down on the pile of pillows. "Being right here sounds perfect."

Izzy had to bite her lip to stop herself from laughing at how quickly he scrambled up beside her. He stretched out next to her, sliding his hand in hers and intertwining their fingers. "Belle, being anywhere with you is perfect." He whispered the words, but they had the effect of a powerful windstorm.

"It's been way too long since we've done this."

Tanner stayed silent for a long time after her comment, and part of her wondered if she shouldn't have said anything. She chewed on her bottom lip and tried to think of anything she could say to ease the sting.

Finally he propped himself up on an elbow. "How long, Belle?"

She turned her head slightly, and the earnest look

on his face made her scoot closer to his side. "At least three years," she said softly. "With the kids and work, we were just too busy."

Tanner leaned down and brushed his lips across hers. "Not we. Me. Dammit, Belle, I'm sorry."

She reached up to bury her fingers in his hair and pull his lips more firmly against hers. The taste of his lips drove her to wiggle her body beneath his. His scent wafted over her, and she barely contained a groan. She was finally surrounded by Tanner in every way and she never wanted it to end.

"Belle." He murmured her name against her lips and began to kiss down her jaw, planting moist kisses along the column of her neck.

Izzy pulled Tanner until he was fully on top of her and her thighs were locked around his waist. When she lifted her hips and pressed against the evidence of his need, she felt a gasp against her neck where Tanner had been licking and biting softly.

His hands slid under her shirt, caressing her back and drawing her closer to him. Tanner lifted the shirt over her head and began making a path of hot kisses across her bare chest. She arched into him again, her fingers tugging on his hair to bring his mouth back up to hers.

"Tanner." She whimpered his name in between kisses, the soft cotton of his shirt rubbing against her skin, teasing every overly sensitized inch.

She'd always loved playing with Tanner's hair and gave her fingers free rein to get reacquainted with each strand. When his hands skimmed down her sides and flicked the button open on her waistband, she couldn't help but shiver against him.

His mouth curved against hers. "You like that, sweetheart?"

She hadn't realized until this moment just how much she missed his touch and his lips leaving a scorching trail along her body.

His hands.

His mouth.

And one week ago they had been kissing someone else. Holding someone else. Touching someone else.

Ice trickled down her spine, freezing her movement. She pushed Tanner away and scooted to the far corner of the mattress. She grabbed her shirt and held it against her chest. *Why didn't I put on a bra?* she chastised herself.

Even in the darkness she could see his face fall. "Belle, what's wrong?"

"I can't." She sobbed and gripped the shirt tighter against herself. She waved her free hand in a sweeping gesture. "Tanner, this is beautiful and perfect, and you gave me the most amazing gift...but I can't stop thinking about *her*. And you." Her heart splintered. "And you don't feel like mine anymore."

She tugged her shirt on over her head, jumped out of the truck, and ran toward the dimly lit house in the distance as fast as she could.

***

Izzy had already found Orion four times and Perseus once, but it didn't stop her from searching the ceiling again for more familiar constellations. She didn't want to close her eyes and sleep. This was far better than any dream.

She'd dreaded her birthday ever since her parents' divorce. It had become just another reason for them to bribe her into loving one more than the other, to fight over whose turn it was to have her, or to badmouth the other parent. Each year made her feel exhausted and manipulated, but mostly unloved.

A smile spread across her lips. That was all before Tanner.

His arm came over her stomach and he pulled her next to him. "I'm gonna take that down if you don't stop looking at it and get some sleep, sweetheart." His voice was sleep-roughened and possibly the sexiest thing she'd ever heard.

Izzy rolled onto her side and moved even closer against him. "This was the best birthday I've ever had." She leaned forward and pressed a soft, moist kiss on his bare chest. Neither had the energy to pull their clothes back on after a thorough birthday celebration under the star-lit ceiling.

Eyes still closed, Tanner's lips curved up. "Yet, sweetheart, yet. That was just the beginning. I've got a lifetime of birthdays to spoil you."

Nothing lasts forever. The voice that always lingered in the back of her head seemed to be louder and much more insistent tonight. Maybe, just maybe, if she could keep Tanner happy, maybe this could last. "You really are the perfect boyfriend, baby."

"We're perfect for each other."

Keep Tanner happy. The thought raced through her mind again. An idea started to form and she smiled. He definitely should get some reward for all his hard work.

He rolled onto his back and pulled her against his side. Even though she was still slightly sore nearly everywhere from lots of undivided and oh-so talented attention from Tanner, the moment she pressed her bare skin against his, the smoldering embers ignited. She bit her bottom lip, slowly tracing the muscles on his stomach with her finger.

His face remained completely expressionless and his eyes stayed closed, but his muscles contracted beneath her touch, giving her just enough motivation to lightly trail her hand further down. When she wrapped her hand around the smooth skin below, she was finally rewarded with a groan.

Izzy's confidence grew, and she moved her hand up and down softly, reveling in every twitch as he responded to her touch. She slid her body down his, following the path of her fingers with her mouth and grinning against his skin at his sharp intake of breath.

"Belle." Her name left his mouth on a hiss just as her tongue ran up the silky length her hand abandoned. He clamped her wrist tightly and dragged her up his body. "Sweetheart, what the hell are you doing?"

Her heart plummeted. She did it wrong. Tanner wasn't happy. "I-I…" she faltered, not ever dreaming she'd need to explain herself. She scrambled off his chest and sat up, tucking the sheet around her. Fine time to be naked.

Tanner sat up to face her, an inscrutable expression on his face. She hated it when she couldn't read him. "I didn't mean that. I know what you were doing, sweetheart. I just want to know why." He flicked his gaze to the ceiling and waved his hand. "This is a gift for you, Belle. Something I wanted to do because I love you and it would make you happy. Not something you need to pay me back for."

A tear streaked down her cheek and she cursed it. Why did she feel the need to ruin everything by crying? "I just want you to be as happy as I am so that you're mine forever." Izzy clapped a hand over her mouth as soon as the words tumbled out.

The color drained from his face, and Izzy's stomach turned, hot tears falling in earnest now. Why did she have to wreck the best birthday of her life by saying that to him?

Tanner put his hands on her cheeks and lifted her face, his thumbs swiping at the wet streaks on her face. "Belle, sweetheart, I'm yours. Forever. I have been since the first day I met you. Happy, sad, angry, doesn't matter. I'm not going anywhere without you."

Her hands fell away from the sheet and she launched herself into his arms. Tanner's arms. The safest place in the world.

He made soothing sounds and ran his hands down her hair. After several moments, he lightly pulled her away, just far enough to look in her eyes. It had been over a year that she had spent completely spellbound by those sapphire pools, but the duration didn't lessen the impact, even though they were barely visible in the nearly dark room.

His hands slid down from her shoulders and he held hers captive. "Now repeat after me: 'Tanner is mine forever.'"

"Tanner is mine forever," she parroted back dutifully. Her fears quieted for the moment, she couldn't help but smile. He really was perfect.

"'And very, very soon I am going to finish everything my soft little hands and talented mouth started tonight before Tanner dies of anticipation.'"

Izzy threw her head back and laughed. Maybe she didn't do it wrong after all. "And very, very, *very* soon I am going to finish tasting every part of Tanner I can think of and a few more I can't."

She pulled her hands from his and climbed into his lap, the sheets tangling around them. Tanner groaned when her lips found the soft patch of skin at the juncture of his neck and shoulders. "Holy hell, Belle."

She nipped at the sensitive spot and smiled. Tanner was hers.

Chapter Twelve

Tanner

He sat frozen in the bed of the truck, his mind struggling to catch up. *What the hell just happened?*

A long time after Belle's back disappeared over the hill, Tanner jumped out of the truck and began pacing.

It was perfect. Everything went exactly as planned. No, better than planned. The weather was ideal. His brother actually showed up on time with minimal sarcasm. Belle loved her gift. She was reminded of all the happiness they'd shared together.

And then she left. Ran away.

He landed a left hook on the rear fender of his truck and immediately regretted the decision as pain shot through his hand and the skin split. Shit. He probably broke something.

Just then his eyes landed on the telescope and his anger surged. *Break something.* He kicked the stand and it crashed to the ground. He was trying. He

111

lifted it over his head and slammed it down with as much force as possible. Pieces of glass and plastic splintered. Dammit, he was trying to fix everything. He stomped on it over and over before kicking it thirty feet away.

She was being stubborn and pig-headed and completely unreasonable. Yeah, he screwed up, but she wasn't listening and wasn't giving him a fair chance. He braced both hands on the bed of the truck, the breath leaving his body with a sharp gasp as pain shot through his left hand with the pressure. He barely noticed the blood pouring from his knuckles.

If she would have just talked to him instead of running away. If she would have let him slow things down. If she…

Well, hell.

Tanner's knees buckled and he dropped to the ground. His forehead rested against the wheel well, and he cursed the unfamiliar feeling of tears streaking down his face. She didn't do a damn thing wrong.

He wasn't just a grade A, number one asshole for…that, but here he was promising Belle that he was going to fix it all and prove he could be the same guy she fell in love with, and what did he do? Started blaming her. And losing his temper like a damn kid. Why the hell was she even giving him a second chance? She'd be better off with someone else who wouldn't forget how special she was. Someone who wouldn't take her for granted.

Blood began streaming down his forearm, pulling him from his self-destructive thoughts. He wasn't giving up. He still had thirty-six days and many more dates planned for Belle.

Tanner stood slowly, cradling his hand against his abdomen. Dammit all to hell, he was going to need stitches. Maybe a cast.

He climbed in his truck and guided it carefully around the bulk of the debris left behind from his temper tantrum and made a mental note to come back and clear the field. For a brief moment he debated on asking Belle to drive him to the hospital before dismissing the thought with a stern shake of his head. No, Dean could pull his happy little ass out of bed and drive him.

The entire ride to and from the emergency room in Dean's absurdly small sports car, and every minute in between while he sat getting ten stitches put in across his knuckles, he rehearsed what he'd say. It had only been a week. What the hell was he thinking?

The first fingers of light were touching the sky as they walked through the front door. Dean pushed past his brother with an added shove. "I'm claiming your bed for the next six hours at least. Don't disturb me again."

"It's not my bed." He refused to think of it as anything other than the guest room. Even if he slept in there every night.

Dean chuckled as he ascended the stairs. "It is until you get Izzy to forget what an asshole she married," he called over his shoulder.

Tanner scowled at his brother's back. He was exhausted and wanted nothing more than to curl up on the nearest horizontal surface, pop a few of the pain pills they had given him at the hospital, and pass out for several hours. But that wasn't going to happen any time soon. It was Sunday morning.

He pulled out pans and ingredients as quietly as possible. He hoped to hell he wouldn't wake Belle. When had he stopped making breakfast on Sunday morning? He beat the eggs in the bowl with more force than necessary with a self-derisive snort. She should have kicked him out long ago.

His eyes caught the blood stains that had formed on his shirt and jeans and he sighed. He needed to go shower before Belle saw. She'd worry. His heart stopped. She always worried about everyone else, especially him.

As quietly as possible, he snuck into the guest room, grabbed some clothes, and took as fast a shower as he could, holding his left hand out of the water. Hell, he missed everything he'd taken for granted just a week ago. His wife, his family, and even the damn shower in the master bedroom.

He threw on a pair of athletic shorts and tugged the sleeveless shirt over his head before racing down the stairs. He had to at least get everything started before…

Just as he rounded the corner, he saw Belle filling the coffeepot. His first thought wasn't for the breakfast that would no longer be a surprise, but on the light streaming through the kitchen window picking up the flecks of gold woven through her dark brown hair. His gaze traveled over her profile unnoticed. Dammit all to hell, when had he stopped noticing that Belle was the sexiest thing on two legs?

"Tanner." Her voice caught. So maybe she had noticed his unabashed staring. Her eyes followed a similar path down his body as his had done to her, stopping when she saw the stark white bandage. She abandoned the can of coffee and rushed over to pick up his hand, concern filling her face. "What happened?"

Honesty. The word that had repeated over and over in his mind as he thought of what he would tell her while he was focusing on anything other than the searing pain of the doctor sewing his hand back together. "I'm a damn idiot that lost his temper."

Tears collected in the corners of her eyes as she cradled his hand in both of hers. Her head tilted down and two drops plopped on the cotton covering his stitches. "It's my fault." Her words were barely a whisper but managed to pierce his heart.

He hooked a finger under her chin and forced her to meet his gaze. Damn those gorgeous chestnut eyes that could see through all the way to his soul. "Sweetheart, don't you dare. I was pissed because I'm a pathetic asshole who screwed up the best thing in my life. None of it was your fault."

Belle lifted his hand to her mouth, a stray tear still falling down her cheek. "But I don't want to see you hurt."

Dammit all to hell. After everything he'd done to her, she wanted to take care of him. Tanner moved his hand up to her cheek. "Let me keep trying, sweetheart. Don't give up on me yet. That would hurt more than hitting my truck."

Her lips twitched, and he could see she was holding in a laugh. "You hit your truck?" Her

115

eyebrows shot up with the words. "So your obnoxious yellow truck has an obnoxious dent in it now?"

Tanner narrowed his gaze, but a smile played about his lips. He captured a strand of her long hair and twisted it around his fingers. "It's not obnoxious."

Belle's teeth clamped down on her bottom lip. "I'm not giving up."

Relief flooded through Tanner's body, and he planted a light kiss on her lips. "Good. Now sit down so I can make French toast. It's Sunday."

***

Well, hell.

This was not going as planned. Tanner bit the inside of his cheek and tugged the kitchen window open, hoping the smoke would disperse outside before the alarm could kick in and wake Belle. That would be one sorry-ass first attempt at a breakfast in bed.

He dumped the blackened pancakes in the trash and began running the pan under water. If he ruined her cookware, she would be pissed.

With a heavy sigh, he looked at the plate on the counter. The eggs were runny and the bacon was limp. He couldn't give this to Belle. She served him his favorite meal cooked better than any gourmet restaurant he'd ever been to. The least she deserved was an edible breakfast.

Tanner snorted. She deserved a lot more than breakfast in bed. Hell, she deserved a lot more than him, but for whatever reason she chose to love him. And he needed to make sure every day that she didn't regret that decision.

Breakfast in bed for Belle on Sunday mornings seemed like a good place to start. Except for the tiny fact he couldn't cook. The food he thought was so simple confounded him more than Global Corporate Responsibility with Professor Hoover.

This time Belle's breakfast would have to consist of muffins, bagels, and coffee from the shop on the corner. He tugged on some shoes, grabbed his keys and wallet, and softly clicked the door closed behind him.

Next week he'd make breakfast. Maybe he'd start with frozen waffles, though.

He ran as fast as he could to the coffee shop and back, but his heart fell when he saw Belle scrubbing the pan in the sink. "Dammit, sweetheart, I was going to do that." He kicked his shoes off and set the bags on the table.

When she turned around to face him, there were tears in her eyes and he felt sick. Shit. He should have cleaned everything before he left.

But instead of screaming at him for ruining her pan or leaving a mess in the kitchen, she jumped into his arms. "You were making me breakfast," she whispered against his ear, her arms and legs tighter around him than he ever remembered before.

"I was trying, Belle. And I promise I'll get you a new pan if that one's beyond hope. I didn't mean to leave a mess for you, I was just getting—" Her lips found his and cut off his words.

After a long time, she finally released his mouth

and he sucked in a deep breath. "I don't care about the mess, and I definitely don't care about the pan." She kissed him again, softer than before. "Baby, you were making me breakfast. I love that."

Tanner's chest puffed up. All right then. "Damn straight I was, sweetheart. And you better get used to it because I'm going to make you breakfast in bed every Sunday."

"Every Sunday until when?"

If he could figure out a way to punch her father and not ruin their relationship, he'd be damn near giddy. This beautiful, loving, caring woman should never have to question how long their relationship would last. If it was one day longer than forever it still wouldn't be enough for him.

He carried her toward the bedroom, more determined than ever to give her breakfast in bed even if he had to tuck her back in it himself. "Every Sunday until you get tired of me and my attempts at cooking."

She laughed when he lightly tossed her on the bed. "Since that'll never happen, it looks like you've got a lot of cooking in your future, Mr. Carlisle."

Her dark brown hair spread out on the pillow around her and her eyes twinkled. He didn't have words for how much he loved her. As much as he wanted to cover her body with his and give her a little taste of the forever he had in mind, he forced himself to focus on taking care of her physical hunger. For now.

"Stay put." He pointed at her with mock seriousness as he backed out of the room.

"Breakfast in bed requires being in bed."

She smiled softly and his heart almost stopped beating at the sight. "I'm not going anywhere, baby."

Chapter Thirteen

Izzy

Four days. It had been four days since Tanner had created the single most perfect date and given her a gift so thoughtful her eyes welled every time she thought of it. He hadn't done anything that special since college.

And she blew it.

Her toe touched the porch and set the swing in motion again. She picked up her cell phone from the small table and reread the text message for the tenth time today.

Tanner: I'm yours forever. And then a few days after that.

Tanner had sent her the same message every day after he left for work. Every day her heart constricted as soon as she read it and every day she didn't respond. She read it over and over and willed herself to believe the words the way she used to.

120

Izzy's grip on the glass in her hand tightened. No matter how hard she tried, she couldn't erase the image of Tanner kissing someone else from her mind. Of someone else touching his arms, his shoulders, his back, his...

The dark thoughts were interrupted by the deep, throaty sound of Tanner's truck coming down the driveway. She frowned and glanced at the thin silver watch around her wrist. Four o'clock. On a Thursday. Tanner had always complained Thursdays were his busiest day, everyone wanting to tie up loose ends and take a three-day weekend. Everyone that wasn't Tanner, of course. He hadn't taken a three-day weekend in at least two years and would never, ever leave work early on a Thursday afternoon two weeks in a row. Except—here he was.

A small voice from the deep recesses of her heart reminded her he was trying. He was genuinely sorry for everything and he was working hard to do better. He was fixing things she had long ago accepted.

But the voice of eight-year-old Izzy echoed in her mind. The voice that reminded her that she had been traded in once before. That the only example she had of marriage ended in failure, and why should she believe hers would turn out any differently than her parents' had?

She stood, crossed to the edge of the porch, and supported herself with the post at the top of the stairs. "What are you doing home so early?" She asked the question as soon as he closed the driver's door.

Her words caused his steps to pause for a brief moment, his smile faltering slightly. Just as quickly as it left, the grin showed back up on his lips, and he walked over to stand at the bottom of the stairs. "It's family movie night. The kids and I need to go get dinner and a movie. We're getting Chinese tonight. Ava's request, naturally."

Izzy's brows drew together, and she took two steps down toward Tanner. "You still want to do that?"

Tanner matched her movement, now only one step separating them. "Belle, I still want to have family movie night when we're watching them with our great-grandkids."

Swallowing the emotion that bubbled at his words and forcing that incessant voice of caution in her mind to be quiet, she stepped down the last step separating them. The slight elevation advantage she had nearly put her at eye level with Tanner.

Two weeks ago that comment would have made her wrap her arms around him, offer deep kisses, and make all kinds of promises of the things she would do to him later. She would never have hesitated, never have thought twice about it. But today her hand shook slightly as she reached out to stroke his cheek. Her smile wobbled just before she leaned in for a kiss.

For several long moments, Tanner's hands stayed at his side, and when the realization hit Izzy that he was letting her set the pace, she wanted to cry. *He's trying*, her heart reminded her.

She ran her tongue along his bottom lip and wound her arms around his neck. The deep moan from the back of his throat made her smile as she continued to tease him. Finally she felt his arms encircle her waist and her heart soared. In spite of everything that happened, being held by Tanner made her feel loved.

She had no idea how long they would have stayed fixed in that spot, doing nothing more than enjoying each other, if not for the thundering arrival of their children behind them. Izzy couldn't help but laugh at Tanner's disappointed groan when they bounded out of the house, chattering away at the same time.

He lifted a hand to her cheek once more and gave her a last lingering kiss, chuckling at the disgusted noises the kids made behind him. "Sesame chicken, right?"

Izzy had no idea why she was surprised he remembered her favorite take-out dish. She nodded dumbly, words failing her at that moment and the beating of her heart reminding her once again that he was trying.

Tanner scooted Ava and Noah into the truck and paused beside the door, suddenly looking uncomfortable. "I, um, I'm not going into the office tomorrow. I have a few errands to run and stuff so, uh, if you need anything, just make a list tonight."

She had to have heard him wrong. "You're…you're taking Friday off? You're taking a non-holiday required three-day weekend?"

He grinned and nodded. "Perks of being the boss, remember?"

Izzy wanted to tell him that being the boss hadn't offered any perks in the past few years. She wanted to say she couldn't remember the last time he'd been willing to miss this much work. She wanted to tell him that she was terrified that in thirty-two days everything would go back to the way it had been. And she was only just realizing that the way it had been hadn't been as great as she thought.

Instead she smiled and nodded. "Yeah, I remember."

***

"I'm sorry, Iz. You're a great employee, but I can't show you any favoritism."

Izzy chewed the inside of her lip and nodded, quietly thanking her manager before fleeing his office. She should have known she couldn't get any extra hours at the coffee shop.

Of course she could never top Tanner's birthday gift for her, but she wanted to make it special, and for that she needed some extra cash. Not to mention the fact his birthday was just a few weeks before Christmas and she was screwed.

She leaned her forehead against the steering wheel of her car. If only her dad hadn't cut her off from everything, this wouldn't be an issue. She sighed before reluctantly starting her car to head home. That really wasn't an option anymore. Being with Tanner was far and away more important. She'd just have to make this work.

Her teeth worried her bottom lip the entire drive and as she trudged up the two flights of stairs into the apartment. At least Tanner had football practice and she'd be able to figure out a plan before he...

"Hey, sweetheart," he greeted brightly when she walked through the door. His gaze swept over her, and his brows pulled together. "What's wrong, Belle?"

So practice was done early tonight. Great. "Just a busy day, baby." She smiled and lifted up on her tiptoes to plant a kiss on his cheek. "I'm going to go take a long, hot shower and climb in bed with a sexy football player who is home much earlier than expected."

Tanner offered a small grin, but the lines on his forehead stayed in place. She skirted around him into the relative sanctuary of the bathroom. Izzy stripped her clothes off as soon as she shut the door, a sigh filled with a mixture of relief and frustration escaping her lips. She closed her eyes beneath the hot spray, willing the water to give her the answer she was looking for.

She stood there for a long time, lost in thought. Getting a second job would be her only solution, but how would she explain that to Tanner? And how could she possibly manage her course load and two jobs?

Izzy felt the movement behind her before she even heard the curtain being pulled aside. She couldn't stifle the gasp of surprise as she spun around to see Tanner. "Baby, what are you doing?"

Without a word, he gathered her close to him and lowered his head to claim her lips. Every worry disappeared from her mind at the very first touch from Tanner. His fingers trailed down her spine and she shivered, stepping as close to him as possible.

"Tell me what's wrong," he said breathlessly

when they finally both pulled away for air. "Just tell me what's wrong, sweetheart. I'll fix it."

She swallowed and shook her head. "You can't fix everything, baby."

His arms locked around her waist and he lifted her so she was level with his stormy gaze. A small squeak escaped, and she wrapped her legs around him. Tanner turned to the right and pressed her against the wall. "The hell I can't. Tell me."

Before she even had a chance to answer, his hands cupped beneath her and his mouth began trailing hot kisses along her neck and shoulder. "Tell me, sweetheart," he murmured against her skin.

Izzy arched her back, pushing into him. Feeling the physical proof of his need for her was a heady sensation. "I-I can't." She barely gasped out the words.

Tanner lowered his head, making a path down from her collarbone with his tongue. "Yes you can, Belle. You can tell me anything."

She shook her head against the tile. Did he honestly expect her to think at this particular moment, much less carry on a cognitive conversation? She struggled to catch her breath long enough to answer as his fingers began teasing her. "I, oh geez, Tanner." She whimpered and bit down on his shoulder in frustration. "I can figure this out on my own, baby."

Every muscle in his body stilled. After several long beats, he shifted her slightly and raised a hand to hook a finger under her chin. "I know you can, sweetheart." His passion-laced voice softened as he spoke. He brushed his lips across hers. "You are strong and smart." He quirked his lips into a smirk and pressed hard against her again, close enough she groaned from the torture. "And sexy as hell. But you don't have to do a damn thing alone anymore. I'm yours forever, remember?"

In spite of the passionate haze surrounding them, as soon as he said the words, Izzy couldn't stop her own from tumbling out. "I wanted to do something really special for your birthday, but I can't get any more hours at work and I don't know how I could fit in a second job. And you gave me the most amazing—"

His finger landed on her lips and a smile spread across his. "Now was that so difficult?" Tanner's hand dropped and maneuvered its way between their bodies, stroking a gentle line that caused Izzy to bite her lower lip. "Hell, that's easy, sweetheart."

He returned his attention to her chest, softly kissing his way back up to her mouth, sliding inside her just as he reached her lips, both of them groaning simultaneously. Tanner broke the kiss and pressed his forehead against hers as he moved slowly in and out, taunting and tormenting them both. If he kept this up, she might die of need.

"You're going to listen to me when I tell that you don't need to pay for a damn thing in this apartment. Not the bills. Not the food." He moved slightly faster. "Not one damn thing. You're gonna work as much or as little as you want and you're gonna let me take care of you."

Izzy could do little more than nod in agreement. He finally kicked his pace up, and with one final thrust, their cries intermingled just as the water began to cool.

Tanner gathered her close to his chest and, with a strength she found impressive, carried her to the bedroom. They both stretched out on the bed on their sides, ignoring the water they dripped on the comforter.

Looking in his eyes, she finally spoke the words haunting her heart. "I don't want you to think I'm using you. Y-you're the perfect boyfriend and I…" She shrugged helplessly.

The hand that had been stroking her cheek stilled and the smile cleared from his face. "Sweetheart, you are normally right, but you got this all wrong." He sat up long enough to tuck a blanket around them. He laid on his back and pulled her against his side. "You keep saying I'm the perfect boyfriend, but everything I do is because of you. There's no way in hell I'd wallpaper a ceiling or cook anything for anyone else. It's just what you do to me."

She smiled and pressed her lips against his chest. She wanted to argue with him. No one had ever taken care of her as well as he did, not even her parents. "I-I'd kinda like to let you take care of me." She cleared her throat and firmed her tone. "Even though I can take care of myself."

Tanner's chuckled slightly, his breathing slowing. "I know and that makes you even hotter," he mumbled just before he started snoring.

Chapter Fourteen

Tanner

Despite his mounting frustration, Tanner turned on a placating smile. "I understand you usually have people select one of your packages, but I want my wife to be able to choose whatever she wants."

The young girl with sleek blonde hair and an overly made-up face batted her lashes at him and it was all he could do not to roll his eyes. "Well, isn't she a lucky woman."

"Hell, no." The words popped out before he could catch them. He was rapidly losing patience and had no desire to negotiate. This certainly wasn't the only spa in Asheville. "Listen, my wife is going to have a guest with her. I'm going to give that person my credit card and you're going to take it without complaining."

Instead of his words inspiring a level of respect or professionalism, the clerk behind the counter only kicked up the flirting a notch. Shit. He should have sent Dean to do this. He was more than happy to spend Tanner's money.

"Sure thing, Mr. Carlisle." She practically cooed his name and leaned over the counter. "We will happily take care of anything she needs."

He shot her a glare. "Thanks." The single word came out dryly and he made a quick exit.

What the hell was all that? An overly affectionate blonde had gotten him into this situation to begin with; he certainly had no desire to deal with another one.

Tanner muttered curses under his breath the entire way to his truck. His lips curled into a sardonic smile at the dent in the rear fender. Maybe he should leave it there as a reminder to not be such a total and complete asshole to his wife again.

If he still had a wife at the end of this. His stomach clenched as the familiar reminder rolled through his mind. No. This was going to work. This had to work.

He hit the button for the window to roll down as the air conditioner worked to cool the cab of his stifling hot truck from an hour in the sun. He grabbed the notebook off the passenger's seat and checked off the spa. When the hell had he turned into the guy who needed a friggin' to-do list?

Oh right—when he decided to break every promise he ever made to his wife.

Tanner leaned back on the headrest as the cold air began pouring out of the vents. He'd always regret each decision that led up to the moment his brother dragged him out of that bar, but a small part of him couldn't help but feel a small measure of gratitude. He hadn't realized how detached he had become from everything, especially Belle, until he started this plan to win her back.

And he had to admit, despite the overwhelming fear that he couldn't fix this, he was actually having fun. Trying to invent creative dates that would make that sparkle light up her eyes and that soft smile curve her lips and...

How the hell could he have ignored her for so long?

With a sigh, he glanced at the list again before tossing it on the seat beside him and pulling out of the parking lot. A grin tugged at the corner of his mouth. The florist was next. All right, maybe having flowers delivered at the spa was a bit of overkill, but she'd love it. Her cheeks would turn pink and she'd close her eyes and bury her nose in them, breathing in deeply.

Damn. He shifted uncomfortably in his seat. Just thinking about Belle was driving him crazy. No matter how busy he'd been, when he crawled into bed at night she would curl into him and show him exactly how much she'd missed him. He'd never gone longer than a couple of days without touching her and tasting her.

And now it had been two weeks. Dammit.

He pulled himself under control long enough to order an obscene arrangement of roses and daisies. As an afterthought, he ordered a small yellow pitcher filled with sunflowers to be delivered with Belle's flowers tomorrow. His mom always was a sucker for gifts from her boys.

And he damn sure needed every bit of help he could get. His entire family would happily kick his ass to the curb if Belle couldn't forgive him. But if he was going to have a chance in hell of making this work, he'd need a little more help.

Tanner repeated the speech he'd spent half the night planning as he turned up the long driveway leading to his parents' house. If the past two weeks had taught him anything, it was how to beg, and he had no problem begging his mom to do one tiny favor.

He snorted. Only his mother would require begging to go for an all-expense paid spa trip.

He'd briefly considered calling Belle's best friend to join her, but she hadn't talked about Caroline much lately. Maybe they'd had a falling out and he'd been too distracted to notice. Yeah, asshole fit.

All the preparation in the world, however, couldn't have prepared him for his mother's reaction when she agreed before he even told her the entire plan. "I'd love to, son," she calmly stated, interrupting his grand speech.

He stood with his mouth gaping open for several long minutes. "Y-you would?"

Tracy Carlisle wiped her flour-covered hands on her apron and tilted her head to pin her son with an irritated glare. "As much as I don't think you deserve to have Izzy forgive you, I don't want to see you two…" Her voice trailed off, and he was dumbfounded to see tears collecting in the corners of her eyes. "She's just as much my daughter as if I'd had her myself, and I want her to be happy. For some reason I really don't understand anymore, you make her happy. Even when you're barely home or off screwing around."

Tanner sighed and hung his head. "Hell, Mom, why didn't you ever tell me?"

She shrugged and picked up her rolling pin once more, attacking the dough in front of her. "Because you're a grown man who shouldn't have to have people telling him how to behave?"

Well, hell. The reminder this wasn't just about what happened at some bar in Nashville hit him between the eyes once again. This was about years of Tanner screwing up his marriage. He wanted to punch something. Or kick something. But the itching from his left hand reminded him what happened when he lost control of his temper.

"So you'll go with her tomorrow?" He repeated the question, stuffing down all the thoughts surfacing of just how long he'd been disregarding his family. If Belle could forgive him, he'd never fall into that trap again.

A smile kicked up the corners of his mother's mouth as she laid the flattened dough across the pie pan. "What woman in her right mind wouldn't love an afternoon at the spa and having her son foot the bill?" She raised one eyebrow at him. "Just don't expect to have me to spend the whole time extolling your virtues to her."

Tanner couldn't help but chuckle. "I'd never dream of it."

***

Where was she?

Where the *hell* was she?

133

Tanner paused in front of the couch to grab his cell. Ten thirty-seven. He tossed the phone back on the couch and resumed the path he was wearing in the carpet. He'd never felt closer to insanity in his life.

She could have had an accident. She could be hurt. She could be lost. She could be…

An icy feeling spread from his head to his toes. She could be with someone else. She'd never once given him a reason to doubt her, but wasn't he always the one saying she was the hottest thing on two legs?

Just as he reached down to pick up the phone for the tenth time in the past twenty minutes, he heard the knob turn and the squeak as the door swung open. Belle practically burst through the door, her cheeks rosy and her eyes sparkling. Damn if she wasn't the most gorgeous thing he'd ever seen.

He crossed the room in a few large strides and pulled her close. The relief at finally seeing her, at finally knowing she was okay, superseded his anger. For a moment. After he'd assured himself she was physically okay, he held her at arm's length. "Where the hell have you been?"

She grinned. She friggin' grinned. His temper shot through the roof.

"Baby, I told you I had my study group tonight." She stepped out of his arms, dumped her book bag and coat on the couch, and walked into the kitchen.

He clenched and unclenched his teeth. "That was supposed to be done nearly two hours ago. Where were you? And why didn't you answer your phone?"

Belle rooted in the refrigerator for a minute before popping her head up and fixing him with another smile. Why the hell was she smiling? Couldn't she tell he was worried? Pissed?

"I'm sorry, baby, our group went over and my phone was dead so I couldn't call you. Did you eat? Do you want me to heat you up some leftovers? I'm starving." She continued to pull out containers from the refrigerator before spinning around to pull two plates down from the cabinet.

Tanner closed his eyes in disbelief for a minute before storming into the kitchen and grabbing her upper arm. "Don't you understand? Don't you get that I was worried about you? That I was going out of my mind not knowing where the hell you were or what the hell you were doing? This is a big deal, Belle."

Regret filled her face, and she bit down on her lip. "I didn't mean to worry you. But I told you this morning I was going to my study group. You knew where I was and what I was doing."

"Oh yeah? Is that all you were doing?" He folded his arms over his chest and leaned a hip against the counter.

Belle scoffed, scooping some of the leftover lasagna onto a plate. "I'm going to ignore the implication and chalk it up to you being worried about me."

A small voice at the back of his mind told Tanner to shut the hell up and walk away before he said something he'd regret. He wasn't very good at listening to that particular voice. "Or are you avoiding answering it because I'm right? Because you were out doing whatever with whoever?"

She sat the glass container down on the counter with a loud clatter and turned to face him with a glare. "That's pretty funny coming from you."

His eyebrows shot up. "Me?" His deep voice jumped two octaves with the single word. "What the hell have I ever done?"

A mocking laugh answered his question. "You mean besides spending four and five nights a week from August through January with cheerleaders prancing around you? What have you done other than have half-naked fans throwing themselves at you outside the locker room every time you're leaving the field?" She rolled her eyes. "And don't even get me started on the girls who watch baseball practice in cut-off shorts and bikini tops."

He slammed his fist down on the counter. "And I don't look at a single one of them! I come home to you. I wait for you. I don't stay out until ten-thirty at night and leave you at home to worry about me, and I sure as *hell* don't ignore your phone calls."

A look of fear filled her eyes, tinged with anger. Her voice dropped, thick with emotion. "You honestly think I would cheat on you? After everything I've told you about my family, after everything we've done?" She pushed both hands against his chest. "If you don't trust me, then why are we still together?"

Tanner swallowed deeply. "I don't know."

He spun away and grabbed his coat, shoving his arms in the sleeves. He had to get out of here before he said or did something he'd regret. The last thing he needed was to put his fist through the wall.

"Where are you going?" She wrapped her arms around herself and gnawed on her lower lip.

His heart urged him to stop, to shut the hell up and hold her. But his pride was stronger and louder and propelled him to leave. He paused, halfway through the door. "Anywhere that isn't here. Don't worry, *my* phone's charged."

He closed the door quietly behind him and raced down the stairs before he lost his nerve. He'd never yelled at Belle before and definitely never walked away from her.

It only took going twenty feet from the apartment building before he began calling himself every kind of asshole he could think of.

Chapter Fifteen

Izzy

Crossing the threshold of the spa made Izzy feel like she was stepping into a dream world. Had Tanner somehow conjured up her every fantasy and brought it to life? First, a night under the stars and now this?

She had tried to maintain poise and composure as she entered the spa with Tanner's mom, but that was practically impossible. Even the reception area oozed luxury and decadence. The plush ivory couches and soft bamboo flooring tastefully accented the teal walls and black and white oversized prints hanging on them. The scent of jasmine filled the air, and it was as if a switch was flipped and every muscle in her body had permission to relax.

Two women dressed in ivory slacks and teal polo shirts approached them, each carrying a robe in one hand and a brochure in the other. Izzy had to hold back a laugh at the realization the color scheme

138

carried over into their clothing.

She was shoved out of her depth as the women explained various packages and services they offered and asked her what treatments she wanted that day. She raised her eyebrows and looked to her mother-in-law for guidance.

Tracy smiled at the staff helping them and threw Izzy a wink. "Everything." She handed over Tanner's credit card nonchalantly and followed the women into the back, beckoning Izzy to follow.

"What do you mean everything?" She whispered the question to Tracy. "That will take all day and cost a small fortune."

Just as they reached the changing rooms, Tracy turned to her and grabbed her hand. "Honey, my son is an idiot. Truly he is. And I have no intention of selling you on him or begging you to forgive him. But for the first time since Michael handed the company over to Tanner, I'm seeing a glimpse of the guy who brought you to our house for Thanksgiving a dozen years ago." A sly grin spread across her face. "And I think we need to enjoy every second of his guilt and have a wonderful day together."

Izzy just stared at her for a long moment. "But what if everything goes back to the way it was?" She hadn't dared to let herself think about that too often and certainly hadn't voiced her concern to Tanner, but she had always felt closer to his mother than her own. And she finally found the strength to voice her fear.

Tracy Carlisle wrapped her arms around her daughter-in-law and pulled her in for a close hug, the fluffy robe falling off her arm. "Oh Izzy, honey." She rubbed a hand up and down her back soothingly before pulling away to look in her eyes. "I can't predict the future, Iz, all I can do is tell you I've never seen my son this devastated, or this motivated, in his life."

A smile tugged at Izzy's lips, and she wrinkled her nose. "Is it wrong that I'm just a little happy to hear that Tanner is completely devastated?"

Laughing, the older woman squeezed her shoulders again and shooed her into the changing room. "Not at all, honey, not at all."

Six hours—and more money than she cared to admit—later, Izzy drove home, more relaxed than she'd ever been in her life. The sunlight dropping lower in the sky caught the glitter in the blue nail polish on her fingers, identical to the shade on her toes, and Izzy couldn't help but grin.

When Tanner proposed the idea of taking forty-three days to prove himself to her, she expected lavish gifts, expensive wine and fancy dinners. She never dreamed of family nights, a picnic at Wake Forest, or a night under the stars. She certainly never dreamed Tanner would plan a "date" and then completely exclude himself from it. She cast a quick glance to the vase overflowing with roses and daisies beside her. Well, almost completely exclude.

She pulled her car into the garage and sat for just a few moments. A thought had been running through her head the entire day as she lay with a facial mask in place or having each knot in her shoulders firmly massaged.

She missed Tanner.

It was something she hadn't allowed herself to think when his nights at the office grew later and later or his business trips increased in frequency. She'd rationalized it all because he was trying to prove he was as good as his father. As capable, as dependable, and as successful. So she'd supported him and never complained.

But she missed Tanner.

In the past two weeks, she had started to feel a glimmer of hope. The Tanner that could read her like a book, the Tanner that begged her to let him slay every dragon, the Tanner that had been gone for more than three years, was finally showing up.

She was equal parts thrilled and terrified. And she wasn't sure she could ever touch him, kiss him, or even look at him without thoughts of *her* intruding.

But she still missed Tanner.

The idea started to grow and a slow smile spread across her face as she finally forced her legs into motion and walked into the house. She stopped, dumbfounded to find Tanner in the kitchen, putting dishes away.

He turned and pinned her with the smile that still curled her toes. "Hey, sweetheart. How was your day?"

She dropped her purse on the island and stood a few feet away from him, leaning her back against the counter. "It was…" She rolled her eyes up to the ceiling and searched for the right words. "Amazing. I don't know how you manage to give me things I don't even know I want."

Tanner closed the overhead cabinet and folded

his arms across his chest. He lifted one shoulder. "I'm paying attention now, Belle." He shook his head and looked at the floor. "I know I wasn't for a long time, but I am now."

"I, um, I wanted to talk to you." She looked around, suddenly realizing the house was exceptionally quiet. "Where are the kids?"

He chuckled and propped his hip on the counter. "Asleep. We spent the entire afternoon at my parents' house. In the pool, riding the horses, cleaning the stalls—"

Izzy held up a hand. "Ava and Noah? They cleaned the stalls?"

Tanner shrugged again with a mischievous smile. "They helped. And after all that, they were happy to go to bed early."

She pushed off the island and took a couple of steps closer to him. "I miss you."

His hands fell to his sides, and he took a step toward her, so close they were nearly touching. "I'm right here, sweetheart."

Her gaze fell and she saw the muscles in his hand twitch. He wanted to touch her, to hold her, but she knew he wasn't going to make the first move. She met his stare and laced her fingers with his.

"I know and I…" She bit her bottom lip. The nerves overwhelming her at the prospect of asking a simple question were ridiculous. He was her first love. Her husband. The one person on the earth who knew every part of her better than she did, and she really was going to ask him this? Izzy took a deep breath. "I wanted to know if you'd like to…sleep with me tonight? I-I don't m-mean like that. I'm not ready for that. I-I just—"

"One condition." He cut her off and held up a finger.

She couldn't resist grinning at him. "That business degree rears its ugly head again. Okay, Mr. MBA, what's your counter offer?"

He lifted their joined hands and placed a soft kiss on her knuckles. "That I get to hold you."

***

The soft click of the door latch echoed like a gun shot in Izzy's head, and she couldn't help but jump.

He left.

Her mind replayed their fight over and over as she stared at the closed door. He yelled at her and then he left.

The tears began to fall, and she felt like the air had been sucked from her lungs. She stumbled over to the couch and fell into it, gasping for air. They fought. He left. They were over. This was how relationships ended.

Over. The word repeated in her mind like a broken record. She clapped her hands over her ears to try to avoid hearing the single word.

A new thought popped into her brain that caused her barely beating heart to suddenly race. Where was she going to go? She'd only gotten student loans to cover tuition and books. Even if she had the money, there were no available dorms. She couldn't possibly ask her dad. That bridge was burned. There was no way her mother could afford the thousands

143

needed to get her own apartment.

She couldn't avoid the hysterical laughter that bubbled up. Tanner promised to take care of her. Begged her to trust him and take a chance on him. And now she was going to be homeless.

At least she wouldn't have to worry about packing the cookware if she was homeless.

Izzy felt like she was going to throw up. She felt like she was going insane. She felt like her world had just spun into another orbit.

Three deep breaths later, she finally found the strength to stand, square her shoulders, and dry her tears. What had she always told Tanner? She could take care of herself. Even if that meant doing it with a broken heart and living in her car for the next two months while she finished school. She would take care of herself.

She stared at the closet and chewed on her bottom lip. There was no way she could fit all her clothes into the two suitcases she owned. Her gaze fell on the black dress Tanner had bought for her birthday and suddenly her cheeks were wet again. She swiped at them angrily. She couldn't afford to cry. She needed to pack and leave before Tanner came back. If he came back.

She shook her head to dispel the avalanche of thoughts that followed. Where was he? Would he come back tonight? She gulped back the threatening sobs. Would he even miss her when he did?

There wasn't time to think about that. She had to figure out what to do with her clothes. Garbage bags. Whatever didn't fit in the suitcases would go in garbage bags. She barked out a hollow laugh. A homeless bag lady. Perfect. Her father would be so proud.

Izzy began stuffing clothes from the closet in bags, carefully avoiding the black dress. That would definitely be staying. She moved to the dresser and began to fill the suitcases with the clothes she wore most often, hoping to keep them relatively wrinkle free.

She scoffed at herself. She was losing her home, any possessions she couldn't fit in her car, and more important than either of those things, she was losing Tanner. And she was worried about her clothes.

"What the hell are you doing?"

She hadn't heard the door or his footsteps. The shock from hearing his voice made her drop the stack of shirts she was valiantly trying to fit into the first suitcase. "I-I'm s-sorry. I was h-h-hoping to be done b-before you got back." The stupid tears began to collect at the corners of her eyes and she cursed each one, not wanting to show Tanner how much leaving hurt.

He stalked across the room, picked up the shirts from the floor, and put them back in the dresser. "It's a damn good thing you weren't. I'm too tired to spend the whole night chasing you down and bringing you back." Tanner folded his arms and leaned his back against the doorframe. "You're not going anywhere."

Izzy waved a hand around the room helplessly. "I-I can't afford to stay here on my own."

His gaze narrowed. "Who said anything about you staying here on your own?"

She rubbed her first two fingers up and down her

temple and shook her head. She couldn't understand a word he was saying, and she certainly couldn't keep looking at him. Her heart was ripped to shreds and he was standing here like they were having a perfectly normal conversation about...what? Becoming roommates?

Her stomach lurched at the thought of sharing an apartment with Tanner and seeing him bring home a parade of different girls. Hearing their screams coming from their bedroom—no, *his* bedroom. She really was going to throw up.

Her chin quivered and she gave up holding back the tears. "Tanner, there is no way I can become your roommate after...everything. We-this-us..." She sighed as the tears streaked down her face. "It makes sense that I'm the one that leaves. I promise I'll be gone soon."

In three large strides, he crossed the room and gathered her in his arms. If she thought her heart was broken before, now it was shattered. A goodbye hug? Is that something people did? Her parents certainly hadn't parted amicably. There was only screaming and bitterness. Did normal couples end their relationships like this?

She couldn't stop her arms from encircling his neck or her tears from soaking the shoulder of his shirt. Tanner wasn't just her boyfriend. He was her best friend. Losing him meant losing so much more than a first love.

When his hands gripped her sides and pushed her away, she felt gutted. Broken. "Sweetheart, we had an argument." His voice was soft and soothing. "This doesn't change a damn thing and it sure as hell doesn't mean you leave. The only thing that happens right now is I apologize for being a complete and total asshole and beg you to forgive me. But nobody leaves."

Izzy froze. That's not how it worked. Was it? Her parents fought, her dad left. That's how it happened, right? You didn't yell at someone you loved. You didn't fight with someone you wanted to spend your life with. Fighting meant you were over…didn't it?

"You said you don't know why we're together," she stuttered out between hiccups.

Tanner winced. "That's where the apologizing for being an asshole thing comes in, sweetheart. I sure as hell know why I'm with you. You are smart and strong and the sexiest damn thing on two legs. I have no clue why the hell you put up with me, though." He sighed and tightened his grip on her waist. "I don't have an excuse for anything I said or did. I was worried, I was tired, and I couldn't think clearly. I'm sorry, sweetheart."

Disbelief swept through her, followed closely by hope. "W-we're not over?"

The color drained from his face. He pulled her tight against his body, lifting her feet off the ground. "No. *Hell* no. We aren't over. We are a forever thing, sweetheart. Unless you can't forgive me for being a sorry son of a—"

Izzy grabbed the sides of his face and kissed him deeply. Her chest swelled and her not-so-shattered heart finally started beating again.

Tanner lowered her down slowly, not breaking the kiss until her feet reached the floor. "Belle, I can't promise we will never fight again and I can't promise I'll never act like a total prick again, but I promise you that a fight doesn't mean we're over. It doesn't mean anyone leaves."

She nodded rapidly and struggled to find the words she needed to say. "It's just...I just..." She heaved a sigh and wrapped her arms around his waist, pressing a cheek to his chest. "I don't ever remember my parents fighting until the day my dad left and I-I just thought..."

He hooked a finger under her chin. "We aren't and never will be your parents, sweetheart. That I can definitely promise."

Chapter Sixteen

Tanner

Tanner did everything he could think of to keep himself awake. He didn't want to risk falling asleep just to find out it was all a dream. Belle's apple shampoo filled his nose. He hadn't realized how much he'd missed the smell, the feel, and the warmth of Belle beside him all night until he finally got it back again.

Eventually the exhaustion of the day, and the sheer ecstasy of having Belle close to him, took over and he drifted into the most peaceful sleep he'd had in more than two weeks. Since the very first night he'd spent in her dorm at college, he'd always slept best when Belle was next to him.

The bright sunlight streaming in the window pried his eyes open. Relief swept through him when he looked down and saw that Belle hadn't disappeared. His breathing stuttered when he realized she had turned during the night and now was facing him, cuddled into his chest, a small smile curving her lips. She'd slept that way for years, but he didn't pay attention.

Her long lashes rested against her cheeks and he picked out a dozen freckles that were barely visible, but pretty damn cute. Her left hand rested on his chest beside her face and he grinned at the glittery nail polish she had chosen. He could spend the rest of the day lying here, exactly like this.

But today was Sunday. And Tanner was on a quest to stop being a self-centered asshole, which included making the gorgeous creature sound asleep next to him breakfast.

He slowly began to pull his arm from under her head, being as careful as possible not to wake her.

But Belle clung to his white shirt with the first movement, snuggling deeper into his embrace. "Just five more minutes."

Tanner grinned and kissed the top of her head. "You can stay here as long as you want sweetheart. But I need to go make breakfast."

"I release you of all your culinary duties for today." Her eyes stayed closed and she kept a firm grip on his shirt. "Because I'm just too comfortable and I've missed you too much."

Her words struck him in a way he knew she never intended. "You could have told me, Belle." He held her closer, just to remind himself she was really here, in his arms. "You could have told me I was gone too much. That I'd stopped doing all the important stuff. That I wasn't…"

She released the death grip she had on his shirt and smoothed her hand over it. She propped her chin on his chest and fixed him with an open expression. "That you weren't Tanner anymore?"

He swallowed. Well, hell. That was one way of putting it. "Sweetheart, I—"

Belle covered his mouth with her hand. "Bathroom. Now."

She clambered over top of him and tugged his arm until he got out of the bed and followed her. "Belle, I mean, hell, I've missed you too and I've really, really missed…but I don't think the shower is best…" He stopped talking when she plopped his toothbrush in his hand, generously covered in toothpaste. "Wait, what's this?"

Her eyebrows shot up and white foam trickled out of her mouth as she grinned around her toothbrush. "Ith your toothbruth," she mumbled. She spit into the sink and the running water swirled the mixture down the drain. She lifted her eyes expectantly, toothbrush poised to attack her teeth again. "We both have morning breath, but I want to kiss you, so get to brushing."

Tanner laughed as he obediently began scrubbing his teeth. But his laughter died when Belle hopped up onto the counter between the double sinks. He spit into the basin and wiped his mouth with the small hand towel she held out to him. He stood in front of her and ran a hand over the bare length of thigh visible under her short nightgown. "You want to kiss me?"

Belle's eyes widened and her hands slid up and down his arms. "Mmmhmm."

He took a step forward and her legs automatically parted. Damn, that was a gorgeous sight. He dipped his head down and paused, his lips

151

a breath away from hers. "Are you sure, Belle?"

Instead of answering, she wound her fingers through his hair and pulled his mouth to hers. When her lips softened under his, he groaned and deepened the kiss. His fingers trailed over her body from her soft, silky thighs up to her already heated neck and back down. Next they journeyed under her nightgown, and her responding gasp made him smile. "Do you like that, sweetheart?"

Belle's only reaction was to tighten her thighs around his legs. He dropped his mouth to her ear and sucked on her earlobe. "How about this, Belle?" His lips trailed down her neck. "Is this okay, sweetheart?"

"Y-yes," she whispered. "Yes, Tanner."

He tugged her nightgown over her head before any rational thoughts could stop him. The very breath was ripped from his body as he looked at every inch of her body.

After several long minutes staring at her, he raised a tortured gaze. "Stop me if—"

"No stopping," she answered before claiming his mouth again.

His greedy hands felt every part of her soft skin, remembering each spot that made her gasp and moan. His mouth moved to her neck and he lightly started sucking where her pulse was thumping in time with his heart. Tanner's fingers outlined her panties before finally sliding in and stroking the sensitive skin.

Belle whimpered under his touch. "Tanner, please."

His lips curved against her shoulder as he left a

path of light kisses. Every teasing swirl of his fingers made her breath grow shallower. He sealed his lips against hers just as she started to scream his name, only sliding his fingers out of her when her breathing slowed.

Tanner picked her up, carried her back to their bed, and gently laid her down. He propped himself on his elbows over her, planting soft kisses on her cheeks, her nose, her lips. "I love you so much, sweetheart," he whispered against her skin. "I love every little sigh you make, I love the way your skin tastes, I love the way your fingers feel on my body."

He ran his tongue in a long line down from her neck to her chest and after a few minutes of undivided attention continued making a path down to her navel, dipping his tongue in and grinning at her sharp intake of breath. "Tan-ner." Her voice broke over his name.

As much as his body screamed at him for relief, he forced back every desire and focused on her. *His* Belle. She deserved so much more, but right now he was determined to take care of her. Just her.

He peeled her underwear down slowly, replacing it with his mouth and his hands, reveling in the feel of her fingers toying with his hair. She always loved playing with his hair and he always loved playing with her.

His physical need grew to painful proportions with every sound she made and every drop of her on his tongue. But his need to show her that for the first time in a long time he was making everything about her overrode the demands of his body. When she finally cried out, he rested his sweat-slickened forehead against her abdomen, breathing deeply and desperately, trying to gain some measure of control.

Belle tugged on his head to bring him back up to her mouth. Her cheeks were tinged with pink and her eyes wide. "Tanner, th-that was…I-I mean…y-you need—"

He cut off her words with a kiss. "I need to go make you breakfast, sweetheart." He grinned and walked away before his overwhelming need for her kicked in.

***

Welcome   to   Wake   Forest University School of Business.

He read the subject then read it again before even opening the email. It was already February and he was certain he hadn't made it into the MBA program when week after week passed with no response. The tightness that had been present in his chest for so long finally eased.

The truth was, he was far less concerned with making it into graduate school than he was with leaving Belle. The very thought of going to a different school made him nauseated.

His very first instinct was to grab his backpack and laptop and run from the lecture hall to call her. Make plans to celebrate. But graduating with his Bachelor's was kind of required for graduate school and leaving in the middle of class certainly wouldn't endear him to the professor standing twenty feet away, droning on about international business ethics.

Twenty long minutes later, he slipped his phone from his pocket and pulled up Belle's number without even looking. "Hey sweetheart, where are you?"

"Umm, I'm just leaving the library. Why?"

Her tone immediately brought a frown to his lips. "Everything okay, sweetheart?" This didn't sound like Belle. He got the distinct and extremely uneasy feeling she was keeping something from him.

"Everything is great, baby, what's up?"

This time her voice was far too chipper and did nothing to lessen his discomfort. He pushed it aside with a shake of his head and leaned his back against the wall, allowing everyone to pass him in the hall. "I got in, Belle!" His proclamation came out far louder than he'd intended. Clearing his throat, he lowered his voice. "I got into the MBA program and we need to celebrate, sweetheart."

There was a slight pause that Tanner was certain was only a few seconds long, but it felt like much longer. "Congratulations, baby!" Her voice seemed fake, and he could swear he heard someone else and a door closing.

What the hell was going on?

"Belle, are you sure—"

"Tanner, baby, listen, I gotta go but, um, don't you have practice tonight? So you won't be home until after seven or something, right?"

His confusion quickly turned to anger. She never asked when he'd be home and she certainly never tried to get off the phone with him. "Yeah,

155

sweetheart." The endearment, spoken out of habit, was clipped. "I'll be home after seven." He clicked the phone off and stormed out of the building toward his next class.

Hell to the no. She was hiding something, and there was no way he was going to screw around at some stupid baseball practice.

For the next three hours, Tanner's mind ignored everything the professors said in his last two classes and raced from one possibility to another with the most insistent thought being someone else in his home with his Belle. The thought that had been hanging at the back of his mind since he picked her up from class and noticed the eyes of her classmates following her out. The thought he voiced when she came home late from study group two weeks ago. And the same thought that created their first fight.

His mind conjured up the image of Belle packing her bags, and that cooled some of his anger. Some. He sat in his truck for a few minutes, allowing his temper to cool before slowly driving away from campus and reminding himself repeatedly there was no reason to break the speed limit on the way home. And he certainly didn't need to entertain any notions of breaking down the apartment door.

Dammit all to hell. He had no reason to be jealous. They had been dating for nearly a year and a half. They lived together for crying out loud. Belle was as loyal as anyone he'd ever met.

But she was oblivious to the fact she was the sexiest damn thing on two legs. Never noticed the looks she got nearly everywhere they went. Hell, she didn't even know that his own brothers drooled every time she walked in their house.

Tanner, however, wasn't. Not in the slightest. He'd made sure the guys on both his teams kept their thoughts, their eyes, and especially their hands to themselves where she was concerned, but he couldn't control the whole campus. Hell, the whole world.

And that realization coupled with the memory of half of the male population in her class checking out her tight little ass when she left the room had been driving him insane for the past month.

He forced himself to take the stairs one at a time instead of racing up them at double speed. He took a deep breath and checked his watch before turning the knob at their apartment. He was home two hours earlier than she expected. Whatever she was up to, he'd find out soon enough.

There wasn't a calming technique around that could have prepared him for the sight laid out before him when he walked through the door. Dozens of unlit white candles of various shapes and sizes were placed around the room, a black cloth with a strip of gold material running down the middle covered their small coffee table, and two champagne flutes sat on top. Balloons with the word "Congratulations" emblazoned across the front were attached to a weight in the middle of the table.

Well, hell.

His backpack slid to the floor with a thunk, and at that moment it registered that he could hear the shower running. If he turned around and left right then, Belle would never know he had been here.

Never know his mind had spiraled him into another jealous fit and—

The water turned off and, before Tanner could make up his mind, she emerged from the bathroom with a small shriek when she saw him. Dammit. Why did she have to be wrapped in nothing but a towel? His body immediately reacted to that little tidbit of information, despite his best efforts to bank his desire.

Her face fell, and he cursed himself. "Tanner, I, um, I didn't expect you home. I-I..." She swallowed, and tears collected at the corners of her eyes. "I wanted to surprise you."

Stupid, distrustful, short-tempered, son of a bitch. He smiled as he cursed himself silently. "Sweetheart, you did surprise me. This is amazing and thoughtful and..." He crossed the room to gather her in his arms and pulled her close. "Wait, how did you get all of this together so fast?"

Pink tinged her cheeks, and she focused on his chest. "I-I didn't. Remember when my study group went late?"

Tanner nodded, feeling his guilt amplifying. Their first fight. And if he told her the truth, he had a sneaking suspicion they'd be gearing up for their second.

"Well, I wasn't totally honest." She sighed and finally raised her eyes to his. "This one guy in my group is the teacher's assistant for the Dean of the business school, and he told me you got in that night. I-I didn't want to tell you. I wanted you to get the letter, but I wanted to be ready..."

Well double hell. He really didn't deserve her.

He lowered his mouth to hers and felt her lips curve before she pulled back. "It's a little out of order," she stepped back and tugged at the knot on the towel, letting it pool at her feet, "but since I'm more appropriately attired for the end of our celebration and you're so very clearly ready…" She grabbed his hand and pulled him toward their bedroom.

Chapter Seventeen

Izzy

What just happened?

Her arms felt like lead and she couldn't open her eyes.

She counted to ten, then twenty, then fifty before she finally forced herself out of the bed and into the shower. The entire time she wavered between berating herself for needing Tanner so badly and reveling in the warmth still lingering on her skin from his touch. She couldn't help but avoid eye contact with herself in the mirror while she blow-dried her hair, certain she wouldn't like whatever she saw reflected back.

She tugged on a pair of cut-off denim shorts and a blue tank top and let her gaze travel down the length of her body with a sigh. Maybe she wasn't trying hard enough. Maybe she should start wearing sexier clothes, making sure her makeup was flawless, and doing something with her long brown hair besides throwing it in a ponytail.

Maybe then Tanner would be home more.

Maybe then he wouldn't have wanted someone else.

Maybe.

Ava's giggles coming from the kitchen pulled Izzy from the migraine-inducing thoughts as she trudged down the stairs. She leaned against the entryway to the kitchen and grinned. Tanner had swept Ava off her feet into a bear hug and was smacking kisses on her cheeks.

"Daddy! Your beard tickles!" She barely gasped the words out through her laughter.

Tanner unceremoniously plopped her on the stool before leaving one more kiss on her cheek and ruffling Noah's hair. "You realize that Daddy only does round pancakes right? None of this hearts and stars stuff. Mommy is in charge of being creative."

"Oh, I am, huh?" Izzy playfully called out.

A smirk settled on Tanner's face as he looked up from the batter he was pouring in the pan long enough to throw her a wink. "Well, good morning, sweetheart."

She couldn't help the pink that crept onto her face and was grateful the kids were young enough not to pick up on it. She crossed the kitchen to stand next to him and dropped her voice, hoping Ava and Noah would be so wrapped up in their chatter they'd ignore their parents. "We need to talk, Tanner. About that. About this morning."

His smile faltered for the briefest of moments as he flipped the pancakes. He nodded to the kids and flicked his gaze over to her before fixing it on the pan in front of him again. "Yeah, but...later?

161

Besides, I need to ask you something."

Izzy frowned slightly. Okay, talking about their two mind-blowing encounters—and all the reasons they would not be happening again for at least a little while—would have to wait until the kids were out of the room, but she wasn't sure she liked the look on Tanner's face. "About?"

He pointed the spatula at a piece of paper with a streak of ketchup across the top. "I dropped your favorite knife in the trash accidentally and I found that when I was digging it out. Why aren't you going, Belle?"

She picked up the flyer and quickly scanned over the advertisement for the painting night fundraiser for Noah's baseball team. "It's on a Wednesday night," she stated matter-of-factly before crumpling the paper and tossing it back into the trash can.

"And?" Tanner carried the pan over to the island and slid a pancake on each of the two plates, barely pulling back before the kids doused them in syrup and practically inhaled them.

Izzy rolled her eyes. "And," she exaggerated the single word, "it starts at five o'clock. What will I do with the kids?"

He set the pan back on the stove, poured enough batter in for three more pancakes, and turned to her with a grin and a mischievous glint in his eyes. "Hi, my name is Tanner. I'm their father and sometimes can be considered a responsible adult."

She failed at keeping a smile from covering her face. "Nice to meet you, Tanner, and those are very true facts, but at four o'clock in the afternoon on a Wednesday, when I need to leave, you'll be in the office. Talking to someone in California. Or Beijing."

"Nope." He flipped one of the pancakes. "Beijing is twelve hours ahead, so it would be four in the morning there. Plus, I'll come home early so you can go."

Izzy's teeth clamped down on her bottom lip, and she leaned the small of her back against the counter beside Tanner. "Why?"

Her heart began to race when the supremely confident smirk slipped back in place on Tanner's face. He braced his hands on the counter on either side of her, standing just far enough away that they didn't touch but close enough to feel the heat radiating off his body. She folded her arms over her chest to disguise his effect on her and simultaneously prevent her hands from reaching out to pull him closer.

His head bent down close to hers, but he stopped a whisper away from her mouth. "Because I think you want to go, but you'd never ask." His breath tickled her lips as he spoke the words in a low tone. "Because I'm fairly certain you'd create a masterpiece. And because I'd love nothing more than to steal it and hang it in my office."

A chill ran down her spine and she couldn't help shivering. Tanner's grin widened as he stepped back and put the pancakes on a plate, holding it up to her. "Here ya go, sweetheart."

The entire day, Izzy couldn't help but marvel at the normalcy. Tanner hadn't planned any crazy date nights and there were no surprises waiting in the wings. But several rounds of various games, a dinner of hot dogs roasted over a fire, and early bedtimes for two exhausted kids later, Izzy found herself sitting on a log, snuggling close to Tanner and feeling completely at peace.

His arm wrapped around her shoulders and pulled her even closer. He kissed the top of her head softly. "Belle, I-I just wanted to ask, I mean, I just want to be sure…"

She picked her head up from his shoulder, watching the flickering lights from the fire dance over Tanner's face. His uncharacteristic apprehensive tone caused warmth to spread through her chest.

"Where do you want me to sleep tonight?"

Izzy slid onto his lap, and his body relaxed around hers. "The same place I always want you to sleep, Tanner. Next to me."

***

The container of ketchup slid across the shelf in the refrigerator and bumped against the back wall. Izzy slammed the door shut and wiped an angry tear from her eyes.

The red numbers of the digital clock on the stove mocked her as it ticked off another minute.

This morning Tanner had promised her he'd be home by eight. When eight had come and gone, she called his office and he assured her that he would be home before nine. Now it was after ten o'clock. The meatloaf was ice cold, the mashed potatoes were congealed into a sticky paste, and the green beans had shriveled.

Finally, after she had put away the last part of the meal, she heard the click of the door being unlocked. Just as Tanner rounded the corner into the kitchen, she blew out the candles.

"Uhhh." His eyes darted from the mostly melted lumps of wax to the bottle of wine on the counter before finally resting on her face. "Did I forget something, sweetheart?"

Izzy rolled her eyes as she brushed past him. "No, Tanner. Not at all."

His hand closed around her upper arm. "Talk to me. Don't walk away."

She pulled out of his grasp and took three steps away from him. "Talk to you? When, Tanner? I'm doing my student teaching the entire day so I can graduate in two months and then I come home and do my lesson planning at night. You spend your mornings in the classroom and your nights in that little office space your dad leased for you that was *supposed* to help you be home more." She threw her hands in the air. "I don't ever see you to talk to you."

He closed his eyes and leaned his head back. "Do you honestly think I *want* to be gone this much?" When he finally opened his eyes to look at her, the exhaustion evident there was tinged with anger and she felt a pang of guilt. "Do you think I want to spend six hours a day sitting in a classroom and another ten learning how to run the company? Exactly what part of all of this sounds like fun to you?"

Izzy folded her arms across her chest and frowned. Any sympathy she felt when she saw the dark circles under his eyes quickly disappeared. "And what part of this do you think is fun for me? Tanner, you promised you'd be home by eight. Then nine. It's nearly eleven now."

His hand slammed against the wall, and she jumped at the sound. "I'm working to build a future for us! To make sure I don't bankrupt the company and destroy everything my dad built over the past twenty-five years. I'm going to be in charge of the entire company in just a few years, and I am going to have fifty employees on top of my family counting on me to do things right. Don't you understand, Belle?"

She stepped in front of him and poked a finger in his chest. "I understand that unless you start spending just a little more time with me, there isn't going to be an us to build a future for."

The color drained from his face. "Do you mean that?"

"I-I-I…" She stammered as the words she said solely out of anger sank in.

"Dammit, Belle, do you mean it?" He grabbed the finger that was still resting against his chest and held her hand close to his heart. His voice sounded strained and hoarse. "Do you mean you want to leave me? To give up on us?"

She licked her suddenly dry lips. "It means I don't want to be alone in a relationship."

Before he could respond, she pulled her hand free from his and ran into the bedroom. She closed the door and slid down it in tears.

The questions he asked echoed in her mind. Did she mean it? Did she want to break up with him because he was working too much?

By the time her tears finally slowed, her head was throbbing and her back hurt from the uncomfortable seat against the door. She crawled between the sheets, not bothering to take off her t-shirt and jeans. She pulled his pillow close and took a deep breath of the cedarwood and musk scent that clung to it.

Just before she drifted off, the door creaked open and the bed dipped beside her. She couldn't help but breathe a sigh of relief knowing Tanner was lying next to her. Without a second thought, she turned and cuddled into his arms, resting her cheek against the soft cotton of his shirt. "Nobody leaves?"

He kissed the top of her head softly. "Nobody leaves," he affirmed.

Chapter Eighteen

Tanner

Tanner took a quick bite out of his sandwich and returned his attention to the computer screen, entering more numbers into the spreadsheet and hoping it would make sense this time. He had a deadline tonight and he'd be damned if he would be late.

A tap on his office door pulled him out of the columns of numbers swimming before him and he looked at his guest with a mixture of confusion and concern. "Dad?" His brows drew together. "What's wrong?"

Michael Carlisle had declared himself semi-retired three years ago, choosing to spend most of his days golfing or fishing rather than showing up in the office. His father took the seat across the desk from him, wearing an impeccably ironed shirt and his favorite tie. Tanner immediately tensed up, dreading whatever crisis was about to be discussed. He absolutely did *not* have time for this.

"Get her to forgive you yet?" His father leaned back in the chair, resting an ankle on the opposite knee, and folded his hands over his abdomen. His bushy eyebrows raised a fraction as he waited expectantly for an answer.

Tanner rolled his eyes and took another bite of his lunch. "What do you need, Dad?" he asked around a mouth full of food, pointedly ignoring his father's question.

Mike lifted his shoulders slightly. "I am still president of the company. I need to see what's going on around here."

"Yeah, and I'm the CEO." He shook his head and chuckled lightly. "This place is a well-oiled machine and you usually only show your face in here once or twice a month. This is the third time in the past two weeks. Why are you really here?"

His father sighed and straightened in his chair. "Because I think I forgot to teach you some important things about running Carlisle International." Mike's gaze fixed on the mahogany desk separating them, and a thoughtful expression descended over his face. "Probably the most important thing."

Tanner sighed and closed his eyes. He counted to ten in his mind and mustered all of his patience. He had a list of things to get done before he could get home to Belle and his father wasn't helping his time constraints. At all. "Listen, Dad, unless this is something urgent—"

"I didn't think it was until you acted like a damn fool and tried to ruin your marriage. I tried to give you space, son. I figured you'd be as stubborn and pig-headed as me, but that you'd figure it out on your own eventually." He scratched the back of his neck. "I guess I should've said something sooner. Told you that you were being as big of an asshole as I used to be."

Obviously his father wasn't going to leave anytime soon. Rather than fighting him any further, he waved him on, feeling irritated to be on the receiving end of another lecture. "I have a feeling this is going to go faster if you just tell me all the things I'm screwing up."

Mike's open palm slapped down on the desk. "Don't act like such an arrogant son of a bitch."

Shocked at the display of blatant anger from his father, some of Tanner's ire slipped. Both of his parents had been strict and stern while he was growing up, but at that moment, Mike Carlisle was radiating fury, something Tanner wasn't accustomed to. "Dad, I—"

"No." He cut his son off again and stood. "You're going to sit there and listen to me."

Tanner swallowed back the words that were on the tip of his tongue as he watched his father pace back and forth in the space in front of his desk. Several minutes ticked by as Mike continued to march resolutely, seeming to gather his thoughts.

Finally he turned and leaned over Tanner's desk, bracing his hands on the smooth wood surface. "You don't get to ignore your family because of this." He waved a hand around the room. "You don't get to act like a reckless teenager and you damn sure don't get to break her heart."

Mike's voice thickened with emotion. "This

company is not worth more than your wife and your kids. I had to learn the hard way, and I almost lost your mom because of it. I hoped you'd be smarter than me."

Tanner leapt to his feet and his black leather chair hit the bookcase behind him with the movement. "Twenty-five years, Dad." He walked over to the window and stared out unseeingly for several long minutes. "Twenty-five years ago you brought me here for the first time. You had just built this office and moved out of that tiny building on Crescent."

He ran his hands through his hair and locked his fingers behind his neck, turning to face his father. "You brought me here on the first day of summer vacation when I was eight and told me one day I would be the boss. I would be in charge. I would be responsible for the company and the family. You brought me to work with you all the time. You trained me for this."

His eyes lifted to the ceiling, and he barked out a mirthless laugh. "And the first time in thirty-three years I decided to just have fun and be as irresponsible as Wyatt...it blew up in my face. I was miserable, I missed Belle and the kids like crazy, and I woke up with a hangover from hell, knowing I'd just made the worst mistake in my life."

The color drained from his father's face and his mouth fell open. "Son, I never meant...I never wanted you to feel..." He scrubbed his hands over his face and sighed. "Well, hell."

Tanner's hands fell to his sides. "I didn't want to

disappoint you. The last thing I ever wanted to do was disappoint you." He sighed and nearly collapsed into the chair his father had been sitting in earlier. "But that's exactly what I did. I disappointed you and Mom and, hell, I broke Belle's heart."

Mike took the seat next to his son and rested his elbows on his knees. He kept his gaze fixed on his interlaced fingers for a long time. "Tanner, I don't understand why you never said anything before this. Son, you know you can come to me for anything."

A hollow smile curved Tanner's lips. "So you'll give up the Thursday morning golf games if I need to start taking some time off?"

He quirked an eyebrow at Tanner. "How about we do one better than that?" He circled around the desk and took up residence in Tanner's seat. He quickly located a blank piece of paper and pen and began scribbling furiously. After five minutes, he slid the paper across the desk. "How does that look? We can make adjustments as we go."

Tanner's eyes scanned over the page, and he grinned. "Hey, the old man's still got it."

His father pinned him with a stoic expression. "The 'old man' built it. And don't you forget it." Finally the veneer cracked, and he offered his son a wink and a smile. "Now I think that means you need to get the hell out of here."

For the first time in longer than he cared to remember, some of the tension drained from Tanner's shoulders. "Thanks, Dad."

Before his father could even respond, he grabbed the rest of his lunch off the desk and all but sprinted out the door.

***

He peeled back the blue sheet that was covering her and began trailing kisses from her wrist up to her shoulder, never taking his eyes off her face. Just as his mouth moved over her elbow, her eyelids fluttered and he couldn't help but grin. "Good morning, Sleeping Beauty," he murmured against her skin.

Belle rolled onto her back and smiled at him. "Good morning, baby." As soon as the words left her mouth, clouds formed in her eyes and she bit down on her bottom lip. "Tanner, I'm sorry I said—"

Tanner shook his head and ran his tongue up the column of her neck, silencing her thoughts and eliciting a soft moan. "No, sweetheart, you were right. I've been working too damn much." He nipped the sensitive skin between her neck and shoulder lightly before pulling his head back. "And we're gonna make up for some of that today."

A mischievous glint lit up her eyes. "That sounds like fun."

He chuckled softly and planted a kiss on her forehead before jumping off the bed and taking a few large steps to the dresser. His greedy little vixen was going to tempt every ounce of his self-control and they'd never wind up leaving the apartment if he didn't refocus. He grabbed a dark green shirt and a pair of cutoff denim shorts from her drawers and tossed them on the bed. "Here ya go, sweetheart."

Her full lips turned down into a pretty little pout that begged to be kissed. Shit. Tanner had to look away before he climbed on top of her and…

"What's this?" She looked from the clothes on the bed to him and back again. Then a slow smile started to spread across her face. Belle stood on her knees on the mattress, turning to face him, and crossed her arms in front of her, catching the hem of her shirt. "So you want me to get dressed?"

At the sound of her voice that somehow had dropped an octave, Tanner couldn't help but lift his eyes just as she whipped her shirt over her head. "Dammit all to hell." The words sounded hoarse in his own ears and he couldn't stop himself from crossing to the bed and pushing her back down against the mattress. "We're gonna be late."

She ran her hands up the back of his blue cotton shirt and gave a throaty laugh. "Just ten minutes, baby." Her words ended on a moan as his tongue made a path down the front of her body. "Okay, maybe fifteen."

Two and a half hours later, they stood on the landing overlooking the Lower Cascade Falls. The roaring waterfall was even more beautiful than he had anticipated, and the look on Belle's face when she caught her first glimpse of the falls caused his heart to swell.

Tanner wrapped his arms around her waist and held her back close to his front. He planted a kiss on the top of her head. "I love you, Belle."

Her hands covered his and her head tilted back against his chest. "I love you too, Tanner."

He turned her around in his arms and slowly

174

backed her against one of the square stone posts. He bent his head down and brushed his lips across hers. "Promise me you'll tell me if I'm working too much again."

A sheen of unshed tears covered her eyes, and she ran her hand over the light growth of facial hair covering his cheek. "Tanner, I didn't mean it." A fat drop escaped and trailed down her face. "You, me, us…" She shook her head and kissed him. "We're a forever thing, right?"

Tanner swiped his thumb under her eyes, clearing away any hint of the tear. He couldn't help but grin when she used his words on him. "Hell yeah, we are. Sweetheart, listen, I promise you I'll try my damndest to make you happy. Every day. But you gotta tell me when I screw up, okay?"

She smiled back up at him. "And what makes you happy, baby?"

His mouth covered hers for several long minutes before a desperate need for oxygen forced them apart. "This. You. In my arms." His breath came in stuttering gasps as he tried to pull air into his lungs. "Belle, when the team went through the worst damned losing streak ever, when I thought I was gonna fail my midterm, hell, when I was certain I'd screwed up the biggest account my dad had…" His forehead rested against hers. "Sweetheart, I didn't give a damn about any of that because I'd come home to you and you'd throw in some ridiculous movie and sit in my lap, and suddenly nothing else would matter."

Her tears began to fall in earnest, and Tanner brushed his lips over each wet cheek. "If I promise to keep trying, will you promise to keep letting me?"

"Tan-ner," his name broke on a hiccuping sob as she wrapped her arms around his neck and held him tight, "I promise."

Chapter Nineteen

Izzy

"It's three o'clock."

The mischievous smile—that did nothing to lessen her suspicion—spread across his face. "I know." He sauntered across the living room to stand in front of her, his hands clasped behind his back. "But I've got a surprise for you."

Izzy tilted her head and narrowed her gaze at him. "A surprise?"

His one arm snaked around her waist, and she couldn't suppress the small shriek. Or the way her hands clung to his shoulders. "A surprise," he confirmed, nuzzling against her neck. "Well, two surprises actually."

Her fingers trailed up his neck and into his hair. "Um, and w-what would those t-two surprises be?" A wave of need rolled through Izzy, despite the fact it was the middle of the day and the kids could barrel through the back door at any moment.

Tanner's hand slid down farther, cupping

beneath her, and pulling her tightly against him. All of the air left her lungs on a hiss. She tugged at his head and brought his mouth to hers.

Finally.

Ever since Sunday morning, Tanner had done nothing more than give her sweet, but all too chaste, kisses and hold her at night. Triumph mixed with desire as his mouth slid from hers along her jawline to her ear and down the column of her neck.

Three days of his mouth staying in very G-rated places. Three days of his hands not straying beneath a single article of clothing. Three days of sheer torture.

His lips trailed back up and he nipped her earlobe. "Close your eyes, sweetheart." The tickle of his breath from the whispered words caused a chill to run down her spine.

Every logical thought fled as she obediently closed her eyes. Tanner was always so good at surprises. But when something small and square landed in her palm, her eyes flew open and her brow furrowed. "A box?"

Her eyes collided with his amused sapphire gaze. "A box." He nodded toward the unopened package. "It's yours, ya know. To open."

Izzy looked from Tanner to the gift several times before finally pulling the lid off. Her eyes welled up at the sight of the necklace lying on the satin inside. "How did you…" The words were barely more than a whisper.

Tanner pulled the silver chain from the box and fastened it around her neck. Her fingers immediately flew to the silver pendant scrolled to

178

look like a waterfall with an aquamarine stone nestled inside. Her mind raced with memories of the promises they had spoken that day at the waterfall. A pang hit her heart when she realized she broke her promise.

Just as she stood on her tiptoes to kiss him on the cheek, the sliding glass door at the back of the house whooshed open and Ava and Noah raced inside. Their delighted cries mixed together at the unfamiliar and exciting sight of their father in the middle of the day.

Izzy couldn't help the laughter that bubbled up before her eyes fell on the large bronze clock hanging on the living room wall. "I, um..." She pointed helplessly at the clock.

He winked at her as the kids jumped on him, begging for attention. "Go get ready, sweetheart. And have a great night."

Have a great night played on repeat in her brain the thirty-minute drive to the painting studio and the five minutes she spent in the car working up the nerve to walk in. Somewhere over the past three years, she felt like she lost every ounce of confidence. Every drop of Isabelle Ricci's sassy New York attitude. And she was just now noticing it.

Squaring her shoulders, she looked resolutely at herself in the rearview mirror. "Your girl is from New York, Tanner. She can take care of herself." Whispering the words to herself that she had spoken to him so long ago calmed a few of her nerves and brought a smile to her face.

"Izzy!"

179

The high-pitched squeal nearly made her jump before she even crossed the threshold. Her closest friend—who she'd forged a bond with under life-altering circumstances—bounded over and pulled her into a quick but tight embrace. When she pulled back, she tucked a strand of her short dark brown hair behind her ear.

Izzy fought the urge to fall apart right there. Seeing Caroline again after far longer than she'd care to admit felt just as good as it hurt. She'd missed her friend.

Her enthusiasm was contagious, and Izzy's smile grew at the greeting. "Caroline, I'm so happy to see someone here I know." She shook her head, thinking back over the past season. "It seems like all the kids from T-ball have gone on completely different teams."

"Honey, you have been too busy runnin' those kids in twenty different directions. You'd never be able to pick out the team from a line-up."

Izzy opened her mouth to argue, but she came up short. Her friend was right. Tanner's constantly increasing workload changed every aspect of their lives, and she often dropped Noah at baseball with just enough time to run Ava to gymnastics before coming back to pick him up at the end of the game.

Caroline's expression softened as her eyes scanned Izzy's face. "Iz, do you…"

Before she could finish, the teacher standing on the small stage called out for everyone to find a seat. Caroline linked her arm through Izzy's and pulled her over to one of the long tables on the right. "You are definitely sitting beside me. It's been far too long since I've spent any time with you."

Izzy moved her brush over the canvas as the petite blonde at the front of the class instructed, finding herself laughing in between at Caroline's constant moaning over her less than desirable artistic acumen. She was putting the finishing touches on the shading of a petal when the teacher made her rounds, offering advice, and stopped at Izzy's painting.

"This is lovely." Her voice was soft. She leaned in close to Izzy's head, and a blonde curl brushed Izzy's shoulder.

The seemingly innocuous encounter made Izzy's stomach roll. She quickly excused herself and made a mad dash in the direction she hoped she'd find the bathroom. She gripped the sides of the sink, tears streaming down her face. All it took was a lock of blonde hair and she couldn't think, couldn't breathe.

She barely registered the door opening and gasped when she saw Caroline standing next to her. Blatant shock registered on her friend's face.

"Izzy, honey, what's wrong?"

Izzy wanted to be strong and resolute, but she fell against Caroline's shoulder. "He cheated on me." The words that had silently taunted her over and over for the past several weeks hurt even more when they were finally spoken aloud. "H-he w-went out with his b-brother a-and he kissed some other g-g-girl."

Caroline's hands ran up and down her back as she made soft, soothing noises. Once Izzy had finally calmed down, her friend leaned back and caught her eye. "I knew something was wrong as soon as I saw you. Iz, honey, why didn't you call me?"

She sniffled and lifted a shoulder. "I don't know." But once she started speaking her heartache out loud, she couldn't stop. "I've felt so alone for so long. Tanner is always working, and I can't just leave the kids with his parents all the time to go have coffee or go shopping or anything we used to do. I just couldn't burden them like that. And then I just seemed to have lost touch with everyone and…" Her voice broke off on a hiccup. "A-And he cheated on me."

"Are you okay to drive home?"

Izzy nodded and sniffled some more. "Yeah, but Caroline, how am I going to go back out there? They will all see my face and know I was crying and—"

"And I will give them your deepest apologies and explain you've got an awful stomach bug and need to get home as soon as possible. When you get home, you are going to send me a message that you're okay. And then tomorrow at one, you're going to come to this address in comfortable clothes." She pulled a business card from the pocket of her khaki capris and slid it into Izzy's palm, grasping both of her hands.

"Thank you," Izzy whispered softly. She quickly escaped the bathroom and the studio, letting her chocolate brown hair create a curtain to shield her from anyone's inquiring gaze. As she opened the door and stepped into the muggy summer air, she could hear Caroline's voice launching into the story and she couldn't help but smile.

She pulled the SUV into the garage and sighed as she threw it in park. Her head hit the back of the seat and she pulled the business card from the cup holder where she had tossed it when she fled the studio.

Balance Yoga was printed across the front of the cream-colored card in a dark maroon script. *Caroline Thompson, Instructor* was written in block letters below.

A small smile tugged at the corners of her mouth. Maybe Mike and Tracy wouldn't mind babysitting tomorrow afternoon. Just this once.

***

"Whose brilliant idea was this whole high school history teacher thing anyway?" Izzy muttered to herself as she climbed the stairs to the apartment. "And why did Tanner think a walk-up was a good idea?"

After five months of full-time teaching, the career path she had chosen so carefully in high school didn't feel as right as it once did. She was miserable, the students never listened, and she couldn't speak a word of it to Tanner. He'd want to swoop in and fix it all and probably remind her she didn't even need to work in the first place.

As though that would actually happen.

She flicked the sleeve of her winter coat back and glanced at the thin silver watch. Even with staying late to get the kids on the correct buses— and that really was an absurd job to require in high school—she was home long enough before Tanner to squeeze in a relaxing bath.

Or maybe not.

She barely had time to close the door behind her before she found herself pushed against it, with Tanner's hot mouth covering hers. Any and all thoughts of complaining fled Izzy's mind as her purse and tote bag slid from her shoulder and onto the floor. Her hands locked behind his neck, and an involuntary moan escaped her lips.

Several long minutes later, he finally pulled his head back. "You're late."

Izzy sucked in several deep breaths. "I had bus duty."

Tanner chuckled and nuzzled her neck. "High school kids are old enough to get on the damn bus by themselves."

She captured her bottom lip between her teeth, her hands falling to her sides as Tanner slid her coat off her shoulders. "I know, baby, but what are *you* doing home this early?"

He lifted his head and offered the smirk that never failed to make her weak in the knees. "Well, sweetheart, if I need to tell you what I'm doing, I guess I'm not doing it right." Tanner hooked an arm beneath her legs and easily held her against his chest.

Izzy squeaked and planted a soft kiss on his neck. She toed her ballet flats off as he carried her through the living room. "Mmm, maybe I need just a small example to make sure we are on the same page."

His chest rumbled with laughter and she felt the

vibration all the way to her feet. He gently lowered her to the ground beside the bed and cupped her cheek. The look in his eyes stole every molecule of air from her lungs. Time stood still as she stared into the sapphire pools that radiated more love than she'd ever seen. "Tanner?"

He leaned his head down and brushed his lips across hers softly. Reverentially. "I love you, Belle," he whispered against her lips before deepening the kiss. "So much."

Tanner peeled her purple shift dress over her head and stared at her. She had a sudden burst of self-consciousness, clad in only black satin bra and panties as his eyes slowly roamed from her face down to her feet and back up. A blaze of heat radiated through her body that followed their path.

She slid her hands under his Henley shirt and pulled him closer. "I love you too, baby." The corners of her mouth quirked up. "I think you're wearing too many clothes."

Faster than she imagined, his arms crossed over his front and he threw the shirt across the room. But he didn't return her smile. His eyes continued to bore holes through her, and a moment's concern swept over her. Before she could question him, he lifted her in his arms again and lowered her onto the mattress.

The words of worry died on her lips when his jeans joined the shirt on the floor and he hovered over her on his elbows. He rocked against her, barely touching her, but she still gasped at the power of his need. His mouth worshipped her body, slowly taking the last remnants of her clothing with him as he went.

His soft facial hair tickled the inside of her thighs, and she felt like she would melt into a puddle. His tongue ran a scorching path, dipping deep inside for far too brief a moment, and she was certain she would die from pleasure.

Two fingers joined his tongue and Izzy looked down, shocked to lock her eyes with his. Every single time with Tanner felt special in its own way, but as she forced her gaze to stay fixed while she screamed her ecstasy combined with his name, she felt closer to him than ever before.

Her body still trembling, she reached down to pull him back up, face to face with her again. "Tanner." Her voice shook as she spoke his name. She searched her mind for the words she wanted to say, but she could only think of one thing. She rolled her hips against him. "I need you, baby."

His Adam's apple bobbed once. Twice. In what seemed like a single movement, he slid his boxers off and entered her with such tenderness moisture collected in the corners of her eyes. Izzy trailed her fingers up his arms, shoulders, and into his hair as she tugged his lips down to join with hers.

Several long, smooth strokes later, he groaned his love for her once more against her mouth just as she lost all ability to think or speak.

Tanner fell back against the pillows, pulling her tightly against his left side and tucked her head on his chest beneath his chin. Some of her earlier questions began to bubble to the surface again. Today felt so different than every other time they had made love. And she couldn't imagine a good reason for Tanner to be home this early.

But then she felt his jaw clench and unclench several times and her stomach turned. Tanner was nervous. Frustrated. Or mad.

She propped her chin on his chest. "What's wrong, Tanner?" She offered a strangled laugh. "Are you hungry?"

"You try every ounce of my patience."

Izzy was certain she stopped breathing. "Wh-what?" She scrambled to sit up and tug the blanket up to cover her, tucking it under her arms. Why did this always seem to happen when she was naked?

Tanner sat on the bed, a small smile tugging at the corners of his mouth. "I tried to wait to meet you, but I couldn't. I tried to wait to kiss you, but I couldn't." He turned away to retrieve something from the nightstand before facing her again. "And I tried like hell to wait until I pulled together something big, something special, something romantic."

Her mind raced trying to keep up with everything he was saying. It certainly didn't sound like he was breaking up with her, but... "Wait for what?"

He opened a small, maroon box and held it out to her. The round center diamond caught her attention immediately. Tears forming in her eyes made the pavé set diamond crossover and white gold band blur. When she finally met his gaze, the question and uncertainty she saw reflected there left her speechless.

"Belle, I love you more than I thought it was possible to love anyone. You're smart, strong, and you're from New York so I know you can take care of yourself." The corners of his eyes crinkled with his smile. "I love when you try to negotiate with me. And more than anything, I love that we have just as much fun lying on the couch reading in total silence as we do screaming our lungs out at a football game." He grabbed her hand and held it tightly. "Sweetheart, will you marry me?"

She launched herself into his arms, sobbing into his neck.

Just like always, Tanner held her close. Just like always, Tanner stroked his hand down her hair and offered soothing sounds while she cried. And just like always, Izzy knew that in his arms was the only place she wanted to be.

When her tears finally slowed, he kissed the crown of her head. "Sweetheart, you're making me nervous."

With a gasp, Izzy pulled back and clapped a hand over her mouth. "Oh, Tanner, baby, I-I'm...*yes*! Yes, of course I'll marry you."

He chuckled and pulled her hand from her mouth. He kissed the third finger on her left hand before sliding the ring on.

Izzy gripped the back of his neck and kissed him deeply. "I love you," she whispered against his lips as she pushed him back on the bed. Dinner could wait just a little longer.

Chapter Twenty

Tanner

His hands skimmed down her side, her skin smoother than the satin sheets clinging to their sweat-slickened bodies. The faint scent of salt water wafted through the open window, but Tanner didn't pay any attention, choosing to breathe in her scent instead. Apples and sun and perfection.

"Oh, baby." She whimpered the long forgotten endearment into his shoulder as he slowly started to thrust in and out. "Oh, baby, yes."

Her heard her breath catch on the end of the word and grinned as he nipped the skin at the base of her neck. "Is that good, sweetheart?" He murmured the question as he made a trail of kisses from one shoulder to the other. "Damn, Belle, I've missed you so much."

Before she could answer, her eyes widened and her mouth fell open. He felt the hot coil tightening in his belly, almost to the point of being painful. She screamed his name and he rolled his hips

189

forward again, so close…

"Tanner." Her voice sounded softer suddenly, farther away. He pushed the thought from his mind. *So close…*

The entire bed began to shake. What in the actual hell? An earthquake? On an island in the middle of the Caribbean? This couldn't be happening, could it?

"Tanner!" This time Belle's voice was sharp and right next to him, and he bolted upright in bed. His bed. Their bed. In their house. No island, no earthquake, and sure as hell no hot sex with his wife.

"Tanner, you're late." She hissed out the words, still shaking his arm despite the fact he clearly wasn't asleep any longer.

He swept a hand across his sweaty brow and squinted at her. The last tendrils of his lusty dream hung on, and he wanted nothing more in that moment than to lay Belle down on the bed and remind her exactly why they were so good together. "Late for what?"

She rolled her eyes, still kneeling next to him on the bed. "For work? Tanner, it's almost eight and…"

Yeah, he forgot to mention that detail yesterday. He smirked at her and saw a cloud of suspicion cover her eyes. "And it's my day off."

Her hand fell from his arm, and she rested back on her heels. She shook her head and drew her brows together. "Y-you don't take days off." She ran her fingers through her long, chocolate brown hair and Tanner had to stifle a groan. Damn, she

190

looked good first thing in the morning. "You work late nights, you work weekends, but you definitely don't take days off."

Tanner's heart constricted with her words and a spark of irritation flared. "I do now." His voice was harder than he'd intended, but dammit, he was getting tired of the reminders of his failures. He was fixing it, wasn't he?

Belle lifted her eyes to his and nearly all of his frustration melted away at the fire he saw reflected back at him. "You do?" She walked forward on her knees and straddled his lap. "So every Thursday you'll be home?"

Oh, holy hell, was she really doing this or was he still dreaming? He swallowed down the sarcastic words that had been on the tip of his tongue just a moment ago. "Y-yes. And Tuesday afternoon."

A small smile curved her lips and her fingers trailed up his arms to rest on his shoulders. She sat in his lap, and as soon as the physical result of his far too realistic dream brushed against her inner thigh, her eyes flared, and he sucked in a breath. Well, damn. His greedy little vixen was back.

When her tongue ran along her bottom lip, he thought he'd die right there. He tried to keep his hands at his sides. He tried to let her take control. He wanted her to be certain. Needed her to be ready. But the feel of her mouth against his ear nearly destroyed every ounce of self-control he had in his body.

"You were having a really good dream, weren't you?"

Honesty, he reminded himself again, *total*

honesty. "I had your tight little body beneath me." He grasped her thighs. "And your sexy legs holding me tight against you while you screamed my name. Hell yeah, it was a good dream."

His hands traveled under her shirt. She gasped against his neck where she had been planting tiny kisses. He made lazy patterns on her back with his fingertips before circling around to her navel.

She pulled back slightly, staring at him for several long moments before tugging his shirt over his head.

He grinned as her unabashedly needy gaze swept over his chest and her tongue darted out to lick her lips again. "You see something you like there, sweetheart?"

Belle's eyes flew up and caught his. Something had changed and his smile slipped away. Seconds before what had been pure desire blazing in the chestnut depths now mixed with a love and adoration he hadn't seen in a long time.

Tanner lifted a hand to her face, running a finger down her cheek. The haze of passion that had clouded his vision became something much stronger.

She wrapped her hands behind his head, lowering her forehead to rest against his. "Tanner, I—"

A sharp rap on the door accompanied by a small whiny voice cut off her next words. "Mommy, we're hungry," Noah pleaded from the other side.

With a light chuckle, she closed her eyes, then placed a soft kiss on his cheek. She scrambled off the bed, but Tanner grabbed her wrist before she could step away. When she turned back, she pinned him with a dazzling smile that took his breath away. Words failing him at that moment, he kissed the inside of her wrist before letting her go.

Ten minutes later, he braced his hands on the wall of the shower, his head hanging down as the icy blast did absolutely nothing to cool the fire Belle stirred.

He pulled one hand back and slapped an open palm against the smooth tile. He was trying so damn hard to be patient. But waiting was so much harder than it had been in college. He knew what she felt like, what she tasted like, what she sounded like…and dammit all to hell, he wanted that back.

With a growl, he turned off the water, unsure if his mounting anger was toward Belle or himself, and that only fueled his irritation. Tanner tugged a fresh t-shirt and shorts on with much more force than necessary.

He marched down the stairs resolutely. He needed to talk to her. Needed to know that she saw the changes he was making. That she knew he was sorry and that he'd never make those kinds of mistakes again.

And his conviction held firm until their eyes collided. The concentration that had filled her face while she poured orange juice and scooped scrambled eggs onto the plates dissolved into a sparkle that wiped away his frustration.

She lifted a shoulder, and a light blush stained her cheeks. Twelve years together and she still blushed. "Hey."

So she wanted to flirt? He threw her the cocky

smile he knew she loved. He could absolutely play this game. "Hey yourself, sweetheart."

Tanner dropped a kiss on Ava's cheek and gave Noah a high five, feeling Belle's gaze on him the entire time from where she stood with her hip propped against the counter. He crossed the room to stand as close to her as possible. He trailed a finger down her arm. "So what do you want to do today, sweetheart?"

Some of the playfulness disappeared from her eyes. "I, um, I didn't expect you to be home and, well, I was going to ask your parents to watch the kids to go to a yoga class. With Caroline. She, um, she invited me last night."

On the last word, Belle captured her bottom lip between her teeth. Tanner reached up and pulled it free, smoothing his thumb across it. "That sounds like a great day, Belle." He touched his mouth against hers in the barest of kisses before leaning down close to her ear. "And an even better night if we get the kids to bed early."

He turned away to join the kids at the table, smiling to himself. But he couldn't resist throwing a wink at her flushed face as he took his seat. "Hey, guys, Mom has some stuff to do today, so I was thinking we could go ride horses at Grandma and Grandpa's."

***

The screaming from inside the apartment hit Tanner's ears before he got his key in the lock. What in the holy hell was going on in there?

Belle sat on the couch, eyes closed, mouth drawn down. The raised voices coming from where her phone sat on the coffee table seemed to get louder with each exchange. A single tear trailed down her cheek.

He dropped his case on the chair and took a seat beside her, insults and sarcasm still blaring from her phone. She turned her head and fixed him with an empty gaze. At times like this, he really hated her parents.

"They're fighting over who is going to pay for my shoes." Her voice was so soft he had to lean close to hear. "My shoes, Tanner. We are having a three-way phone conversation just so they can have a screaming match over my shoes."

Summoning every ounce of calm he could, Tanner cleared his throat. "Carla, Jerry, I just got home and Belle and I need to work on some things so she's going to have to call you back." He pressed the red button on the touchscreen before either of her parents could respond.

How two such self-centered assholes could create something as beautiful and special as the girl falling apart in his arms astounded him. He wouldn't change a thing about Belle, but he hated that her childhood was a constant cycle of shouting and selfishness. She deserved better. And he had every intention of giving her just that for the rest of their lives.

She mumbled something against his navy polo shirt, and he set her away from him slightly, smoothing back her hair. "What'd you say, sweetheart?"

"Let's elope."

If she had told him she was actually an alien in disguise, he couldn't have been more shocked. Since the day he proposed, she spent nearly every night skimming bridal magazines and websites, shoving various pictures in his face when she was exceptionally excited. And he feigned interest every time because damn, she was cute when she was eager.

She wanted an autumn wedding. She wanted a four-tier wedding cake. She wanted a damn tiara. She didn't want to elope.

"Sweetheart, I don't—"

Belle covered his mouth with one hand. "Don't say it. The dress, the venue, the cake…none of it matters. What matters is that we are married and we love each other and we love *our* day." Fresh tears collected in the corners of her eyes. "And there is no way I can enjoy my day with that. So please. Let's elope. Tonight. Tomorrow. I don't care."

Her words did a better job of silencing him than the soft palm resting against his lips. His mind raced. Damn, he wanted to do the right thing. He wanted to make her happy. He wanted her to have zero regrets. He wanted…

"Please." Belle's hand slid from his mouth to his cheek, her voice soft and pleading.

Well, hell. "Where to?"

Within four hours, Belle had booked a flight to New Orleans, they had packed their bags, and they were driving to the airport. Their trip through security, at the ticket counter, and even the wait to board the plan seemed to fly by. Tanner stored their luggage in the overhead compartment and settled in beside Belle for the two and a half hour flight.

Before he finished buckling his belt, she slipped her arm through his. "In less than twenty-four hours, I'm going to be your wife."

His chest swelled with an unexpected pride, but he couldn't ignore the small voice of doubt that warned she may regret this decision in a week or a month or a year. When his brothers got married. When they were invited to a wedding. His stomach churned with worry that one day she would wish they had a big wedding.

"Hey." Her soft voice cut through his thoughts just as the plane leveled out. "What's wrong?"

Tanner had a brief internal debate on exactly how he should answer before closing his eyes and heaving a sigh. Screw the macho crap, he'd always be one hundred percent honest with her. "I'm scared you're going to regret this one day."

Her lips curled into a sensuous smile. "You're pretty sexy when you're all insecure and stuff." She nuzzled close to his ear. "There is not one second of our time together I've ever regretted, and this certainly won't be the first one."

Tanner finally let go of the last reservation and turned slightly in his seat toward her. "So tomorrow is going to be a great day, right?"

Belle's hand, as it always inevitably did, drifted into his hair, playing with each short strand. "And it's going to be an even better night."

Chapter Twenty-One

Izzy

"Focus on your breathing, in through your nose and out through your mouth." Caroline's voice was soft and melodic as she spoke to the group. "Take this opportunity to set an intention for yourself. Maybe you need to find compassion. Gratitude. Forgiveness. Feel free to revisit this intention at any point during your practice."

After several minutes of calm, comfortable silence, she stood and pushed a button. The soft instrumental music surrounded Izzy as she moved from one pose to the other. Occasionally Caroline would circulate through the small class and gently guide arms and legs into the correct position.

Every movement pushed Izzy just a little past her body's ability to bend, but with each pause, she relaxed a little further and her emotions calmed a little more.

Right up until Izzy followed one of Caroline's last instructions and assumed the pigeon pose, folding her right leg at the knee in front of her and extending her left leg behind her. The first few seconds put all the muscles in her hips on an extreme stretch. After nearly a minute, she adjusted to the position, but unexpected and unprovoked tears began to track down her cheeks.

Her friend came behind her and firmly grasped her shoulders, running her hands down her upper arms. Caroline's voice was soft and low, meant only for Izzy's ears. "It's okay, Izzy. Let it out, honey."

The very last thing Izzy had expected as she alternated her legs was for a fresh round of tears to fall in a classroom full of strangers. But she couldn't seem to find it in herself to be embarrassed or ashamed. Only peace rolled through her with each tear that escaped.

And the word that had immediately struck her at the beginning of class filtered through her mind once more. Forgiveness.

Twenty minutes later, she pulled into the garage, and Caroline's voice replayed in her head. *It's normal, it's expected, for the deep hip exercises to let go of some emotions you've been holding onto.* Caroline pulled her into a tight hug. *It's why I wanted you to come today, Iz. You needed this.*

A small smile pulled at Izzy's mouth and stayed fixed throughout her shower and dinner with Tanner and the kids. When Tanner popped in the latest animated release for their family movie night, she moved just a little closer to him than she had in the past few weeks.

Caroline was right. She needed that release and to let go of everything that had left a constant ache in her heart for so much longer than even she had realized. But she needed Tanner even more.

And when they finally lay side-by-side in bed, she fit herself as tightly against him as she could. "Tanner, I need you." She brushed her lips across his and tightened her grip on his white shirt. "I need you so much."

His fingers dug into her hip a little, and even in the dark room she could see his Adam's apple bobbing. "Are you sure, sweetheart?"

She slid her hands down the front of his shirt and grabbed the hem, tugging it over his head. "I'm so sure." Her fingers traced along the muscles of his abdomen. "I've missed you so much, Tanner. Please." She drew out the last word, knowing it would be his undoing.

"Belle, if this is too soon, too fast—"

Izzy lifted his hand from her hip and kissed each finger, slowly drawing the index finger into her mouth, keeping her gaze locked on his. "I need your hands on me." She leaned forward and captured his mouth in a hard, brief kiss. "I need your lips on me." She nudged him gently until he was lying on his back and she straddled his hips. "I need every part of you on every part of me, Tanner."

Before he could answer, she pulled off her short nightgown and threw it somewhere in the direction of the bathroom door. The sharp intake of breath from Tanner made her lips turn up in a smug grin. She kissed him again, softer, longer, and slowly made a trail down his chest to his navel, outlining each muscle there with her tongue.

She slid his pajama pants and boxers down with her as she moved down his body. Her mouth wrapped around him with practiced confidence. She heard her name on a moan from his lips and bit back a smile. At one time, she had been hesitant and unsure, but now...now she knew exactly what Tanner wanted.

Her tongue wrapped around him as her mouth glided up and down. Izzy looked up and saw his chest move faster, and she picked up her rhythm in time with his breathing.

A strangled sound came from his throat, and before it registered, she found herself pulled back up until she was face to face with Tanner before he flipped her on her back.

"Oh, hell no, sweetheart." His voice was low and rugged. "No way in hell your hot little mouth is going to take away all my fun."

She wanted to smile, to laugh, to offer a quick retort, but before her mind could catch up, he was crashing into her and the breath was ripped from her body with the movement. Her hands flew into his hair and brought his mouth to hers. She locked her legs around him and found herself spiraling out of control much faster than she'd dreamed.

Izzy broke the kiss and held his face inches from hers, staring into his blue eyes in the dim light. "Tanner, I..." The words ended on an indecipherable scream that was quickly followed by Tanner's low moans.

He collapsed on top of her and, despite his

weight, she held him there for several minutes before he finally rolled on his side and pulled her against him.

The silence stretched out for so long she began to think he'd fallen asleep when his chest rumbled against her cheek. "Are you okay, sweetheart?"

She planted a soft kiss against his chest. "I am now." Izzy could feel his entire body relax next to her, and she smiled against his skin. "Well, I will be."

Immediately he responded by tensing and hooking a finger under her chin. "What's wrong, Belle? Was that too rough? Too soon? Aw, hell, I'm sorry I…"

She rocked forward and planted a kiss on his lips. "You're pretty sexy when you're insecure." Her fingers began walking across his chest and down his stomach. "But I was kinda hoping this wasn't going to be a one-time deal."

His eyes widened at her words and his cocky smile fell right into place. He turned and pinned her on the mattress, grabbing her wandering hand and interlacing his fingers through hers, holding them above her head. "I like the way you think, Belle."

***

One hundred twenty-seven, one hundred twenty-eight…

"You're not going back to sleep, are you?"

Izzy turned her head to the right where Tanner lay beside her on his stomach, one arm thrown over her midsection. "How did you know I was awake?"

He popped one eye open. "Because your breathing changes when you wake up. Because I notice everything about you." He grinned mischievously. "And because your foot has been shaking the bottom of the bed for the past ten minutes."

She scrunched her nose. "Sorry, I thought I was being quiet and calm counting the dots on the ceiling."

Tanner laughed into the pillow. "We probably should get up. Lots to do today."

"All we have to do is get the marriage license." Her brows drew together. "That shouldn't take long, should it?"

With a groan, Tanner leaned over and kissed her shoulder before heaving himself out of bed. "It shouldn't, but we also need to get rings and you need a dress and flowers."

Izzy sat up quickly on her knees on the mattress. "No, I packed a dress. And I don't need flowers. Although you might have a point about the rings…" She waved her hand dismissively. "But we can even get those at some point when we get back home."

He stood next to the bed and planted a kiss on her forehead. "You're getting a dress." He kissed her left cheek. "And flowers." He kissed her right cheek. "And rings." He leaned in a little closer and nipped her earlobe. "But first I think we should get a shower."

Her arms flew around his neck as he lifted her up, and she laughed. "Well, we do have two hours until the clerk's office opens…"

Tanner crossed the few feet into the small

bathroom in their hotel room and lowered her onto the cold white tile floor. "Last chance, Belle. Are you sure this is what you want?"

She wanted to tell him that the wedding itself really was meaningless to her. She wanted to tell him that no matter how their marriage started, being married to him was really all that mattered. She wanted to tell him that starting their lives together happy and uncomplicated was her version of a fairy tale come true.

But she couldn't seem to find the words or the composure to say them. She pointed at herself and then at him. "This is what I want." She tugged her nightgown over her head and shimmied her underwear down in one seamless move with a grin. "And I really, really want to take a shower."

Three and a half hours later, marriage license stashed safely away in her purse, Izzy turned from one side to the other in front of the full-length mirror. Tanner dutifully waited at the front door of the small boutique, insistent on the fact she needed a dress for their wedding.

And she couldn't help but agree as soon as she'd slipped the strapless lavender knee-length dress over her head. She smoothed a hand over the tulle skirt, fighting against the tears collecting in the corner of her eyes. Not that she'd ever admit it to him, but that one simple piece made the day feel real. And exciting. And terrifying.

She traded her basic black flip-flops for flat silver sandals with deep purple gemstones dotting the straps, matching the contrasting sash on her dress. Izzy closed her eyes, took a deep breath, and stepped out from behind the curtain. Tanner stood leaning against the far wall, his legs crossed at the ankles, but as soon as his gaze landed on her, he jumped to attention and crossed the room.

"Belle...I..." He shook his head and gently brought her hand up to his mouth. "You look gorgeous."

Tanner winked at her before he slid a charming smile in place and pinned the middle-aged woman behind the counter with it. "Ma'am, I'm sure it violates some store policy, but is there any way my fiancée could wear these out of the store? We're on our way to get married and..." He let his words trail off and shrugged his shoulders.

Izzy wasn't sure if she wanted to laugh or smack his shoulder. Maybe both.

But every drop of mock irritation fell away when she found herself pulled into a jewelry store three doors down from the boutique. Her eyes were drawn to a matching set of white gold bands with channel-set diamonds encased in the middle of the store. They were exactly what she'd dreamed of, but the attached price tag immediately made her look for another option.

He tugged on the hand held firmly in his, and she spun around to look at him. His other hand cupped her cheek and he rested his forehead against hers. "I saw that look, sweetheart. This is our day, right? All about us and what we want?"

She nodded her head against his. "But baby..."

A smile curved his lips, and Izzy had to concentrate on restraining her mouth from seeking his. "How about we just try them on, okay?" His smile settled into a smirk. "But if they fit and you like 'em, you know damn well I'm going to buy them."

"Pushy jerk."

"But you love me."

Her hand wrapped around his neck, and she planted a gentle kiss against his lips. "More than anything, baby."

An hour after they tried the rings on, they stood before the chaplain reciting their vows. "With this ring," Izzy repeated, unable to stop her emotion from thickening her voice, "I thee wed."

Tanner's deep voice sounded gravelly and rough. A single tear slid down his cheek. "With this ring, I thee wed."

Before the chaplain could finish the command, Tanner leaned down and kissed his wife and Izzy held her husband close.

"Nobody leaves." He whispered their private vow against her lips in between kisses.

"Nobody leaves."

Chapter Twenty-Two

Tanner

"Your ass looks hot in those yoga pants." Tanner let out a low whistle as Belle walked past the foot of the bed.

She popped her hip out, put a hand on it, and lifted one eyebrow. "Excuse me?"

He laughed and jumped out of the bed. He snaked one arm around her waist and drew her close. "I said, have fun at yoga, sweetheart."

Her hands slid up his bare chest and behind his neck. "But you should be thrilled I'm going to yoga." She lifted up on her tiptoes and whispered in his ear. "Think of all the positions we can try with my new…flexibility."

His mouth went dry and the thin boxers he wore did nothing to disguise the effect her words, and her deep throaty chuckle, had on him. His hand slipped

207

down from her waist to cup her firmly against him, and he started to think of all the ways he could encourage her to skip one class. She'd been going every other day for two weeks now; surely she could miss just this once. "Damn, my greedy little vixen showed up again."

Belle pulled back a little and smiled up at him with the same damn smile that never failed to stop his heart. "My husband showed up again." She gave him a peck on the cheek and stepped out of his embrace.

Tanner watched in stunned silence while she grabbed her mat and her bag and trotted out the door, long chocolate ponytail swinging behind her.

Well, hell.

He wasn't done trying to win her back, but no matter what happened last night and every other night this week, comments like that made him feel like he still had a long way to go. He still had two weeks to show Belle that their relationship was worth saving, worth fighting for. And tonight would be another date he hoped she loved.

Tanner stepped beneath the icy spray of the shower. Every night this past week had been…indescribable. He couldn't help the laugh that bubbled up. Five hours ago, he had been tangled up in Belle and yet he still found himself in need of a little help cooling off. Damn, that woman drove him wild.

He groaned at the memory of her hair falling over her shoulder as she climbed on top of him. He closed his eyes and started reciting Italian trade regulations. Hell, that was better than a cold shower.

Finally feeling in control of himself, he stepped out of the shower and quickly dried off. He tugged a dark gray shirt over his head and pulled on a pair of khaki shorts. As soon as Belle got home and showered, they'd be ready to go.

He grinned. Hell yeah, she was going to love their date this afternoon.

His thoughts were interrupted by a tiny voice right outside the bedroom. "Mommy, Noah wants waffles for breakfast, but I want French toast and…" The words died on Ava's lips as she barged through the door. She stopped and stared, blinking a few times, at Tanner. "Where's Mommy?"

He threw his daughter a look of mock hurt before picking her up and tickling her tummy lightly. "She's at her yoga class, sweetpea. What, isn't Daddy good enough?"

Ava giggled and wound her arms around Tanner's neck. "Yeah you are, but Mommy's always here. You're always at work."

Well, double hell.

"Daddy's here today." He kissed her cheek. "Daddy's been home more, right?"

Her small face split in half with a smile identical to her mother's. Her soft chestnut eyes shone brightly. "Yep." She popped the last letter. "I'm really glad you like us again."

An icy feeling, far colder than his shower, started at the top of Tanner's head and trickled through his entire body. "Ava, sweetie, I've always liked you. I love you, you know that right?"

She tilted her head to the side and, as ridiculous

as it was, he felt himself squirm under her intuitive gaze. "But you like work better."

Tanner swallowed past the lump in his throat. "Sweetpea, I've always, *always*, loved you and Noah and Mommy more than anything else. Always. I just…forgot. For a little while."

Her face brightened again, and she kissed his bearded cheek. "I'm glad you remembered. I missed you."

Never once had Tanner thought his heavy workload and need to watch over every detail of the company would affect anyone else. Not Belle and definitely not the kids. But his daughter's innocent comments added another level to his guilt. And reaffirmed his commitment to make as many changes as he needed to fix everything he had so royally screwed up.

He pushed back the strong emotions Ava's words had stirred. "I'm glad I remembered, too." He cleared his throat and forced a smile. "And I'm really glad I didn't forget how to make waffles or French toast." His fingers tickled along her rib cage as he carried her out of the room and down the stairs.

Once both kids were seated at the table with their food in front of them generously coated in syrup, Tanner poured a cup of coffee and sat across from them. "We have something really important to talk about."

In that way only twins could, Ava and Noah looked at each other, and Tanner swore he could almost see their silent conversation. Noah shoved another piece of his waffle in his mouth. "What's that, Daddy?" The words came out mumbled around a mouthful of food.

Tanner quirked a smile. "Don't talk with your mouth full, son." He took another long draw of his warm drink. "I want to do something special with Mommy tonight."

Ava's face fell a little. "Just you and Mommy?" she asked, peeking at him through her long lashes.

"Nope." He winked at his daughter and watched her immediately perk up. "It's going to be something really special for all of us. But I'm gonna need some help. Do you two think you're up to the challenge?"

Ava and Noah exchanged another conspiratorial look, this time ending with a nod and matching grins. "Yes!" they answered in unison.

Tanner grinned. "Okay, but the first rule is, we can't tell Mommy…"

***

Six more weeks.

Tanner marched resolutely up the stairs with a heavy sigh. Six more weeks and they would be moving into a condo in Asheville. He'd close the tiny branch of Carlisle International in Winston-Salem and start working in his father's sleek and modern home office.

As he reached the third floor and walked down the hall to their apartment, a grin spread across his face. Six more weeks and Belle would start teaching at the small private school just outside of town. Damn, she was adorable when she came home from the interview almost giddy at getting an offer right away.

He slid his key into the lock. Yeah, just six more weeks of this, followed by a few years in the condo, and then they would start building their dream house and their family.

What in the ever loving hell?

The sight before him when he walked through the door pulled his lips down into a frown. "Belle, what's wrong?"

She paused her pacing and looked up and him, distress evident in her eyes. "We need to talk."

Tanner dropped his case on the floor just inside the door, stepped out of his shoes, and crossed the room to pull her into his arms. "Anything, sweetheart, we can talk about anything. Whatever is wrong, we can fix it."

"Just…we…I…" She huffed out a breath. "Let's sit down." She stepped out of his arms and pulled him over to the couch.

Her eyes fixed on their joined hands where they rested in her lap. Several minutes of silence passed and Tanner thought he was going to go crazy. She needed to talk to him. Tell him what was wrong. Give him a chance to fix it. He could do that. He could fix anything that was wrong in their relationship. His job, his role since birth, was to take care of everyone. And he sure as hell could take care of Belle.

He hooked a finger under her chin, forcing her to meet his gaze. "We can handle anything, sweetheart. You just need to talk to me."

She held up a white, plastic rectangular object he

hadn't even noticed before. "I'm pregnant, Tanner."

The three softly spoken words slammed into him with the force of a prizefighter's punch. His eyes took in the two pink lines, one slightly lighter than the other, on the pregnancy test she still held in her shaking hand. A tingly feeling spread through his entire body. "Pregnant?"

Belle swallowed and nodded her head. "Pregnant." She lifted her shoulders in a helpless motion. "I-I don't know what happened. I never, ever missed a pill. I took it at exactly the same time every day just like I always have, I just..."

Tanner couldn't help the small smile that curved his lips. And he really couldn't help his eyes drifting to her still-flat abdomen. "Pregnant." He repeated the word in an even lower tone.

Her grip tightened on his hand. "I know this isn't at all what we planned and it's happening so much faster than we wanted and I know we are going to be moving soon, but Tanner even though I'm scared to death, I'm really happy too and—"

His lips brushed across hers and took away her words. "Yes, it's not what we were planning and certainly not what I expected to hear you say, but damn, I'm happy too."

The tears that had been hovering at the corner of her eyes spilled over and tracked down her cheeks. "You are?" Her hands flew to his face, and she slid onto his lap. "Y-you're really happy, baby?"

Tanner chuckled and locked his arms around her waist. "Hell, yeah, I'm happy, sweetheart." He kissed her again, deeper this time, and bit back a moan when her hands speared his hair. Geez, he loved when she did that. "Dammit all to hell, I love knowing you're pregnant with my baby."

He laid her back on the couch and continued to kiss her, moving from her mouth to her jaw to her neck. "Hell, sweetheart, that might be the hottest thing you've ever said." His hand had just started to travel beneath her shirt when a thought stopped his movement.

Wait. What had she said? He propped himself up on his forearms and studied her face. He knew her better than he knew himself and searched for any sign she wasn't actually as happy as she said. "Are you okay, Belle? Be honest with me, sweetheart. I need to know how you feel about this."

A serene smile he'd never seen before made her face look even more beautiful. Something he never thought possible. "First of all, this is *our* baby." She moved beneath him until her legs were wrapped around his waist. "And I was terrified about what you would think and how you would react, but I am so happy."

His stomach clenched. "Y-you were scared of me? Of my reaction?"

Belle quickly shook her head. "Not like that. I just…we had everything planned and I didn't want to disappoint you."

He sat up, pulling her with him, and pressed his lips hard against hers. "Never." His voice sounded rough and thick, even to his own ears. "Never think that. You'll never disappoint me. I love you, Belle. And I love *our* baby."

She kissed him back, holding his face in her soft hands. "I love you too, Tanner."

He stood up and hooked an arm underneath her with a grin. "I think this requires a celebration."

Her eyes widened, and she clasped her hands behind his neck. "I like that idea, baby. Does that mean we're going out to dinner?"

Tanner threw his head back and laughed, carrying her to the bedroom. "Sweetheart, if you have enough energy to get up when I'm done, then obviously I haven't done my job right."

Chapter Twenty-Three

Izzy

"Are you sure about this?" Izzy wrinkled her nose at the green mixture in the glass.

Caroline tilted her head back and laughed. "Trust me, Iz. It's a cucumber mint juice that will help you rehydrate and refresh."

She quirked a disbelieving eyebrow but obediently took a small sip, quickly followed by a larger one. "First yoga and now this. I really should blindly trust everything you tell me."

Her proclamation was met with another round of laughter from her friend, and they lightly clinked their juice glasses. "So if I tell you that I think you should become a yoga instructor, you'll just do it without arguing?"

Izzy nearly choked on the mouth full of juice. She grabbed a napkin from the dispenser on the counter, coughing into it and waving a hand at the attendant who came over to see if she was okay. "Me? Caroline, it's only been a couple of weeks. You can't possibly think—"

"I think," Caroline cut in, "that you grabbed the mats and started cleaning them at your second class. No questions asked. And when Rosa called off, you manned the front desk for me and, frankly, you were probably nicer to the clients than she ever has been." She rolled her eyes.

Izzy laughed and opened her mouth to say something, but Caroline continued. "And more than anything, I think that I've seen you happier and lighter the last two weeks than in the past three years. I know Tanner is a big part of that, but, Iz, I think you've found some of *you* again. This is the girl I first met when we were standing in the NICU and you were screaming at the doctor."

Izzy couldn't help but blush at the memory. Right after she had gotten done lecturing the arrogant, offensive doctor, a harrowed Caroline had run up to her and wrapped her in a big hug before introducing herself. Over the next three weeks, Izzy and Caroline had bonded over beeping monitors and growing babies.

The words sank in and she had to admit, only to herself, that for the first time in a very long time she felt confident. Self-assured. And it felt…good.

Caroline fiddled with her straw before sighing and looking at Izzy. "I'll be honest, Iz. I do believe that you would be a fantastic instructor. You are naturally calming, and with your teaching background, you have lots of patience and a genuine desire to help people learn. But I also have a selfish reason."

Izzy drew her brows together. "I don't understand."

She lifted her one shoulder and readjusted the tie-dyed headband holding her short brown hair back from her face. "The company that owns the building just raised the rent on my studio space. If you become certified, you could become my partner and we could offer more classes."

Hurt and doubt tried to creep into Izzy's mind as she processed the new information, at first allowing herself to believe that her friend didn't really think she was good enough to be an instructor, just that she needed the extra help.

Before she could politely decline, a new thought occurred to her. Caroline had opened her own studio a year ago. She may need another teacher, but she certainly wouldn't risk her reputation on having an instructor that wasn't competent leading classes. And what was that last thing she said?

"Partner?" Izzy squeaked out the single word. "Did you say partner?"

Caroline bobbed her head excitedly. "It would be great, Iz! You'd be perfect and we'd get to spend more time together. And maybe Prince Charming will help us with marketing and stuff."

She snorted at Caroline's nickname for Tanner. Unwilling to commit right then, Izzy promised to think about it. But the hopeful smile that had taken up residence on her face didn't fade on her drive home as she considered the idea.

Her thoughts and, she was sure, her expression

turned much more suspicious when she walked into the living room and spied two very well-behaved children sitting calmly on the couch, flanking their father, giggling at an animated television show.

Noah caught sight of her first. "Mommy's home! It's time to go on our date!"

Tanner tilted his head back and chuckled, the sound of the deep rumble making Izzy's toes curl. "Mommy has to take a shower and get changed first." He threw her a wink and a lopsided grin. "Isn't that right, sweetheart?"

She should be immune to this by now, shouldn't she? She shouldn't feel excited butterflies in her stomach at his smile. She shouldn't feel a rush of heat when her husband flirted with her. And she really shouldn't be wishing the children were spending the night with their grandparents tonight.

She sped through her shower, trying to calm the excitement churning in her stomach and temper the trepidation. She was loving each and every date Tanner planned. The creative ones and the simple ones. Even more, she loved the nights they spent with the kids watching movies and the Sunday mornings sitting around the table eating whatever Tanner had made for breakfast.

But was this all just temporary? The day after their anniversary, would everything go back to exactly the way it had been? And would Tanner feel the need to look for whatever he was missing in the arms of someone else again?

Thoughts of *her*, which Izzy was surprised hadn't plagued her for days, began to bubble to the surface again as she stepped out of the shower and dried off. She wrapped the towel around herself and knotted it at the top, pushing the dark thoughts from her mind and focusing on what to wear when she had no idea where they were going.

Thinking of the light blue shirt and khaki shorts Tanner was wearing, and wearing so well, she began rummaging in her dresser drawers for something casual and flattering. She curled her top lip in irritation at her body that refused to tighten despite the hours she logged on the treadmill and in yoga.

Izzy was holding the cream-colored top up, debating internally on the wisdom of wearing something so easily stained, when Tanner burst through the bedroom door. As soon as he saw her, still clad only in a towel, he skidded to a halt and his eyes grew wide.

She loved that look. "I'll be ready in a few minutes."

"We don't need to leave just yet." He sauntered the few feet to stand in front of her and slid a hand between the folds of the terrycloth, resting it on the bare skin of her back and pulling her close to him. "The festival is going on until eleven. It's okay if we don't leave for another ten minutes." He buried his face in her neck, planting soft kisses. "Or twenty."

Izzy fitted herself closer to Tanner and twined her arms around his neck with a small laugh. "We're going to the festival? We're gonna eat funnel cake and corn dogs and ride a Ferris wheel?"

"Later." He mumbled the single word against her shoulder before lightly sinking his teeth into the flesh, making her breath exit on a sigh.

She bit her bottom lip. "How about we make a deal, Mr. MBA?"

He pulled his head back, giving her the crooked grin that made her heart forget to beat, his eyes twinkling mischievously. "I thought I burned those damned textbooks."

Lifting up on her tiptoes, Izzy intended to plant a soft kiss on Tanner's cheek, but he turned his head just then and captured her lips with his, tightening her arm around her waist. Her mouth opened against his as she gasped at the contact. His tongue slid inside, wreaking havoc on every ounce of self-control she was trying to muster.

She flattened her palms against his chest and pushed him away. "Ring toss."

Tanner blinked a few times with a small shake of his head. "Ring toss?"

Izzy nodded, stepping away to release the knot on her towel and dress as slowly as possible. "We play the ring toss game." She did her level best to affect a nonchalant tone, reveling in Tanner's obvious agony as she slowly dressed. "I win, I choose. You win, you choose."

His Adam's apple bobbed twice. "Choose what?"

She buttoned her denim shorts and flashed him a smile, pointing at the front of his shorts. "Choose where and how we take care of that little issue."

He folded his arms across his chest and furrowed his brow, but his blue eyes twinkled mischievously. "Little? Sweetheart, that isn't what you were saying last night."

***

The first stab of pain made Izzy sit upright in bed.

The second followed closely and took the breath from her lungs.

When the third stroke of searing pain ran across her abdomen, she shook Tanner's shoulder.

This wasn't right. She'd read dozens of books, talked to countless other mothers, and felt she had a pretty good idea of what labor, at least early labor, was supposed to feel like and it wasn't this. It shouldn't feel like this, and it shouldn't be happening now. She still had eight weeks to go.

"Tan-ner." Her voice broke over his name as a sob rolled through her. "Tanner, baby, wake up. Something's wrong."

Before she finished speaking, he'd thrown back the covers and turned on the light. The sight of bright red blood covering her nightgown and the sheets made her throat close. She reached a shaking hand down to touch the pool of red surrounding her—warm, sticky, and far too real.

No, no, no. This couldn't be happening. Her hands covered her swollen abdomen and cradled it protectively.

Tanner pulled her head against his shoulder with one hand while the other dialed 911. She barely registered his careful, measured tone. Something was wrong with her babies and there was nothing she could do. Nothing Tanner could do.

She hiccuped and her body shook violently in his arms. Her teeth even chattered, the loud echoing in her ears, but she was helpless to stop it. She couldn't tell if he was still on the phone, but she couldn't prevent the screams coming from her mouth. "Tanner! Fix it! You need to fix this!"

His grip tightened around her. "The ambulance is on its way, sweetheart. The babies are fine. Nothing is going to happen to them or to you."

Part of Izzy wanted to believe every word he said. Tanner had always taken such good care of her. But another side wanted to scream in his face there was no way he could know that the babies were okay. No way he could possibly promise that nothing would happen. Bad stuff happened all the time and bad stuff was happening right now.

Instead she soaked the front of his white shirt with her tears, reminding herself how to breathe in between choking sobs.

After what felt like an eternity, the sound of an approaching siren had Tanner releasing her. He smoothed the hair away from her wet face and cupped her cheeks. "I'm going down to let them in, but I will be right back, Belle. Thirty seconds, tops. I will be right back, sweetheart." He planted a kiss on her forehead and raced out of the room.

Breathe, she reminded herself once again, *you need to breathe*. Within minutes, hulking men in navy blue uniforms invaded their small bedroom. Her mind struggled to keep up with the questions. How long had this been going on? Was she dizzy? Was she still in pain? Where was her pain on a scale from 1–10? Was she allergic to any medication?

Her chest constricted further. Where was Tanner?

"Tanner?" Her voice sounded shaky to her own ears, ignoring the interrogation from the men towering over her. A bubble of hysteria began to rise in her throat. "Tanner?"

The bed dipped to her right. "Right here, sweetheart. I'm right here."

She turned to look at him, grasping for his hand, and the tears that had momentarily dried began to fall again. "I-I-I…"

He held tightly to her hand, never letting go as the paramedics slid a board beneath her and lifted her onto the gurney. "I'm right here. I'm coming with you, sweetheart. I'm not leaving your side."

Izzy's mind stalled through the ride to the hospital. She could register little more than the feel of Tanner's hand stroking her hair and the low murmur of his voice even though the words didn't make any sense.

Finally, after an IV was placed in her hand, a fetal monitor attached around her stomach, and more annoying questions were asked, Tanner and Izzy were left alone in the small cubicle. The tightness in her chest began to ease with the first whooshing heartbeat she heard.

She slid to the far side of the bed as much as possible. "Baby, I need you to hold me." She spoke in a whispered tone, illogically afraid the slightest disturbance in the atmosphere of the room would cause the modicum of peace she felt to disappear.

Before she could blink, he was lying next to her, one arm under her head, the other hand on top of her stomach. His touch seemed to set off a flurry of activity, and Izzy found herself being kicked from seemingly every angle.

A haunted smile tugged at her lips. "They love their daddy."

He hooked a finger under her chin and forced her to meet his gaze. "They love their mommy, and they are going to be fine. And you are going to be fine. And in a couple of months when we are walking around like sleep-deprived zombies, we are going to forget that this ever happened."

The cubicle door slid open and Dr. MacMillan walked in, an obviously disapproving look on his face when he saw Tanner and Izzy laying in the small hospital bed together. Izzy glared back, silently daring him to say something.

He cleared his throat, glancing over at the monitor beeping beside her. "Mrs. Carlisle, after reviewing your tests, it appears that you are in preterm labor. It isn't uncommon in a multiple pregnancy, but you also have placenta previa, causing the bleeding. Your contractions aren't responding as well to the medication we've given you as we'd like, and we feel it's in your best interest to have a Caesarean section in the near future."

Izzy's throat closed and she felt the grip Tanner had on her shoulder tighten. She could only hear a faint buzzing sound in her ears. Every so often a word would make its way through the haze and register in her brain: "NICU," "lung development," "breathing problems." Her heart slammed against her rib cage.

Then her fear began to give way to anger. Anger at her body for failing her and her children. Anger at the middle-aged doctor standing at the foot of the bed with a monotone voice and detached expression. Anger at the stupid machine affixed to her bicep for choosing that moment to take her blood pressure yet again.

Her teeth ground together and she sat upright in the bed. "I don't care what you have to do, you save my babies." She spat the words. "There is not a single person in this hospital I want you to focus on other than my children, do you understand me?"

Dr. MacMillan's eyes widened, and he backed out of the room. "The nurse will be in to administer the first dose of betamethasone." He spoke from the safety doorway before retreating.

When the door swooshed closed behind him, Izzy's anger dissolved and she melted back into Tanner's arms.

Chapter Twenty-Four

Tanner

Chestnut eyes sparkled up at Tanner. "I win."

In spite of the throngs of people moving around them and Ava and Noah standing between them, every muscle in his body tightened at the seductive tone. He loved when she negotiated deals with him, even more when she got her way because damn she was cute when she gloated.

She put a hand on his shoulder and raised herself up on her toes. The whisper of her breath against his ear sent shivers down his spine. "I get to choose. When, where, and how."

Well, hell.

He could do little more than trail behind as Belle led the kids away to the funnel cake stand, trying to reign in his body's reaction to the greedy little vixen swinging her hips in front of him.

Tanner hadn't realized just how much he'd missed her playful nature until it showed back up in his life. He knew with certainty it had been much more than a few minutes in the arms of another woman that caused it all to disappear. Long hours at work, more business trips than were actually necessary, and completely screwed-up priorities were all to blame.

But now that he saw it all with such devastating clarity, there was no way in hell he'd ever take this, take *them*, for granted again.

He moved close behind Belle where she stood placing the order, pressing against her back and sliding money across the counter. He bent down so only she would hear his words and feel his desire. "I do love your ideas, sweetheart."

Tanner heard the sharp intake of breath and a grin spread across his face. Who knew flirting with his wife could be so much fun?

Just then, a hand fell on his shoulder, and he spun around to meet a pair of blue eyes identical to his. "Wyatt? What the hell are you doing here?"

His brother managed to lean his head back and offer a deep chuckle without dislodging the tan cowboy hat perched on his head. The perfect finishing touch to Wyatt's uniform of a button down western shirt, slightly tighter than necessary Levi's and scuffed boots.

"It's nearly the Fourth of July, brother. You know I'd never miss competing in my hometown."

Tanner's jaw immediately clenched when he heard an excited squeak behind him. "Wyatt!" Belle wrapped her arms around his brother's neck, stirring his jealousy. "Oh, it is so good to see you."

Wyatt grinned and pulled back slightly. "I missed you too, Iz."

As irrational as it felt, the words stung. Had he said that to Belle when he'd come home from business trips? Had he ever told her how empty his arms would feel when he laid in a hotel room without her by his side? His stomach turned. It felt like the more he tried to fix things, the more his shortcomings came into focus, and dammit all to hell, he hated failing.

He cleared his throat and pulled Belle from his brother's arms, fitting her back against his chest and holding her tightly around the waist. "Get your own girl, asshole." He intended the words playfully, but he couldn't help the slight bite that accompanied them.

Wyatt held his hands up, palms forward, and took a step back. He threw Ava and Noah a wink and grin, the adoring gazes they graced their uncle with only furthering Tanner's irritation. "I'll catch you two cowpokes tomorrow at Grandma and Grandpa's house." He exaggerated his drawl to a degree that made Tanner roll his eyes before touching the brim of his hat and tipping it at Belle. "Evenin', Izzy."

The light tinkle of laughter from Belle at his brother's overt flirting caused Tanner's nostrils to flare. It was nothing new; Wyatt had been doing the same thing since the first time he'd brought Belle home to meet his family, but this time was different. Their relationship was still too fragile, too recently rebuilt. And it pissed him the hell off to see any other man lay eyes on his Belle, much less his selfish, conceited brother—

A soft hand on the back of his neck pulled him from his thoughts, and he looked down to see Belle had turned in his arms and was facing him. "You're really sexy when you're jealous, but…Wyatt? Really?" Her eyes darted down to the kids standing beside them before pinning him with a lusty stare and quirking a brow. "I think they're ready to go home and go to bed, don't you?"

He had no clue about Ava and Noah, but he knew for damn sure he was ready to find out what was going through her mind and what plans lay hidden behind her smile. Her hand slid down his arm and her fingers laced through his.

His mind couldn't stop contemplating all the options during the drive home and as she climbed the stairs to tuck in two exhausted children. She had always loved showering with him. And more than once they'd been unable to make it beyond the couch when watching a movie. What could his sweet little Belle have up her sleeves tonight?

Tanner decided to brew a cup of Belle's favorite chocolate mint tea while he waited. She'd love that. She loved all the little things he'd been forgetting to do so much more than any grand gesture.

"Hey there, handsome."

Three words. Twelve years together, eight of them married, two kids and yet all it took was three words falling from her lips to make Tanner forget his own name. "H-hey yourself." Did he just stutter?

He leaned his back against the counter and

braced his hands on either side. He was calm and nonchalant. He certainly wasn't dying of anticipation.

Belle glided across the room until she stood in front of him with a small smile. Her hands wound around his waist and under his shirt. "I don't think you're gonna need this." She grasped the hem of his shirt and pulled it over his head.

Tanner's eyebrows shot up. "Here? Now?"

She planted a soft kiss in the middle of his chest and nodded. "Here. Now."

Before his mind could catch up, her hands dropped to his waistband and began unbuttoning his shorts. The hissing of the zipper pulled the air from his lungs. When she fell to her knees in front of him, he was fairly certain his heart stopped beating.

His grip tightened on the edge of the counter. "Belle, I…you…dammit all to hell. Sweetheart, you don't have to do this."

She licked her lips and looked up at him. "But I want to, Tanner. So much. I miss the taste of you."

Her tongue created a hot path, touching every inch and making his heart pound out of his chest. When her mouth encircled him, his knees started to buckle and the edge of the counter bit into his palm. Her hand held him tightly, meeting her lips with each devastating stroke.

Belle locked her eyes with his as she moved. Her pupils were dilated and ablaze with desire.

How could he have forgotten how soft her lips were, how hot her mouth was, and just how damn good she was at swirling her tongue around him and making his heart forget how to beat?

He wanted to whisper his love. He wanted to tell her he hadn't even realized how much he'd missed their connection until he felt it again. He wanted to drag her up by her shoulders and bury himself deep inside of her until she screamed his name.

But he was helpless to do more than throw his head back and groan with the last flick of her tongue.

Several minutes ticked by before his breathing evened and he found the strength to open his eyes.

She offered a Cheshire cat grin, still positioned at his feet. "I do so love negotiating with you."

***

Thirty hours they'd been in the hospital. Tanner's parents had peeled him from her side yesterday just long enough to go home for a quick shower and change of clothes. He packed a bag while he was there to bring back, determined not to have a reason to leave again.

Belle's long dark lashes rested against pale cheeks. She'd had three doses of the medication that was supposed to help the twins' lungs develop enough to be delivered and each time she'd been violently ill. When he thought his heart couldn't possibly hurt anymore, another wave of nausea would hit and he'd sit beside her in the bathroom, helpless to do anything other than rub her back.

He did little more than move his gaze back and forth from her sleeping face to the monitors beeping at her side. The babies were stable. Belle was stable. The contractions had slowed a lot but not stopped.

The new doctor, a younger and kinder doctor, who had taken over when Dr. MacMillan's shift ended, entered the room and Tanner reached over to squeeze Belle's hand. "Hey, sweetheart, Dr. Cook is here."

The woman took a seat on the foot of Belle's hospital bed and laid a hand on Belle's blanket-covered leg. "How is Mom feeling today?"

Belle's face brightened, and Tanner felt an overwhelming desire to send the doctor a huge bouquet of flowers simply for making his wife happy. "I'm good unless you tell me I need another round of those steroids."

Chuckling, Dr. Cook shook her head. "No. No more medication." Her features sobered. "But you know we haven't been able to completely stop the contractions. And even though your babies are stable right now, I don't think it's in their best interest or yours to wait any longer. I had them hold your breakfast this morning so we could take you down for a Caesarean section today."

Belle's grip on his hand tightened painfully. Her eyes widened and Tanner could see the tears collecting in the corners. "But they are eight weeks early."

Dr. Cook nodded and tucked a stray piece of her short brown hair behind her ear. "Yes, and they will need to be in the NICU for a period of time once they are born, but we've come to a place where we can do more for them on the outside than the inside."

Her gaze flew from the doctor to Tanner's. "But Tanner can be there, right?"

233

"Damn straight I'll be there," he answered, before the doctor could speak. No force was strong enough to stop him. His wife needed him. His kids needed him. He'd never let them down.

The doctor pinned him with an irritated gaze before smiling at Belle. "Yes, he can be there during the surgery."

The phone encased at his hip rang out an alert just at that moment. After a cursory glance at the screen, he squeezed Belle's hand once more before standing. "That's them. I'll be right back, sweetheart." He kissed her forehead and nodded a silent farewell to the doctor.

He jogged over to the elevators and repeatedly tapped the down arrow. As soon as the doors opened, Tanner punched the G button and crossed his arms as the elevator lowered him to the ground floor. His parents were huddled just to the right.

He had debated calling Belle's parents the night they came to the hospital, but fear of the stress her family would cause made him dial his parents instead. Within minutes they were there, waiting in the wings until Belle was ready for visitors. He'd never felt more grateful for their unquestioning support or the love they showered on Belle. She'd practically dissolved into his mother's arms the second she crossed the threshold.

Tracy's eyes were filled with concern. "How is she today, son?"

"Tired, hungry, sick, and getting ready for surgery it sounds like." He closed his eyes and let his shoulders drop, reality sinking in as he spoke the words out loud.

Needing no further information, his mother marched resolutely to the elevators, sparing them little more than a backwards glance. "Well, come on then."

By the time they reached her room, the doctor had left. Belle looked so small, so desolate in the hospital bed it made Tanner's heart drop to the floor. He crossed the room to drop a soft kiss on her lips. "Hey, sweetheart, told you I'd be right back."

Her eyes were filled with fear, but a small smile curved her lips. "Our babies are going to be here today."

He matched her smile with his own and took a seat on the bed beside her. "Yeah, they are. And they will be as strong and as smart as their mama."

Her eyes fell on his parents, hovering just inside the doorway, her bravery not faltering in the slightest. "I hope you guys are ready to be grandparents because they will be back in an hour to take us down."

She lifted a hand to grip the one Tanner held against her cheek. "You stay with them, okay? When they take them to the NICU and evaluate them and everything. You stay with them."

"But sweetheart…"

Belle shook her head, cutting off any further argument from him. "I'll be fine but I won't be able to see them right away." Tears began to fill her eyes again and her voice shook. "Baby, I need you to stay with them."

His instinct was to never leave her side. He'd promised her that more than once. But he could never refuse her anything. And if he wasn't with the

235

twins, she would be worried. A war raged inside him at the very idea of walking away from his wife while she lay on the operating room table.

Before he could answer, a hand landed on his shoulder. "It's okay, Tanner. I'll wait right outside the door for Izzy."

Belle nodded and squeezed his hand. "See, baby, I'll be fine."

He wanted to fight it, every cell in his body screamed that it was the exact opposite of what he should do, but then a smiling nurse in light blue scrubs entered the room. "We're going to get you ready to head downstairs and meet your babies, Mrs. Carlisle!"

Tanner followed behind, only half hearing the chattering nurse's instructions on where he could change into scrubs and what he needed to do next. His stomach churned. He didn't want to leave Belle.

He couldn't shake the feeling this would be the biggest mistake of his life.

Chapter Twenty-Five

Izzy

Izzy carried a tray of drinks outside and set them on the glass patio table. Just then, her youngest brother-in-law performed an unnecessarily exaggerated cannonball into the pool, causing a riot of laughter from her children floating nearby, always entertained by Uncle Dean. She could only roll her eyes in response.

Tanner's arms slid around her waist from behind, and he began planting soft kisses along her neck. "Hey there, sweetheart."

She shivered, annoyed and excited all at the same time. It really wasn't fair the effect he still had on her. In some ways, even stronger than it had been when they were younger. A grin spread over her lips. Her only consolation was knowing just how much she could still tease him.

Izzy turned in his arms and gave him a long, lingering kiss before he broke away, peeled off his tank top with a wink and joined his brother and the kids in the pool. So incredibly unfair.

Valiantly trying to think of anything other than the water dripping down Tanner's broad chest and muscular abs, Izzy wandered over to the grill where her father-in-law methodically flipped the burgers. "Need any help?"

His gaze swept over the all the supplies lined up on the stand beside him. "Naw, Iz, I'm good, honey."

She shrugged and stood on her tiptoes to offer Mike a peck on the cheek. "Okay, I'm going to go check on Mom then."

"It's okay for you to relax too, you know, Iz."

Izzy grinned in response. "Now, what kind of fun is that?"

Just then Izzy spied Tanner in the pool, raking back his wet hair and laughing at something Noah said. Her grin faded and her mouth went dry. Her fingers itched to play with each strand. Her thoughts involuntarily went back to the past few weeks and the reminder of just how much she loved him and appreciation for the effort he put in to changing for her, for *them*, hit her with unexpected force.

She turned to go into the house before she burst into uncontrollable sobs on her in-law's patio or jumped into the pool fully clothed to throw herself into Tanner's arms.

Yes, he had done something wrong. Yes, he had spent the past several years with his priorities so far out of whack it had changed both of them and affected their entire family. And yes, it hurt even worse knowing he had nearly done the same thing her father had so many years ago.

Izzy slid the glass door shut behind her and leaned against it with a sigh. But he wasn't ignoring the problem. He was owning it. Fixing it. And making sure she knew exactly how he felt and where she stood in his life.

She didn't need another week of dates to make up her mind. She already knew.

A grin played about the corners of her mouth. And she would make absolutely sure he knew tonight.

Voices from the den to the left pulled Izzy's attention away from her happy, contented thoughts. She loved all of Tanner's brothers, but arguments and schemes always abounded when they were together, especially on the rare occasions Wyatt was home.

She walked silently to the doorway, intent on finding out which it was and shutting it down before they created any headaches.

"You need to figure out a way to get rid of these, Wyatt."

Her brows drew together. Connor sounded anxious, a strange tone for him. He was usually the peacemaker.

"They aren't mine," Wyatt argued. "I got tagged in the pictures on social media but there is no way for me to get rid of them."

"Don't you have a manager or something that can talk to her? Get her to listen to reason?" Connor's voice was hushed but panicked.

Wyatt scoffed. "You expect some random chick looking to attach herself to me in any way possible to get her fifteen minutes of fame is going to listen to *reason*? Connor, she's only going to pay attention to dollar signs."

Izzy could hear one of them—Connor?—pacing the room. "Then pay her off." His voice rose. "I don't care what you have to do. You weren't here, Wyatt. Things weren't good. But look at them, they're happy. If Izzy sees those pictures…"

An icy feeling washed over her from head to toe. Pictures? Of what? Of who? And then realization hit. Tanner and *her*. She clapped a hand over her mouth, nausea welling inside of her. Her heart and her head went to battle, one needing to know, to see, to gain all the facts and the other wanting to run away and forget she'd ever heard a single word.

Her head won. She marched into the room, one hand extended. "Show me."

Both brothers paled, eyes wide at her sudden presence. Had it been any other time, any other circumstance, she would have laughed at their reaction.

Connor was the first to gain his voice. "No, Iz, you don't need to see these."

She pinned them both with an equally vicious glare. "He is my husband. This is my life. I need to know. I *deserve* to know. Now show me the pictures."

Wyatt gulped and handed his smartphone over with a shaking hand. "Izzy, this can't possibly change anything. You already knew."

But knowing and seeing were two vastly

different things. She swiped her finger to the right, her breath coming in shorter bursts, scrolling through the pictures. The completely innocuous and meaningless ones only fueled her anger, knowing something much worse lay in wait.

And then she saw it. The phone slipped from her grip and fell to the red area rug with a thud. A hand landed on her shoulder but she recoiled from the touch, tears filling her eyes. She backed out of the room needing to escape, needing to leave, needing…something she couldn't even begin to identify.

"Izzy, please." Connor's normally calm voice was anxious. "Please, sit down, let us get Tanner and—"

"No!" She screamed the single word. "No, you are *not* getting Tanner."

She turned and ran through the house, fleeing out the front door. Izzy thought she could move past it, and when *she* was just this mythical thing, maybe she could, but now *she* was real.

And *she* had put her hands in Tanner's hair. The exact same way Izzy always had. The one thing that had always been special, just between them.

She fell to her knees beside the SUV parked in front of the house, leaned her forehead against the hot metal of the door and sobbed. It had been special. It had been hers. And now it was gone.

***

I will be fine. The twins will be fine.
Izzy repeated the mantra over and over, trying to

241

muster the conviction she'd used on Tanner.

She couldn't suppress the giggle that bubbled up when Tanner walked through the door dressed in scrubs, complete with a mask and cap. "Just when I thought I'd seen everything."

His blue eyes twinkling above the mask, he sauntered over to stand in front of where she sat sideways on the operating table. "Maybe I should have gone to medical school instead of that whole MBA thing."

Izzy grasped his shoulders and curved her back outward the way she had been instructed, resting her forehead against his abdomen. "Nope. I love seeing you in a suit. And I love negotiating with you even more." The last word ended on a gasp as the needle pierced her skin.

His hand stroked down her hair. "And I love everything about you, sweetheart."

As soon as the small tube was placed in her back, she felt like a whirlwind of activity broke out around them. Before she realized it, she was laid down on her back, her right arm was strapped down, and a paper sheet hung over her chest, blocking her view.

Izzy turned her head to the left, just as much to make sure Tanner hadn't left as to speak to him. "Baby, remember, you need to go with the twins, okay? Promise. Promise me you will go with them and stay with them until I'm allowed to move."

For several long minutes, his only response was silence, his brows drawn together. "I promise. I'll go with them."

She relaxed then and rolled her head back so she

could stare at the ceiling and continue to remind herself that everything was going to be just fine.

Even though she couldn't feel anything from her chest down, she began to feel an odd sensation of pulling and tugging.

After what felt like an interminable length of time listening to mindless chatter between the doctor and nurses, a tiny, writhing baby was held up over the paper curtain. "Congratulations, it's a girl!"

A fraction of the breath she had been holding released when a squeak sounded from her daughter and they whisked her away to be cleaned and examined.

She turned her head back to Tanner and smiled. "Ava Marie. Don't forget."

He merely nodded in response, and for the fourth time since they first met, she saw a tear escape his eyes. Her heart clenched at the sight and her own threatened to fall, although she could scarcely believe she had a single one left after the past two days of nearly incessant crying.

Moments later, a smaller, much more vocal baby was held up. "And a boy!"

Izzy sought out Tanner's gaze again. "Noah Michael. Don't worry and don't leave them, okay?"

He paused for the briefest of moments, and Izzy was certain he'd argue, he'd say something. But he just nodded and kissed her forehead through the cloth mask before trailing after the two cots already leaving the room, each with their own team affixing tubes and monitors as they went.

She tracked him as long as she could without being able to pick up her head. Her mind began to race with questions. How long before she could go see the babies? They both cried, so that meant they were okay, right? Were there twenty fingers and twenty toes?

Her head felt oddly light and, despite trying to form words, her mouth didn't seem to want to work. Izzy's heart began to race. Why couldn't she talk?

Her vision blurred and she blinked a few times, trying to focus on the ceiling. Her breaths turned shallow, and she was certain she would hyperventilate any moment. The monitors to her right began to ring out an alarm, and she heard an oath from the foot of the bed.

The anesthesiologist that had placed her epidural leaned close to her ear and spoke in a calming tone. "I'm going to put this mask over your face, honey. Take a few deep breaths and you'll start to feel sleepy."

She tried to ask why. She tried to ask what was wrong. She tried to ask why the doctor was yelling out that she needed more A-positive. That was her blood type.

Just before her vision darkened and all the sounds around her ceased, she could have sworn she heard the panicked voice of the doctor saying the bleeding just wouldn't stop and they needed permission from the next of kin…

Chapter Twenty-Six

Tanner

"Ava, Noah, come on guys, time to get out of the pool. We need to go home."

Home? Tanner shook his head to the side, certain the chlorine water filling his ears had affected his hearing.

"But Izzy, we haven't even eaten yet," Mike protested from the grill.

Belle wrapped each grumbling child in their towels and was herding them through the sliding door by the time Tanner climbed out of the pool. And completely ignoring the protestations of everyone around her. His hand wrapped around her bicep. "Hey, give me a minute to dry off and then you can tell me what the hell is going on."

Her red-rimmed eyes looked vacant and haunted. Just as she opened her mouth to answer, Ava spoke

245

up. "Yeah, Mommy, we need to wait for Daddy."

She pinned the brightest and fakest smile on her face Tanner had ever seen and turned to the kids. "Daddy isn't coming with us this time, sweetie. He's going to have a sleepover with Grandma and Grandpa. Just like you guys get to do sometimes."

His stomach dropped to his feet. What in the actual hell just happened? Ten minutes ago, she was fine. More than fine. She was his Belle. His greedy little vixen who loved to negotiate with him and tease him and…

"Belle, come on." He failed to keep the panic from his tone and he cursed himself for it. "You need to talk to me. To tell me what's wrong. Whatever it is, I can fix it. We can fix it. I promise. Just…talk to me, sweetheart."

Wyatt and Connor came racing through the door at that moment, and Belle nodded in their direction, pulling her arm from his slackened grasp. "Ask your brother."

She hustled the kids past his astonished mother and straight out the front door before Tanner could even begin to process what was happening.

Tingling heat spread through his entire body, and he stalked over to Wyatt and Connor. *Ask your brother.* That had to mean Wyatt. He was the only one that was a big enough asshole to ruin everything Tanner had rebuilt with Belle.

He grabbed the front of Wyatt's blue and white striped t-shirt and practically slammed him against the brick wall of the house. "What the hell did you do?"

Wyatt's face turned red with the pressure against

246

his windpipe, and his words came out in gargles. A hand closed around Tanner's forearm. "It wasn't his fault." Connor's voice was calm and clear as always. "Tanner, listen to me. It wasn't his fault. Let go."

The words finally registered in Tanner's brain as did his brother gasping for air. He released his hold and Wyatt fell to his knees, coughing.

Tanner pierced his hair with his fingers and breathed heavily. "Then whose fault was it? What the hell happened? And why is my wife driving away without me?"

Wyatt fished in his pocket, still breathing unevenly, and tapped the screen of his phone a few times before turning it over to Tanner. "She saw these."

Tanner swiped to the left several times, scrolling through the pictures. No, no, no, and *hell* no. She couldn't have. Dammit, he didn't even remember half of the things displayed on the screen in front of him. And he sure as hell didn't remember someone, anyone, other than Belle running her fingers through his hair.

That was theirs. That was sacred.

Every single thing he'd done, change he had made, and realization he'd come to amounted to little more than the smoke from a burning ember whipped away by the wind. He'd violated her trust far worse than he'd thought.

And it was real to her now more than it had been before. It wasn't some faceless woman; it wasn't something she could downplay in her own mind to make it feel better. She had seen practically every event as it unfolded, and it had broken her much more than just the vague concept had.

She left.

He dropped into the wrought iron patio chair, ignoring the water still dripping from his hair and trunks.

She left.

Belle had taken the kids and made sure he knew he wasn't welcome to follow.

She left.

And there wasn't a damn thing he could do about it. For the first time in his life, there was something Tanner Carlisle couldn't fix.

He propped his elbows on his knees and buried his face in his hands. When he finally lifted his head, he was met with tears falling down his mother's cheeks, an angry scowl from his father, and blatant panic written across Connor's face.

"Are you just going to sit here like some pathetic asshole, or are you going to go get your wife back?" Dean called out from the other side of the pool with a smirk tugging at his lips. "'Cause I gotta tell you, brother, the part of the Carlisle family asshole has already been filled by Wyatt and he does a fine job of it, so you need to man the hell up."

From his place on the concrete floor of the patio, Wyatt held his throat with one hand and flipped his little brother off with the other.

Tanner's mouth fell open. It must have just dipped below zero in the depths of hell because his baby brother was actually making sense.

He stood up abruptly, knocking over the chair as he did. "I'm going to need to borrow a car." He looked down at his bare chest and sopping trunks. "And clothes."

***

He knew better.

He knew he shouldn't have left.

And now he was sitting in the hospital room, holding Belle's hand, willing her to open her eyes. They said she was fine. They said after three units of blood, the surgery had ended beautifully. They said her vitals looked perfect. But the enchanting light brown eyes he loved remained closed and he felt like his lungs were as well.

His phone dinged an alert. Every thirty minutes, Tracy Carlisle updated him on the twins and asked how Belle was. And every thirty minutes, he had nothing to report. His head hung between his shoulders.

She was gonna be mad as hell that he was here, but there was no way he'd be anywhere else. Even if she screamed, cried, or threw something at him, he wouldn't leave her side ever again.

He knew he shouldn't have left.

A finger twitched in his grasp and his head shot up. Her long lashes fluttered once. Twice. Belle's eyes darted around the room before her brow drew together and the heel of her palm pressed against her forehead. "Ow." She moaned and closed her eyes again.

"Hey there, beautiful," he whispered softly and reached for the remote affixed to the hospital bed. After pressing the red button to summon the nurse, he hit the two buttons that threw the room into near darkness. "Is that better, sweetheart?"

She nodded slowly and then winced. "What happened? Where are the babies? Why aren't you with them?" Tears collected in her eyes, and she shook her head slightly. "They aren't…"

He reached up to smooth her hair from her face and brushed away the single tear tracking down her cheek. "They are fine, sweetheart. My mom is with them. They are breathing on their own and are shocking almost all of the NICU staff with how strong they are for such tiny babies." He grinned and winked at her. "I told them that's what happens when their mom is from New York."

Belle relaxed back into the bed with a small smile. "Did Noah come out wearing a business suit so he can join you in the board room in the next three to five years?"

Some of the tension eased from Tanner's shoulders. If she was making fun of his MBA, she must be doing okay.

The nurse bustled in the room, flicked on the dimmer light, and began fiddling with the IVs and fluid bags attached to Belle. Tanner stood and moved to the foot of the bed, leaving her plenty of room to take care of his wife.

"How are you feeling, Mrs. Carlisle?"

"I'm fi—"

"Her head hurts," Tanner interrupted, determined not to let her downplay anything in an effort to get to the twins faster. "And don't lie, Belle. I see it when you move your head, and it was even worse when the bright lights were on."

She rolled her eyes with a huff. "Okay, fine, yes. I have a little headache."

The nurse chuckled in response. "Let me get you something to help with that. And how about something to drink?"

Her tongue darted out to touch her lips, and she nodded. "My mouth is really dry."

A heavy weight settled square on Tanner's chest, making it hard to inhale. He needed to tell her. She needed to know. But she was going to be devastated. He closed his eyes and straightened his shoulders. She needed to hear this and hear it from him.

The nurse came in and out of the room a few more times bringing ice chips, a few cans of ginger ale, cups, and straws.

On the last trip, she arrived with a syringe that she injected into the IV tube connected to Belle's hand. "Just a little something for that headache." She winked before exiting the room and pulling the door halfway closed behind her.

He sat on the bed beside her again, pouring a small amount of the soda into a cup for her. "Here ya go, sweetheart."

After a few small sips, she smiled. "Next time we will have a much less eventful birth, okay?"

An iron fist closed around his heart. "Sweetheart, what do you remember? Of the surgery, I mean."

Her lips drew down at the corners, and she rolled her eyes up toward the ceiling like she was trying to pick out the memories. "I...I remember telling you to go with the twins. And...I think I remember seeing them for just a second. Oh!" Her hand flew to his. "Twenty fingers and twenty toes, right? I remember worrying about that."

He laughed and hoped it sounded genuine to her. "Yes, I told you they are healthier than any thirty-two week preemie babies have a right to be. Twenty fingers, twenty toes, four eyes, four ears, two noses, two mouths. All present and accounted for."

Belle sat up a little in the bed and put a hand against his cheek, her expression sober and her gaze locked on his. "Something happened. Something you're not telling me."

He nodded and covered her hand with his. "Yeah, there is. Belle, things didn't go as planned."

"Just tell me, baby." Her voice was strong, but fear was written all over her face.

Tanner pulled her hand from his face and held both of hers firmly in his grasp. "A-after we left, me and the babies, you started bleeding. A lot." He shook his head. "The doctor called it something I can't remember or pronounce. But she said they had to give you blood transfusions a-and they had to put you under general anesthesia and..." His voice caught in his throat as the words the doctor spoke replayed through his mind. "They had to do a hysterectomy, Belle. It was the only way."

The chestnut eyes Tanner loved so much grew wide before they filled with tears and she leaned against his shoulder, her arms wrapping tightly around his neck. He held her for a long time, running a hand down her silky chocolate brown hair.

Finally she pulled back and stared at him, her face filled with desolation. "You should marry someone else. Someone who isn't broken. Someone who can give you more kids."

He cupped the sides of her face. "Don't you say that. Don't you ever even think that, ever again. Belle, don't you understand? You almost died. I almost lost you." He choked on the last few words. "Nothing in this world would matter to me if you weren't by my side. Do you hear me? Not a damn thing."

Tanner held her close to his chest. "Sweetheart, I don't know if I could remember how to breathe without you."

For a long time they both clung to each other, grieving the loss of the future they had planned. Finally Belle pulled away and looked in his eyes with a small smile. "Nobody leaves?"

"Damn straight, sweetheart. Nobody leaves."

Chapter
Twenty-Seven

Izzy

The slamming of the car door made her jump. She grabbed another tissue and rolled her swollen eyes. Why did he have to be so freaking persistent? The least he could have done was to wait until the kids were asleep. They didn't need to hear this.

She sat on the side of the bed, overcome by the same memory that haunted her for more than twenty years. The taillights of her father's car pulling out of the driveway appeared in front of her eyes and her mother's shrill screams echoed in her ears.

She'd always said she wouldn't make their mistakes. She'd sworn she would never let her children deal with the same demons she had. She'd trusted Tanner to stay faithful, to be a better man.

But it was too late for those things now. Clearly history was going to repeat itself, but she didn't know if she'd have the strength to make it through it again.

Her heart pounded as she heard the heavy footsteps on the stairs. Long before she was ready, there was a light tap on the door and it slowly swung open. Tanner stood just inside the doorway wearing gray athletic shorts and a tight, faded blue t-shirt with some indie band logo on the front that she'd never seen before.

The realization that when she drove away she took the duffel bag that held his change of clothes hit and she felt her cheeks warm. Obviously he'd borrowed something from one of his brothers.

"I didn't know." He shifted from one foot to the other. "Wyatt showed me, but sweetheart, I swear I didn't know. I don't remember what happened."

Lifting her hands helplessly, she said, "But it happened, Tanner. It happened and you can't undo it."

She stood up and pointed at him. "*You* made the decision to drive out there, *you* made the decision to follow him to the bar and drink way more than you should have," she choked back her tears, "and *you* made the decision to put your hands and your mouth on someone else."

Izzy wrapped her arms around her midsection. "And now I'm making the decision that you need to leave."

Tanner closed the door with a quiet click before he stormed over to her. He grabbed the tops of her arms and held her tightly. "No. Hell, no. It doesn't end like this. You don't get to walk into my life and make me the happiest man in the world for more than a decade and then throw it away because I screwed up one time. No, Belle. It isn't going down like that."

Mustering all the strength she could, she looked into his blue eyes, drowning in fear and panic and tears. The ones that still could see through to her soul, no matter how much she tried to fight it. "There was one thing. One thing, Tanner, that was special. One thing that was just ours…just mine." She shook her head. "It's not mine anymore. *You're* not mine anymore."

His nostrils flared, and he pressed his forehead against hers. "The hell I'm not. I've been yours since the very first day I saw you and I'm going to be yours until I take my last breath. Please. Please, I've never begged for anything from anyone, but I'll beg if that's what it takes. Just please don't make that decision now."

She offered a hollow, haunted laugh. "And when should I make that decision, Tanner? Tomorrow? Next week? Next month?" She shook her head.

"Saturday. Just wait until Saturday."

Izzy pulled out of his arms. She couldn't be that close anymore. She couldn't feel his skin, his warmth, or the agonizing pain radiating off his body for another second and hope to have any sort of defense. Running a hand through her hair, she took three large steps away. "What's so magical about Saturday?"

If it were possible, he looked even more devastated when she walked away from him. "Our date. Our last date."

She rolled her eyes again and leaned her head

back. "And you really think that this…this *date*," her heart cracked when he winced at the derision in her voice, "is really going to change anything?"

"I *think* I promised you forty-three days of change. Forty-three days to prove how much I love you and how sorry I am that I screwed up the single best thing that ever happened to me." He paused for a minute and rubbed his hand across the back of his neck. "And you said you'd let me try."

She lifted her shoulders slightly. "But that was before…" The images on Wyatt's phone, long red fingernails intertwined through Tanner's hair, danced in front of her eyes and stole the air from her lungs. "Before I knew. Before I saw."

Tanner matched her three steps and fell to his knees in front of her just like he did when he first came home, confessing his transgression. And just like then, her fingers itched to play with every strand of his still damp hair. The desire causing the newest wound to her heart begin to ache even more exquisitely. His hands landed on her hips and he held tight. "Please, Belle, just give me until Saturday."

Her heart and her mind locked in a bitter war. As certain as she was that her heart would never again be whole, the very idea of Tanner's absence from her life made it valiantly urge her to say yes. Ava's piano recitals with each of them sequestered on opposites sides of the auditorium. Noah's baseball games seated at least five rows apart. Graduation. Weddings. Grandchildren. Every single important event yet to happen in their lives, done as two separate, broken people. A far cry from the happily ever after she'd always envisioned.

"Okay."

The single word, barely more than a whisper, made Tanner's head snap up. "Okay?"

She could do little more than nod in response, her brain screaming that he clearly could not be trusted.

He stood up quickly and cradled her face in his hands. He brushed his lips across hers softly, hesitantly. "Thank you, sweetheart." And then just like that, his hands fell away and he left her standing in their bedroom, peeling out of the driveway minutes later.

Her fingers touched her mouth, feeling as cold and vacant as her heart. Izzy fell onto the bed and let go of all the tears she had been holding back, wondering if it was the last time he'd ever kiss her.

***

Izzy folded her arms across her chest and glared at the doctor. She was tired, hungry, and annoyed by the staples still in her stomach eight days after the C-section. The nonsensical comments coming out of the man's mouth weren't helping her attitude in the slightest.

"I really don't care what you think, what the averages are, and what your stupid studies show," she seethed, her voice low and menacing. "My children are not going to have any impairments or disabilities and you can take every pamphlet and paper and shove them up your pompous, insensitive—"

258

He held a hand up in surrender. "I'm simply informing you of probabilities and your options, Mrs. Carlisle."

She snorted and pointed at the door behind him. "I consider myself *fully* informed. Now get out."

Before she reached the plastic cushioned seat carefully placed between the twins' cots, arms wrapped around her from behind, making her jump.

"I'm so sorry." A soft voice spoke from the cheek pressed against her back. "I just needed to thank you for doing that."

Izzy laughed lightly as the other woman released her and she turned to face her. She had seen her in here every day, keeping the same vigil over her son that Izzy did over the twins. Feeding, bathing, changing, all the little tasks most parents took for granted, but things they could only do when their children were stable enough. Healthy enough.

"Hi, I'm Caroline Thompson, and I really am sorry but you said all the things I've always thought but never been strong enough to say." She dropped her gaze to the floor and tucked a lock of hair behind one ear.

Izzy stuck a hand out, feeling just a little foolish at the formal greeting after the other woman had just given her a hug. "Izzy Carlisle. And I'm sorry if I created a scene, I just couldn't listen to another word."

Caroline shook her head quickly, her short brown hair bouncing around her face. "Oh no. He's done that to everyone I've seen so far. And it's terrifying and frustrating and you are so brave."

She raised an eyebrow. "I'm not brave, I just

have a big mouth and an itchy stomach and my husband has yet to magically appear with food."

Izzy noted the dark circles under Caroline's eyes and knew the other woman would have a level of understanding only a fellow NICU mom could have. Something inside warmed at the unfortunate but unique bond immediately created between them.

"So you have twins?" Caroline ventured cautiously. The unspoken rule of the NICU, you never knew what landed someone here, be careful with your words.

Her gaze fell on Ava and Noah, who continued to grow much faster and get much stronger than expected, despite the ridiculous doctor and his ridiculous statistics. "Yeah, pre-term labor with a side dose of placenta previa." Izzy quirked her lips wryly. "I don't recommend waking up in labor covered in blood. It's a little disconcerting."

Caroline laughed lightly. "Preeclampsia isn't a walk in the park either. I didn't think my cankles would ever disappear and he," she gestured to her son's cot, "felt very confident ten weeks early was a perfectly acceptable time to make an appearance. Hopefully any future siblings will decide to stay where they belong for the duration of the ride."

Immediately the smile fell from Izzy's lips and her hand involuntarily covered her abdomen. There wouldn't be any second chances for her and Tanner. She studied first Ava's face, then Noah's. She loved them more than she ever thought possible to love another human being, but knowing there was no chance she and Tanner would have more children of their own, and knowing that decision had been taken away from them, *stolen* from them, shredded her heart. She couldn't stop the crippling pain from forcing her into the squeaky plastic seat and she definitely couldn't stop the onslaught of tears.

Caroline dropped to a knee beside the chair. "Oh, I'm so sorry for…whatever I said. Are you okay?"

Izzy couldn't make her mouth form the words. How could she possibly explain to this woman, this stranger, that she felt broken and useless? That she hadn't had the time to process any of it or figure out her life from this point on because every waking moment had been spent staring at the monitors attached to her babies and anxiously taking any and every opportunity to play the role of a normal parent. That deep inside, despite every reassurance, she felt that Tanner deserved someone better, someone who was whole.

Caroline wrapped an arm around Izzy and pulled her against her shoulder, quickly sealing the bond Izzy felt as soon as she introduced herself. "It's okay, you don't have to explain. If you need to cry, you can just cry."

Several minutes later, Izzy finally felt in control enough to pull away. She waved her hand towards the twins' cots. "They are it for us. We can't…" She shook her head. "*I* can't have any more children. I had complications during the C-section and the doctor wound up doing a hysterectomy."

The other woman's face paled. "Oh honey, I am so sorry."

Izzy shook her head. An overwhelming urge to speak the words she'd been holding in for so long overcame her, and she found herself saying every

261

dark thought to a virtual stranger. "But Tanner, my husband, he…we always planned on having a huge family. Lots of kids." A vacant smile curved her lips. "I'm an only child and he has three brothers. He's used to chaos and I've always wanted it. I just keep thinking he deserves better. He deserves to have his dream."

Caroline grasped her hands. "Your husband? That guy that's here with you every night? Oh honey, he could teach Prince Charming how to treat a woman." Her soft southern accent made Izzy giggle. "That man only has eyes for you. Two kids or twenty."

The frail, fragile heart that had been holding so much fear slowly started to heal. If someone she just met felt this way, why in the world would she question it? "I think you're right."

The wooden door the doctor had exited a few moments earlier swung open and Tanner walked in, still clad in his business suit, carrying Styrofoam containers and paper cups. "Somebody need dinner?"

Caroline popped up off the floor. "I think there is at least one doctor in this hospital who could confirm a hangry diagnosis for your wife here."

His eyes landed on Izzy and all the humor fled. He dropped the containers on the closest counter and assumed the same position on his knees in front of her that Caroline had just abandoned. "What's wrong, sweetheart?" One hand cradled her cheek and the other clamped onto her knee. "Are you okay? Are the babies okay?"

Izzy leaned forward and kissed him. "We are all

fine. I think I just may have scared the doctor though. The self-righteous, arrogant son of a—"

"Hey now." Tanner chuckled. "You never say a bad word. That's my job."

Caroline had taken up residence back beside her son and chimed in. "Your wife certainly took care of that guy. Bad words or no."

Tanner brushed his lips across her forehead. "My wife is from New York. She can take care of herself."

The dull ache still throbbed in the back of her heart, but she felt a new level of peace she hadn't before. "Yeah, but she doesn't have to anymore, right?"

"Damn straight, sweetheart."

Chapter Twenty-Eight

Tanner

In spite of her protestations, Tanner showed up at their house Monday, Wednesday, and today to watch the kids and ensure Izzy went to every yoga class. He made a promise and he sure as hell was going to keep it. Especially now.

When she walked back in the house this afternoon, practically glowing from the exercise, he'd practiced more self-control than ever before in his life to keep his hands to himself. He scoffed at himself. Why the hell hadn't he done that forty-two days ago when he was in that damn bar?

And Belle...his chest tightened at the memory. She'd smiled at him. A real one this time, not just pretending for the kids. She'd asked if he wanted to stay for lunch.

For the first time all week, he'd seen the tiniest

glimmer of hope and he was gonna run with it. He was even more determined that he would make the final date in his plan perfect. Make it everything she deserved. Make it mean enough she'd be willing to give him another chance.

And that glimmer made walking away without touching her and kissing her even more difficult.

But controlling himself around Belle had been easier than trying to put together everything he needed for their final date. Especially when his brothers were involved. He put his hands on his hips and pinned Dean with an irritated scowl.

"I don't have time to screw around with you. This has to be ready by tomorrow night and it has to be perfect. So stop being a total asshole and get over here."

Dean snorted but obediently held the heavy wooden beam for his brother so they could secure it in place. "News flash, big brother, if you would've just kept your hands to yourself, this wouldn't be happening."

Tanner really was getting tired of hearing every single moment of every single day what a screw up he was. "Yeah, yeah. I got that memo. From you, from Mom and Dad, from Wyatt, Connor. Hell, I'm pretty sure the postman left a threatening note in my mailbox."

With a final turn of the wrench, both men let go and Dean held his hands up, palms forward. "Anything is possible. You know for damn sure if you don't make this work, Izzy'll have a line of men waiting to take your place and do a better job of it."

265

Tanner clenched and unclenched his fist several times, breathing heavily. "Shut. Your. Mouth."

Dammit all, his brother was right. And he hated that his brother was right. Belle was strong, smart, and sexy as hell. He'd be a shell of a man without her, but Belle? Shit. She'd move on to someone who would treat her a lot better than him.

No. Tanner shook his head resolutely. That wasn't an option. She wasn't going to be with someone better; he was simply going to *be* someone better. And he'd remind her of all the things he'd done right before screwing up their marriage in such an epic fashion.

"How exactly are you planning on getting this down there?" Dean's question pulled him out of his dark thoughts. "The bed of your truck isn't big enough to carry this."

Tanner rolled his eyes. "Thank you for that brilliant deduction, Sherlock. Wyatt has a friend who is letting me borrow his trailer. So tomorrow morning we are going to load it all up and my three idiot brothers are going to help me set this all up."

"Calling us idiots may not be the best way to enlist our help."

He dropped the next beam on the ground and looked at his brother helplessly. "Fine. You need a reason to help? Here's a reason: you love Izzy. All of you love Izzy. She is just as much a part of this family as I am. And, yeah, I screwed up. I made a horrible, stupid decision and it may very well cost me the best thing in my life. But if I am going to have a chance in hell of saving this marriage, I need help from all of you."

Not usually at a loss for words or a sarcastic retort, Dean simply stared at his brother for several long minutes. "Those are pretty good reasons."

Three much more peaceful hours later, all four brothers carefully loaded all of the supplies Tanner would need into the trailer Wyatt delivered. Swinging the arm into place and locking it to ensure nothing would fall out, Tanner smacked his hand twice against the side.

Connor swiped a hand across his sweaty brow and stood beside Tanner as they watched the sun dip below the mountain behind his parents' house. "This is your last chance, isn't it?"

Tanner only nodded in response.

Connor clapped him on the back. "Okay then." His grip on Tanner's shoulder tightened slightly. "You know, it's okay to make mistakes sometimes."

He quickly held his hands up when Tanner whipped his head around to stare at him with a mixture of shock and irritation. "Listen, I'm not saying *that* was okay. That was stupid and you're an idiot for doing *that*. But everything else, brother, you just lost your focus for a while. And you're fixing it. Just…don't be so hard on yourself, okay?"

Dean joined them, clearing his throat and rolling eyes dramatically. "Are we all finished here? Unlike the rest of you losers, I've got a date."

Wyatt climbed in the front seat of his truck and slammed the door. "Did you finally decide to ask Jill out?"

"Hell, no! She's not my girlfriend."

Connor chuckled beside him. "I think you may

want to tell her that, Deano."

He threw glares to each of his brothers, only making them laugh more. "Oh, whatever. Jilly-bean knows she's my best friend and that is all she'll ever be. You guys are just a bunch of morons."

Dean stormed into the house, grumbling about stopping to buy flowers on the way to his date. Tanner's ears perked up. It hurt like hell leaving Belle this afternoon, but he was trying his damndest to respect her need for space.

A slow smile slid into place. "Thanks." He threw a hand up to Wyatt and Connor before turning and jogging to his truck on the other end of the driveway. "See you guys later."

Okay, so she didn't want him staying there right now, but dropping off a bouquet of her favorite flowers and wishing her goodnight certainly couldn't hurt, right?

***

The sounds of four tiny feet greeted Tanner as soon as he walked through the front door. The three-year-old twins were still light enough that he could carry them both at once.

"Daddy's home!" Ava planted a kiss on his cheek and wrapped her arms around his neck.

"Daddy's home!" Noah echoed just as loudly and laid his head down on Tanner's shoulder.

Belle folded her arms in front of her and gave him a wry smile when he walked into the kitchen. "So, I feel like Daddy might be home, but it wasn't really clear to me."

With a kiss on each forehead, he lowered them to the floor. Once they'd scampered off he wrapped his arms around Belle and drew her close. "Dinner smells good." He buried his nose in her neck. "Mmm, but you smell better."

Her hands crept around his neck and into his hair. "How is it that *I* quit my job and spend all day, every day with them, but *you* get to be the conquering hero when you come home? Very, very unfair."

Tanner pulled his head back and tried to effect the most pained expression he could but failed miserably. "Are you saying I'm not your hero?"

Belle rolled her eyes and patted his chest with one hand. "Let's not feed your already super-sized ego."

This was the best part of coming home. Hugs and kisses from the twins that continued to surpass every expert's opinion of their abilities after such an early and traumatic entrance into the world. Mouth-watering food and an even more delicious wife.

Tanner would never take a moment of this for granted as long as he lived. He knew all too well how valuable this was.

He'd never told her just how close he'd come to losing her when the twins were born. She didn't need to hear the details. She didn't need to know that his father had run to bring him back. She didn't need to know he still woke up with nightmares of the sight of the doctor with blood on her operating gown asking him if he consented to a hysterectomy. And she sure as hell didn't need to know what it felt like to hear the alarms on the monitors going off in the operating room.

He banished the dark thoughts to the back of his mind and kissed the tip of her nose, finally releasing her. "Want me to do anything?"

Belle had opened the oven but paused, arms halfway inside to pull the roasting pan out. She looked over at him, and he realized she caught him checking out her ass. Who could blame him? That woman made everything look good, especially the jeans that were hugging every curve.

She just laughed and shook her head. "If you feel so inclined, you can set the table."

Six o'clock was far too early to put the kids to bed, right? He cleared his throat and shook his head a little. "Sure thing, sweetheart."

Once the plates were in place, he reached into the cabinet for the glasses. "There was something I wanted to tell you…"

Belle looked up from slicing the roast beef with a frown. "Should I be scared?"

"Dad's retiring." He made the announcement quickly, hoping it would be like ripping off a band-aid. "Well, semi-retiring. He's still going to come in to the office sometimes, just not every day. He wants to golf and travel and," he shrugged, "I guess he trusts me."

She dropped the utensils on the counter and stood in front of him, wrapping her arms around his waist. "Of course he trusts you and your super-duper MBA, baby. You've been working so hard and handled everything for him. How could he not trust you?"

She stood on her tiptoes and planted a kiss on his

cheek with a small laugh. "Congratulations, baby. And I really like the beard. I think you need to keep it this time."

This time Tanner rolled his eyes, but he took advantage of the embrace to slide his hands in the back pockets of her jeans. "Are you ever going to stop picking on my degree?"

She tapped her chin thoughtfully. "Um, nope."

He kissed her deeper. "You know, this may mean I have to make a couple of business trips. Not a lot. There's no way in hell I'll be gone long."

Belle grinned. "I know, baby. I trust you. And you're still gonna make sure you'll have Friday mornings free to watch the kids so I can hang out with Caroline, right?"

"Of course, sweetheart. I mean, your weekly date with Caroline is important, but not nearly as important as the book series the kids and I are working on." He winked at her. "And we really need you out of the house for that because I freaking rock at doing all the voices, and if you're around, I'll get distracted."

She tilted her head back and laughed. Tanner wasn't sure if it was the melodic sound or her long chocolate hair tickling his forearms, but a shiver ran down his spine. "Are you sure we've got to do the whole dinner and parenting thing tonight?"

"Yes. Yes, we do. But…" She dragged the single word out and laughed again, this time a throaty, sexy sound, and proceeded to whisper everything they would do as soon as the twins went to sleep. The combination of her promises and her soft, warm breath against his ear wiped his mind clean of everything including his name and made his mouth go dry.

Chapter Twenty-Nine

Izzy

"Tanner." Izzy breathed out his name in shock when she opened the front door. When the chime sounded, she was certain she'd find Wyatt standing on the porch. He'd sent her a text message just a few minutes ago that he was on his way over. "You…rang the doorbell?"

He gave her a self-satisfied smirk and pulled a bouquet of Gerbera daisies from behind his back. "Don't delivery guys usually ring?"

She gathered her heartache around herself like a shield. "Tanner. Those are lovely, but I told you…"

His eyes flickered with hurt at her words. "Not until tomorrow, Belle. No decisions until tomorrow." He thrust the flowers towards her, and she grabbed them reflexively. "I'm sorry for coming over."

273

He turned and descended the stairs, his head hanging down and, in a feat she thought impossible, her heart ached even more. Izzy set the bouquet on the small table beside the door and flew down the steps behind him. She caught up to him just as he pulled open the door to his obnoxious yellow truck. Her hand shook as he touched his arm. "Wait."

When he spun around the look of utter desolation in the blue eyes she loved so much stole the breath from her body. "Th-thank you for the flowers, Tanner. They're beautiful."

His lip curled back and he snorted. "Yeah, well, maybe if I hadn't been such a selfish asshole and done that kind of stuff for the past three years, we wouldn't be standing here."

Without another word, he climbed in his truck and sped away. Izzy just stood watching as the darkness of the night swallowed his taillights and fought the urge to run after him.

Thirty minutes later, she picked her phone up for the fifth time, her finger hovering over his name, needing to talk to him and terrified she'd fall under his spell once again.

Before she forced herself to make a decision, the doorbell rang out once again. "Lived in this house for five years," she murmured under her breath as she walked to the door, "and now people decide to start using the doorbell."

As expected, her brother-in-law stood on her doorstep, dressed as if he'd just stepped off the cover of a western novel. "Are you ever going to drop the whole pseudo cowboy persona?" She gave a heavy sigh.

He swiped his hat off his head and stepped across the threshold with a cocky grin. "As soon as you drop the whole actual hottest chick on the planet thing."

Izzy rolled her eyes at Wyatt's blatantly disingenuous flirting. She turned a cheek up in his direction and he dropped a kiss on it. Her heart ached a little more. She loved Tanner's family. Wyatt, Connor, and Dean quickly became the siblings she'd always wished for growing up. She was losing so much more than just her fairy tale ending.

"So what was so important you had to rush over tonight?" She wrapped her arms around herself. She was so tired of hurting.

Wyatt's smile slipped, and he held his arm out. "How about we go sit down in the living room?"

Izzy was far too tired to argue and nodded as she led the way, sliding down onto the couch gratefully. "I know you're used to keeping late nights," *and corrupting your innocent brother*, "but it's after ten and I am exhausted so can you make this quick?"

He pulled his phone out of the pocket of his shirt, and she felt her stomach roll. What was he thinking? She knew he could be insensitive and thoughtless, but this was a new low even for him.

As soon as she opened her mouth, he held a hand up. "Izzy, I just need you to listen to me for a few minutes and trust me. I promise I'm not going to hurt you."

In the twelve years since she'd met Tanner's family, she'd never seen a more earnest or humble expression on Wyatt's face and that halted her protests more than his words. She simply nodded in response.

"I-I didn't realize what Tanner had told you until just yesterday. Iz, if I'd known, I would have set him straight weeks ago. And if I knew this picture existed, I absolutely would have shown you as soon as you saw those other damned things."

"Wyatt, I really don't want to see another picture…"

He put a calloused hand over hers, where they were fidgeting with the hem of her shirt. "Trust me," he repeated with conviction. "I screwed up a helluva lot in my life, but this is one thing I think I can help fix."

Wyatt pulled his hand away and ran it down the side of his face. "Apparently my genius brother is slightly misinformed. He told me how much he appreciated me pulling him off that girl before he…well, you know."

The bile started to rise in the back of her throat. She knew Wyatt really believed he could help, but so far everything he was saying just made it worse. "Yeah, that's what he said," she confirmed in a hoarse voice.

"That's not what happened."

She clapped a hand over her mouth. No. Oh no. Wyatt didn't stop him in time. Tanner actually…slept with *her*.

Wyatt's eyes widened to a comical size. "No, Iz, no. Whatever you're thinking just…no." He shook his head rapidly. "Tanner, he…" He rubbed his fingers up and down his temple with a sigh. "If this is the shit I've been putting him through for all these years, I don't know how he didn't kick my ass ages ago."

They were getting nowhere, and every little bit of her patience was gone. "Oh, for crying out loud, just tell me, Wyatt." She jumped to her feet. "Or I swear I'll be the one kicking your ass."

He stood with her. "Don't you get it, Izzy? That girl, whoever the hell she was, the second she touched his fuc—" He stopped himself and rubbed the back of his neck. "Sorry, I mean the second she touched his hair, *he* pushed her away. *He* grabbed me and made me leave the bar. *He* sat on the floor of my hotel room all night throwing up, terrified that you couldn't forgive him."

He tapped the screen of his phone and swiped several times. "I didn't do a damn thing. I didn't save the day." He turned the screen towards her. "He did."

Swallowing past the tears that threatened to fall, Izzy reached out to take the phone. Amidst all the pictures from the night she'd already been subjected to there was one she hadn't seen. Tanner's hands locked around the woman's wrists and pushing her away with a sick expression on his face.

A nearly audible click echoed in Izzy's brain. Tanner had ended it. Tanner had walked away. Tanner had come home and immediately went to work fixing things. A small smile fought its way onto her lips. He really was doing a fabulous job.

And he wasn't her father. More than anything, the realization that he wasn't her father settled in her chest. He wasn't running away. He wasn't abandoning her. He was here and fighting for them.

She couldn't tear her eyes away from the image, still aching that it had ever happened, but feeling the warm stirring of hope in her chest.

"Thank you, Wyatt," she whispered, past the tears she couldn't control any longer. She dropped the phone onto the couch and pressed her forehead against Wyatt's chest.

"Geez, Izzy, couldn't you at least ruin one of the shirts I don't like?" He wrapped his arms around her and let her sob all the pain and heartache she'd been holding onto for far too long.

***

Izzy closed the bedroom door softly. Ava and Noah had been asleep for nearly three hours but she didn't want to risk waking them. And there was no way she was simply going to let this slide without a fight. Maybe a loud one.

And then there'd be making up.

"You promised." She turned to face him, trying to ignore the rumpled shirt begging to be taken off or the messy hair she so desperately wanted to play with.

"But it's just this once, Belle. I swear. I told them I didn't do Friday morning meetings, but that was the only day they could meet me."

This was exactly what she'd feared when he said he was taking control of the company. Not that it was a surprise. She'd known since they were dating that Carlisle International was going to wind up in Tanner's hands one day.

But she had no idea it would be this soon. No

idea it would create this many late nights or this many business trips.

She pressed her lips together in a thin line and crossed her arms. "Fine. I'll call Caroline this *one* time to tell her we can't meet. But this is a first and last time thing." She dropped her shoulders a little. "You've been working later, too."

Her voice sounded whiny to her own ears, but she couldn't help it. Tanner wasn't just her husband, he was her best friend, as much as Caroline.

She missed the time they'd spend together after the kids went to bed. She'd stretch out on the couch to read, and Tanner would put a baseball game or stupid action movie on and rub her feet. And inevitably he'd wind up doing so much more.

She missed sharing a bowl of ice cream with him across the kitchen island at midnight. And she really missed the times he'd ask his parents to watch Ava and Noah so that he could steal her away for a surprise dinner.

But it had been nearly six months since any of that happened. He'd been staying later and later at the office, not coming home until long after the kids went to bed.

Clients in different time zones, he'd explain any time she tried to bring it up. Part of her didn't even see the point in mentioning it now except no matter how late he'd been working the night before he'd always managed to spend every Friday morning with the twins, until this week.

"They are going to be really disappointed, Tanner."

He dropped on to the side of the bed and tugged

his tie off. His shoulders sagged and he fixed his gaze on the carpet at his feet. "I'm sorry, Belle. I really am."

It hadn't taken long after they met for her to see that Tanner took far more responsibility on than he needed to. He could be the poster child for the oldest sibling and every issue attached to it. He needed to fix everything for everyone, make sure the business and the family were running smoothly. And he never took a moment to do anything for himself.

That's what she was for. That was their balance. That was how they worked together.

She put her arms around his neck and straddled his lap. "Just how sorry are you, baby?"

His hands grasped her hips, and he swallowed. "Really, really sorry?"

Izzy nodded slowly and grinned. "And can you think of any way possible to show your complete and utter remorse?"

"Oh, you want ideas?" He gave her a smirk and turned so she was lying on her back and he hovered over her. "I love a good brainstorming session."

Her laughter dissolved into a moan as his hand slid under her nightgown. Just as his fingers dipped beneath the elastic waistband of her underwear, a soft tap came from the other side of the door.

"Mommy, I had a bad dream. Can I come sleep with you?"

Tanner's forehead fell against her chest and Izzy couldn't help but giggle. "Sure thing. Just give Mommy a minute."

"Daddy's gonna need more than a minute,"

Tanner grumbled, collecting his sweats and t-shirt from the bottom of the bed and retreating into the bathroom.

Making sure her nightgown was in place and fanning the heat away from her cheeks, she opened to door to a sleepy Noah, holding his favorite stuffed dinosaur. "Come on, buddy, let's see if we can chase those nightmares away."

He had just been tucked in the center of the bed and snuggled against Izzy's side when Tanner reappeared.

"Hey little man."

Noah's eyes, nearly closed just moments earlier, popped open wide. "Daddy! You're home!"

Several long minutes later, Noah snored against Tanner's bicep—which he had adamantly refused to let go of—and Izzy rolled her head to the right to look at Tanner. "Betcha wish you would've come home earlier now?" She threw him a wink and a saucy smile.

Tanner simply groaned in response and Izzy laughed.

Chapter Thirty

Tanner

"You had your hands on my wife." Tanner bit the words out between clenched teeth, and for the second time in a week, he fought the urge to tackle Wyatt to the floor and lay a few well-deserved punches on that golden face of his. The idea gave Tanner all kinds of warm fuzzies. No way he'd land that sponsorship with a broken nose.

Wyatt pushed away the hand that held a fistful of his still-wet shirt. "If you stop and think for one single moment, you'd realize I was trying to help you, you ungrateful bastard."

Tanner's brows shot up. "Help me? Like you helped me when you harassed me almost every day for two weeks until I agreed to drive out to see you? Like you helped me when you challenged me to drink with you? Like you helped me when you put your filthy hands on my wife the first chance you had?"

His brother laughed. "You're ridiculous. I was

282

giving her a hug. I hope like hell that she will forgive you because I'm fairly certain this is driving you crazy."

He hated to admit it, but Wyatt might be right. The very idea of a life without Belle. A life where they would have to be together at times because of the kids. Where he would have to see her moving on with someone better, someone smarter, someone who appreciated her. Yeah, that was enough to make him certifiably insane.

"Why the hell did you go over there, Wyatt?" He ran his fingers through his hair, and the action made his stomach turn. They had been in such a good place until she saw those pictures. "I swear, if you did something, anything, that makes Belle change her mind and she doesn't show up tomorrow—"

"You know, every once in a while I am capable of doing something right." His brother's eyes held a tinge of hurt, and the corners of his mouth turned down. "I went there tonight because you screwed up more than just…*that*."

Tanner's brows knitted together, and he shook his head. "What the hell else did I do wrong? I spent years practically ignoring Belle and the kids when I *thought* I was doing the right thing to keep the company successful and everyone happy. And since that wasn't enough to drive her away, I decided to make out with some chick I don't know and hope to never see again. Oh yeah, and let's not forget there were pictures because she needed to actually see it rather than just hear about it."

Wyatt sighed and threw himself down in the armchair in Tanner's old bedroom. Current

283

bedroom. Temporary bedroom.

"You got it all wrong, big brother." The cocky smirk took up residence on his face again. "Well, not about being a workaholic asshole that neglected the hottest chick in the world. That part you got totally right."

Tanner's nostrils flared. "Don't you dare call her that again."

He straightened his posture and rested his forearms on his knees. "Listen, I'm going to impart the same gem of wisdom to you that I did to Iz. I didn't pull you off that girl."

His mouth went dry and he swallowed a few times. No. No way in hell he had done anything more. No. He'd remember that and there wasn't enough alcohol in the world to make him do *that*. No.

Wyatt continued, oblivious to Tanner's thoughts. "Iz always had a thing for your hair. It's annoying as hell watching you two, ya know? But whatever that means to y'all, it was enough to flip the switch." He stretched his legs out in front of him and crossed them at the ankles, locking his hands behind his head. "You pushed her away. You found me."

Tanner rubbed his temple and shook his head. This made no sense. "I don't remember a lot, but I remember you dragging me away from the bar. I remember you pushing me into your truck."

Wyatt laughed. "I was dragging you because your sorry ass was so drunk you couldn't walk. You were begging me to take you back to the hotel. We really need to do something about your alcohol tolerance, brother. That was damn near embarrassing."

He cued up the same picture he'd shown his sister-in-law. "See, you ended it. Hell, you wanted me to drive you back here that same night."

Tanner studied the picture on the screen, disgust with himself warred with pride that he'd come to his senses on his own. Hope surged, knowing Belle saw the same thing in this picture he did. "And you showed Belle this? What did she say? What did she do?"

His brother shifted uncomfortably in the chair. "The same thing all girls do around me. She cried and ruined one of my favorite shirts." He threw Tanner another arrogant grin, this time looking far more superficial. "After she said, 'Oh Wyatt, thank you, Wyatt,' which is pretty standard too."

He rolled his eyes at his brother. "I think you just bought yourself a free pass on the ass kicking you so richly deserve." He tossed the phone over to Wyatt. "Now get the hell out of this room. I need sleep."

***

Tanner closed his eyes and leaned back in his chair, rubbing the ache that was rapidly forming between his eyes. "Wyatt, I can't come out. I told you that the past three times you called and asked last week and when I answered all the text messages."

"You never want to come watch me. Hell, you haven't even come out the past couple of years when I've been close to home. Izzy and the kids came alone. Twice." His brother let out a heavy sigh. "Come on, Tanner, Nashville is only a five-hour drive, and this is a really important for me."

When Wyatt had set out on this absurd "career path" after high school, he left in true Wyatt fashion with a lot of things undone, unsaid, and one completely devastated auburn-haired girl. But in spite of Tanner's doubts, Wyatt had managed to build a rather lucrative empire through championship wins and sponsors.

And now he actually wanted Tanner to come see his competition? Very un-Wyatt like, but hell, he'd never asked Tanner for anything before, much less this incessantly.

He eyed the schedule on his computer screen and all the meetings, almost back to back, for the next three weeks.

But Jack could handle most of this by himself.

"Okay, but only for the final night," he finally acquiesced.

The relief in his brother's voice was nearly palpable across the line. "Yeah?"

Tanner chuckled. "Yeah. Just let me talk to Belle tonight."

Shit. As he drove home hours later, the sun falling from the sky in front of his truck, he realized he probably should have talked to her first. Tanner dismissed the thought quickly. His Belle was amazing. She took all his schedule changes in stride and handled everything at home. She was the one part of his life he never had to worry about.

She'd be fine.

He wandered around the silent house for a few minutes before he finally discovered her, lying on the couch reading. Her legs stretched out against the gray material, bare beneath the short black shorts, nearly wiped his mind clear. Damn, she was the sexiest thing alive.

"Hey, Tanner." Her greeting was soft as she set the book down and smiled.

He sat beside her on the couch and ran a hand up her leg, grinning when she sucked in a breath of air. "Hey, sweetheart."

Her hands wrapped around his neck and trailed into his hair. "I missed you." She pressed her body against his, brushing her lips across his ear when she spoke.

Damn, she gave as good as she got. Tanner shook his head slightly, not wanting to forget to tell her he'd be taking off in a couple of days. Not that she'd mind. "I need to tell you something. I'm heading out Wednesday. Probably in the afternoon."

She pulled back, resting her arms on his shoulders, and something indecipherable flickered in her eyes. "Another trip? I thought you were clear for the rest of the month."

"No, not a business trip." He tugged her close again, his mouth leaving tiny kisses on her neck.

But she sat back again and he frowned. "Then what is it?"

Tanner dropped his hands from her waist. "Wyatt. He's been asking me for almost two weeks to drive out to Nashville and watch his competition. He says it's important and he really wants me there."

She scooted down the couch far enough to slide off behind him. "Got it, Tanner."

He watched her retreating back as she hopped up the stairs, completely confused by what just happened.

Chapter Thirty-One

Izzy

Izzy leaned against the doorframe and grinned. "You were the last person I expected today."

"That man of yours certainly still has some surprises up his sleeve, I guess." Her best friend beamed with pride, and Izzy knew it had probably killed her to keep this from her all week. She lifted the garment bag in her right hand. "And really good taste in clothes, if I may say so myself. I totally peeked."

Izzy laughed and stepped to the side to let Caroline through the door. "So you're my keeper for the day?"

Caroline brought several bags in with her and walked into the kitchen, laying the garment bag across the back of one of the chairs and reaching into one of the paper sacks to pull out champagne.

"I prefer to think of it as your partner in crime."

She grabbed the bottle from her friend and stared at it. "Was this your addition or his?"

Brows up, Caroline shook her head slowly. "Nope, Iz, everything here is directly from the big guy himself." She gestured with a hand. "I know I've joked about the Prince Charming thing since the early days, but…"

Izzy laughed again. Ever since they first officially met in that dark and scary place called NICU, Caroline had often called Tanner "Prince Charming," thoroughly annoying her own husband in the process. "Yeah, that MBA of his, he doesn't leave anything to chance."

Nothing irritated her more than the sudden onslaught of tears. She was so tired of crying. Hurting. And missing Tanner more than she ever thought possible. But the image Wyatt showed her last night was still so fresh in her mind and right now she needed nothing more than to talk to her best friend about it.

"Every time I think I know the answer and I think I know what the right thing to do is, the rug is pulled out from under me." She sat down on one of the chairs, and Caroline's arm immediately came around her shoulder as she slid into a chair she pulled right next to her.

Sniffling, she took a deep breath. "Wyatt stopped by last night. He said he had something to show me, something to tell me, something Tanner got wrong." She lifted her hands and offered a mirthless laugh. "And it changed every freaking thing I thought I knew."

"Izzy, I don't…I don't understand." Caroline shook her head. "Things were bad when I talked to you last. What in the world could Wyatt have said that would change anything?"

"Wyatt didn't make him leave." Speaking the words made them even more real. Even more meaningful. Giving her heart even more hope and causing even more fear. "Tanner…one of the first things he told me…one of the things he thought happened was that Wyatt saved the day and pulled him away before he could do anything…" She couldn't say it even though she knew it hadn't happened.

Izzy explained the entire story to her friend in detail, feeling relieved to share everything but also even more confused. She looked at Caroline. "What do I do? I was so sure before I saw the pictures that we would be able to go back to normal, well, normal before he started working so much. But when I saw those I just…" She sighed heavily. "I couldn't fathom being with Tanner, living with him, seeing him every day, hugging him, kissing him, and not being in pain."

"And now everything Wyatt told you and showed you made you reconsider."

She shrugged. "Yes? But even before that, he has spent the entire week doing everything he promised he would do. He showed up every day he knew I had class scheduled and watched the kids. He didn't push me, he didn't beg, and he didn't touch me even though I knew it was killing him." She folded her arms on the table and buried her face in them. "Can't you just tell me what to do?"

Caroline laughed and rubbed her back gently. "I can't do that, but I can help you get ready, and the first step is for you to get in the shower."

Izzy groaned her discontent but obediently climbed the stairs, mumbling along the way.

Nearly an hour later, Caroline held a hand mirror out with the practiced flourish of a professional make-up artist. "I declare you ready for Prince Charming."

She carefully stood on the spindly high heels of the blush-colored shoes that matched the short lace dress Tanner had sent with Caroline. She grabbed both of her friend's hands. "It's stupid to be nervous, right?"

A calming smile spread across Caroline's face. "It's completely reasonable for you to be nervous. This is bigger than when you agreed to marry him. You have to decide if you can trust him again. There's really no doubt you still love him, is there?"

Izzy shook her head vigorously and the teardrop pearl earrings tapped against her jaw. "I never stopped."

"I think," she ventured slowly, "trust is so much harder to rebuild and, right now, for you two, maybe even more important than love. You can love him with everything you have, but if you can't trust him again, you'll have a miserable marriage."

Before she could respond, the doorbell rang, and she couldn't help but roll her eyes. "Five years, Caroline. Five freaking years we've lived in this house and that whole time the boys just barged in. Now they decide to start using their manners."

"How do you know it's one of his brothers?" She

laughed as she helped Izzy navigate the stairs without falling.

Izzy grinned when she spied Wyatt and Connor standing on the other side of the door. "I know Tanner."

Connor dropped a kiss on her powdered cheek and informed her he was on childcare duty, and Caroline offered one more hug before pushing her out the door.

Wyatt offered his elbow to her and led her to Tanner's obnoxious yellow truck. "Your chariot, madam." He bowed dramatically as he opened the door, and Izzy laughed.

An hour into the drive, she looked at her brother-in-law. "Not gonna tell me where we're going, are you?"

Wyatt chuckled, resting his wrist on the steering wheel and propping the other arm on the truck door. "Nope. I was threatened with multiple forms of violence if I tell." His features sobered. "For what it's worth, he really is sorry, Iz."

"I know." After several beats, she looked at Wyatt and studied his profile. "Don't you think it's time to try something else?"

He glanced at her with a frown before quickly returning his eyes to the road. "You mean give up bull riding?"

She shook her head, frowning slightly. "No, I mean give up your self-appointed role as the rebel of the Carlisle family. Stop running from whatever you're running from and acting like the jerk you think everyone expects you to be. Because that's not who you are."

His jaw tightened. "What if it is?"

"Don't insult me." She scoffed. "I've known you for too long and seen way too much. I don't know why you think you need to act like this, but I know that's not the real you."

Something in his face softened, and Izzy saw an expression there she'd never seen before. "I'm glad someone thinks so."

***

Kicking the suitcase standing against the closet door would be childish, right?

Izzy huffed and crossed her arms. For someone with an MBA, Tanner was really stupid sometimes. Couldn't he tell she didn't want him to leave? Couldn't he tell that the fact he managed to clear his schedule for Wyatt and some rodeo in Nashville but couldn't seem to come home on time for dinner just one night a week hurt not just her but the kids too? Couldn't he see just how much she missed him?

A small voice at the back of her mind gently asked: *When is the last time you told him?* When was the last time she didn't just simply rearrange everything to fit Tanner?

That question caused her heart to ache even more than the others. There were days she felt like nothing more than a babysitter and housekeeper and cook. Sure, Tanner would curl against her at night, whenever he finally came home. Yes, he would run his hands over her body and ignite the desire that hadn't cooled over their years of marriage. And he would still whisper his love for her before falling into a nearly comatose sleep, but that wasn't enough.

Where was her best friend? Where was the guy who teased her and negotiated with her and used his hands to endlessly torment her while she was making dinner? Where was the Tanner who would put in a stupid movie they both hated just so they could snuggle with each other and make out like teenagers?

This cruise control they'd been operating on for the past three years really wasn't cutting it anymore.

She glared at the suitcase again, and a new idea started to form in her brain. He said he'd be home Friday evening. Her brow smoothed out and her frown curved upward.

Izzy captured her bottom lip between her teeth. She reached in the pocket of her denim shorts and dialed her mother-in-law.

Tracy answered on the third ring. "Hey, Izzy, honey."

"Hey, Mom, listen, I hate to ask this of you guys, but do you think Ava and Noah could spend the night Friday night? Tanner's going out to Wyatt's last show, and I was hoping we could have his first night back alone together." Her cheeks heated. "Only if you guys don't mind, that is. I…"

Laughter trickled over the line. "Oh, Izzy, you know we love having Noah and Ava."

Her eyes landed on the suitcase once again, and this time she smiled. "Thanks so much. I'll drop them off after lunch Friday."

All too soon Tanner strode into their bedroom and the crooked grin she loved so much easily fell into place. "Damn, sweetheart. It's not fair for you to look so damn hot when I don't have time to take advantage of it."

A wave of bitterness rose up at his comment. Oh, really? She hadn't done a single thing differently. Not a stitch of her clothing was new. And she certainly hadn't lost the extra fifteen pounds she was still carrying after the twins' birth.

She bit back every word and kissed his cheek instead. "Call me when you get there and drive safely. And make sure you don't do anything Wyatt would do."

Tanner laughed and pulled out the handle of his suitcase to its full extension. "You got it, sweetheart."

As soon as she heard the throaty sounds of his truck's engine, she sent a quick text message to her brother-in-law, a small half smile curving her lips when he answered within moments.

She gave Tanner a strong head start, nearly thirty minutes, before she poked her head in the playroom. "Hey guys, I need to run to the store for a little bit, but Uncle Connor is coming over to play with you, okay?"

Both kids cheered in excitement. Tanner's brothers may be immature, but the twins adored each of their uncles. And probably were already thinking of all the ways they could manipulate the tender-hearted Connor into feeding them ice cream, cookies, and all the other treats normally off limits before dinner.

As soon as he arrived, she climbed in the driver's seat of her SUV and pointed the vehicle towards the mall. "He always did like when I bought new lingerie." She grinned as she turned from their driveway onto the main road.

Her heart felt light and hopeful for the first time in a long time. As soon as he came home, they'd have a long talk and he'd get a very nice reward.

Chapter
Thirty-Two

Tanner

Tanner shifted on his feet uncomfortably and looked at his watch again. Yeah, he was happy his brother was taking his time and driving carefully, just as he was told, but he was dying a slow and agonizing death waiting for Belle.

Was there a chance in hell she could forgive him? Did Wyatt's little intervention make a difference? Or had she already made up her mind and nothing he did, said, or gave her would change that?

He felt like he was the main contestant on that ridiculous reality show Dean's best friend liked to watch and he was waiting to hand out the final rose.

As soon as he saw Belle standing at the top of the wooden stairs, his breath caught in his throat. His palms grew wet with sweat as she approached, and he wiped them on his black dress pants.

"Damn, you look beautiful." He breathed the words when she reached him. Not at all part of the speech he'd spent most of the night rehearsing but he couldn't help himself. The lace dress hugged the curves that he had memorized. And the soft chocolate curls hanging over her left shoulder made his fingers itch to touch them.

At that moment, he wanted nothing more than to bury his nose into the silky tresses and inhale the fresh scent of apples and summer and Belle, but he had far too much to say.

She looked down, and pink tinged her cheeks. "Thanks. You, uh, decided to go low-key, I see." She waved a hand to encompass the Lower Cascade Falls, roaring behind where they stood beneath the white pergola Tanner and his brothers had set up on the observation deck.

Soft twinkle lights were twisted around each leg and around the periphery of the structure and glowed in the rapidly darkening night. Red rose petals covered the cement pad, and alternating red and white candles flickered along the railing of the deck.

Over the top? Maybe. What Belle deserved? Not even close.

He closed his eyes for a brief moment before fixing them on their joined hands. "Thank you for waiting until now to make a decision and for even showing up here tonight. I swear, sweetheart, I wouldn't have blamed you if you left me standing here alone."

She nodded slightly and gave him the barest of

299

smiles. "This is gorgeous, Tanner. And I love that you picked here." She laughed lightly. "I will never understand how you manage to set this stuff up, though."

He grinned then. "Some secrets are meant to be kept."

Belle's eyes filled with tears, and he swallowed back his own. They had so much between them that was special and unique and only theirs, and he simply couldn't imagine a world where he couldn't utter a relatively innocuous phrase and have her understand.

"I'm sorry, Belle." He felt like he'd uttered those words more over the past forty-three days than he had his entire life. "I'm sorry I ignored you. I'm sorry I took our family for granted. And I am sorrier than I can possibly express that I violated your trust and stole something that was damn near sacred."

"Tanner, wait."

She held a hand against his lips, and his heart stopped beating. She wasn't going to let him apologize. She wasn't going to listen. She was finished with them and tired of his pathetic attempts at making things right.

He'd done too much. Screwed up too badly. This was the final nail in the coffin of his marriage.

Lost in his own head, and so certain nothing would change, he barely registered the feeling of her hand sliding from his mouth to the back of his neck. Or her body pressing against his. Or her other hand twining around his waist.

"Somewhere along the way, we lost us. And I don't just mean us as a couple, I mean you and me."

Her eyes locked on his. "I've realized the past few weeks how much I didn't just miss you, I missed me."

Belle leaned her forehead against his and sighed softly. "It's not all your fault, Tanner. We both lost sight of what's really important. And I...I forgot who you were. You're not my dad. You've never been like him. Tanner, I never should have measured you with his yardstick."

Well, hell.

He gripped her hips tightly. "I will regret what I did for the rest of my life, sweetheart, but I am so damn glad I got a well-deserved wakeup call to put my priorities back in place."

He dropped to one knee before her. When he heard her choked sob, his stomach flipped. Was that a good sign? "Belle, I don't deserve a second chance. The last time we stood here, I made a promise not to work too much. I made a promise to be faithful to you. I made a promise to put you first in my life, and I broke every single one of those."

Her hand clapped over her mouth, and she sucked in a shuddered breath.

"I know I don't deserve it, sweetheart," he repeated, "but I will never again take for granted one second with you if you can possibly find a way to forgive me."

Belle pulled him to his feet and pressed her lips against his. "I forgave you long before I got here."

***

His heart thudded against his ribcage, and he

301

cursed himself. He sure as hell wasn't a virgin and this wasn't his first time with Belle.

But it kind of was.

It was the first time with his new-found appreciation of her. The first time with their fresh start. The first time after they'd fought the biggest battle of their relationship and managed to come out on the other side, scathed but together.

He turned the key in the lock of the heavy wooden door. He wanted to take this slow and worship every square inch of her body, but when her soft hand brushed against his forearm, he fought the urge to push her against the door right on the front porch of the cabin, far too close to prying eyes.

Tanner bent down and hooked an arm under her knees, easily lifting her and cradling her against his chest. Belle let out a small squeak and her arms flew around his neck as he carried her across the threshold, kicking the door closed behind him.

Her lips melded against his, her tongue dancing in his mouth. She was going to test every ounce of his self-control and set fire to his carefully laid plans.

And he really didn't give a damn.

Breaking the kiss, he set her on her feet, her body sliding against his and sending him into a tailspin of desire. She clamped down on her bottom lip and began unbuttoning his shirt with shaking hands.

A tiny laugh escaped Belle's mouth, ending on a huff of frustration. "I'm pretty sure I was more confident the first time we did this."

He hooked a finger under her chin and brought her eyes from his shirt to his face. "You were perfect then and you're perfect now."

She lifted one eyebrow just as she undid the last button. She slid her hands up his stomach and chest to his shoulders and pushed the white linen shirt off his body. "Perfect?"

His hands found the zipper at the back of her dress and he tugged until it hissed its release. "Perfect for me."

Tanner pulled the wide straps of her dress, sucking in a breath when the material pooled around her feet. "Holy hell, sweetheart."

He'd seen her in all manner of clothing from the gown she'd chosen for their wedding to the adorable funky pajamas she slept in and everything in between. But tonight, after making so many mistakes and the undeserved gift of her forgiveness, he wanted to fall before her and spend hours kissing, licking, tasting every part of her.

And the skimpy white lace lingerie set he'd never seen before only amplified his desires. "When the hell did you buy these?"

She blushed again. "The day before you came home from Wyatt's competition."

His heart stilled and his breathing stopped. "You really did come here ready to forgive me."

Belle nodded slightly. Then her hands landed on his belt buckle and he stiffened against a fresh onslaught of need. She dragged his belt through the loops and threw it across room. A saucy grin spread across her face as she unbuttoned his pants. "I've really missed you, Tanner."

Well, double hell.

He locked his arms around her waist and lifted her off her feet, carrying her to the bed on the far side of the open one-room cabin. "I missed you too, sweetheart. So damn much."

Tanner laid Belle across the deep red comforter and stood next to the bed, staring at her for several long moments. He had been too close to losing this, losing her, losing everything that meant something.

Her hands started to cover her stomach, and he reached down to move them away. "Oh, hell no, sweetheart. Don't cover an inch of this gorgeous body."

Tanner laid down on the bed beside her, commanding his body to stay under control. His fingers trailed up her abdomen, traveling beneath her to unhook her bra, sliding the straps down her arms and tossing the undergarment somewhere in the direction of their clothes.

His lips made a path across the warm skin the material had covered and he grinned at Belle's sharp intake of breath. His tongue slipped out of his mouth, desperate to taste the familiar sweetness that was Belle.

Tanner turned until he hovered over her, propped up on his elbows and making trails up and down her body. Her soft sighs propelled him on and drove him to the brink of control.

He hooked his fingers under the edges of her panties and slowly slid them down and over her shoes.

"Let me take those off." She panted out the words, lifting her head and gesturing to the heels.

He grinned and shook his head slowly. "Oh, hell no, sweetheart. I want nothing more than these sexy shoes locked behind my back while I hear you screaming my name. Now lay back Belle. I'm starving for you."

Tanner ran his facial hair along the inside of her thigh and chuckled at the deep, throaty moan. He tempted her with soft kisses everywhere but where he knew she wanted him the most. He thoroughly enjoyed teasing his wife to brink of insanity.

Finally when she whimpered his name, he darted his tongue into the hot, slick flesh and was rewarded with a soft shriek. He traced different patterns with his tongue and slid a finger inside her, moments later—another.

"Tan-ner!"

His lips curved against her and he slowed the rhythm of his tongue but didn't stop until her breathing began to slow. He kissed his way back to her mouth, claiming it and her at the same time, both of them moaning at finally being connected.

He broke the kiss and slowly increased his pace, locking his eyes with her soft chestnut ones, dilated with desire and need.

Tanner thrust two more times and, when the familiar tingling sensation began to build, whispered, "I love you, Belle."

Her thighs tightened around him and her mouth fell open. "I-I-I, oh, Tanner!" She screamed his name as he collapsed on top of her.

Several long minutes later, he rolled off her but pulled her close to his side with the movement. A lot of things were going to happen tonight, but letting go of her was not one of them.

Chapter Thirty-Three

Izzy

Izzy stretched a little, feeling deliciously sore nearly everywhere. Her sleep-fogged brain tried to remember how many times she and Tanner had made love but lost count somewhere between the shower and the couch in the space designated for a living room. The small size of the piece of furniture resulted in a few new, creative positions.

"Good morning, sweetheart." Tanner's voice was soft and rumbly and…There was no way she could possibly be turned on again, was there?

She kept her eyes closed, unwilling to acknowledge the morning or the sun or anything other than more sleep. The thing that hadn't seemed all that important last night. "Not morning. Sleeping."

Tanner's deep chuckle made the bed vibrate. She

shot a hand out to pull him down to lie next to her again, but when she connected with flannel instead of bare skin, her eyes flew open and she sat up. "You're dressed?"

His gaze roamed down his bare chest and pajama-clad legs, then over Izzy and the thin sheet covering her, and he grinned. "Well, maybe more dressed than you, but certainly not fit for public display."

The smile fell from his face, and he swallowed. "Sweetheart...I...you..." He sighed. "There's something you need to do. We need to do."

Her eyes widened. "Aren't you exhausted?"

He threw his head back and laughed. He got up and dug in the suitcase a few feet away. "No, sweetheart, not that. I mean, yes that, but later." Tanner held up one of his shirts and motioned for her to get out of bed. "First put this on, because hot damn, Belle, looking at your body isn't going to help me concentrate."

She obediently stood in front of him, completely naked, and smirked when he sucked in a sharp breath and quickly dropped his shirt over her head. The hem skimmed the tops of her knees and the neck nearly slipped off her shoulder, but apparently it offered enough coverage he could start to breathe again.

Tanner pulled her hand over to the bathroom and sat down on the toilet. She scrubbed a hand over her eyes and tried to understand. She hadn't gotten enough sleep to follow his thoughts. "Tanner, you're gonna have to spell this out for me because I need about a half a pot of coffee to even remember my name right now."

He leaned over to the sink and pulled something off the counter holding it up between them. Her confusion only grew when she realized it was an electric hair trimmer.

"I want you to shave my hair off."

She felt like she'd been punched in the gut. "Wh-what?" She started shaking her head vigorously and immediately her hands flew into his hair wanting to protect each strand from the very suggestion of being shaved. Tanner had never had hair longer than about two inches, but the thought of *nothing* was almost unbelievable.

He set the clippers back on the sink and held her hands, looking up at her with earnest, open blue eyes. "I can't undo what happened, sweetheart, but if you're willing to give me this gift, the least I can do is try to make it as fresh of a start as possible." He released her hands and held the electric device out to her again with a wide smile. "It'll grow back in a few months."

"And then it'll be just ours again." The words barely made it past her clogged throat. She clicked the switch on and jumped at the buzzing sound. Her eyes bounced from the razor to Tanner and back. "A-are…Tanner, are you sure?"

The smile vanished. "Belle, I would lay down my life for you. Do you think losing a few strands of hair is going to bother me in the slightest? And I want you to be honest with me: will this make you feel better?"

There was no way she could answer him. She simply nodded, and the smile spread across his face again. "So I get to have a happy wife and the hottest freaking barber in the world. How exactly is this going to be hard on me?"

Her hand was shaking and she took a few deep breaths to calm herself as much as possible. Was he really offering this?

"Tanner—"

"It's okay, Belle."

She swallowed and made a line through his hair with the razor. Fat tears rolled down her cheeks and landed on his head.

His hands grasped her hips and he gave a gentle squeeze. "Keep going, sweetheart."

Izzy had no idea how long it took to shave the rest of the hair from his head. She stopped several times to use the sleeve of Tanner's shirt to wipe away the tears and clear her vision. When she made the last swipe, she clicked it off and threw it in the sink.

She grabbed a towel from the rack behind her and brushed all the hair off his bare chest and shoulders. As soon as she was done, she sat on his lap, buried her face against his neck, and sobbed.

They sat there for several long minutes before Tanner lifted her against his chest and carried her back to the bed. He stretched out beside her and held her close. She sniffled a few times as the tears began to subside.

Izzy lifted her head and looked in his eyes. A piece of her heart she hadn't realized was still broken slowly began to mend. "Thank you, baby."

Tanner's mouth fell open. "You...you haven't called me that in a long time, sweetheart. I-I missed that."

She pressed her mouth against his. "I know. I love you, baby. And I love that you're mine."

Epilogue

Tanner
One year later

Tanner ran a hand through his hair and watched Belle out the window. It hadn't taken nearly as long as he expected for his hair to grow back. He shook his head and grinned. He didn't give a damn if it never grew back, but it had and it made Belle happy. If anything, she played with his hair even more and it drove him crazy.

There was the added benefit of annoying the shit out of Wyatt since he decided to move back home and was spending more time with them. And desperately trying to get his own second chance with the girl he left behind after high school. Tanner grinned to himself; he'd always liked Georgia, but even more now that she was making his brother jump through half a dozen hoops.

With a laugh, Belle hitched the duffel bag higher on her shoulder and gave her best friend a hug goodbye. Six months ago, she'd gotten her yoga instructor certification and partnered with Caroline at the studio.

Ample promises of private payment from Belle made Tanner all too willing to put his MBA to use to help with their marketing and promotions. He'd been amazed when Belle had taken some of his ideas and made them even better. He offered her a job at his company at least half a dozen times. She was brilliant.

With a little help from Tanner and Caroline and Belle's naturally magnetic personalities, their memberships had quickly tripled and the two women were considering adding another instructor.

She popped up in the cab of his truck and leaned over to kiss him before throwing her bag in the backseat and buckling herself in. "Thanks for waiting, baby."

"You're worth waiting for, sweetheart." He threw the truck in gear and took off down the highway. One of the positives of having so much family within a few miles radius was the abundance of sitters for Ava and Noah when Tanner wanted to steal his wife away.

Belle tossed her head back and laughed, a few strands of chocolate hair falling out of the messy bun on top of her head. "That is definitely a Prince Charming line."

Tanner glanced over at her with a wink and smile. He meant every word he promised her; he would never take her for granted again.

She unbuckled herself, slid into the middle seat, and buckled herself in again, laying her head on his shoulder. "So where are we going?"

He planted a kiss on the top of her head and grabbed her hand, lacing his fingers between hers. "Some secrets are meant to be kept."

THE END

Acknowledgements

To my double A team who are the reason I do this.

To all the hashtags that light up my life:

My #RChat backbone of support, advice, handholding, and loving critiques. You girls made every second of this possible. I do solemnly swear to eliminate "felt" from my vocabulary. Well, mostly.

My #MDO lovelies Marit, Meka, and Evie who provide all the dirty pictures and inappropriate jokes a girl could ever want.

My #BoardmanBitches Hannah & Evie who have made putting ghost peppers, pirate bars, and kilts in the same sentence actually make sense.

And finally to Evie, the very best person I could ever ask for, thank you for understanding every worry and giving the tough love I need it and unfailingly being in my corner. You will always be my person.

About the Author

Books, coffee, and chocolate make up both the heart and body mass that is better known as Amelia Foster. She has been a lifelong lover of the written word, both as a reader and an author, and completed her first manuscript at the ripe old age of five complete with illustrations. Sadly, her art was a medium that never improved over time although thankfully her writing has.

From sweet to salacious the only requirement Amelia has in books she reads–and definitely in the ones she crafts–is an excessively satisfying happily ever after…and then a little bit more.

Facebook:
https://www.facebook.com/amelia.foster.1213986

Twitter:
https://twitter.com/afosterauthor

WordPress:
https://ameliafosterauthor.wordpress.com/

Instagram:
https://www.instagram.com/ameliafosterauthor/

Pinterest:
https://www.pinterest.com/ameliafosterauthor/

Join our Reader Group on Facebook and don't miss out on meeting our authors and entering epic giveaways!

Limitless Reading

Where reading a book
is your first step to becoming
limitless...

LIMITLESS PUBLISHING *Reader Group*

Join today! *"Where reading a book is your first step to becoming limitless..."*

https://www.facebook.com/groups/Limitless Reading/

www.ingramcontent.com/pod-product-compliance
Lightning Source LLC
Chambersburg PA
CBHW051958240626

47153CB00005B/1806